MW00943581

SMOKE
ON THE
MOUNTAIN

A Story of Survival

J. Michael Stewart

"In the woods, we return to reason and faith."

—RALPH WALDO EMERSON

SMOKE
ON THE
MOUNTAIN

1

Get out of the way, you idiot!" Cody yelled as he leaned on the horn and slammed on the brakes. He hated Atlanta traffic—especially Friday afternoon traffic. The city was a maze of super-highways that converged from all directions into a mass of concrete and skyscrapers. He was doing fifty-five miles an hour on I-285, the beltline that ran around the circumference of the city, but he wanted to be going eighty—he was in a hurry, and he was low on patience. He glanced down at the clock on the dashboard and saw it was already three o'clock. He had hoped to be out of town by now.

The red sports car that had cut him off was driven by a man who Cody figured couldn't be a day over nineteen. *Probably some rich doctor's son who got the car for a graduation present.* "Punk," he mumbled under his breath.

He honked his horn again out of frustration, and the teenager returned the gesture with one of his own—a middle finger shoved forcefully skyward out of the driver's side window.

"Relax," Cody told himself as he took a couple of deep breaths and started counting slowly to ten.

The sports car moved on down the freeway, zooming in and out of traffic, and was soon out of sight. By this time,

Cody had counted to ten three times and was already forgetting about the near accident just a minute earlier. Combat driving was a daily occurrence of his commute, so he had learned to deal with it as best he could. It was a necessary, albeit unpleasant, part of his daily routine.

He had left the Forbes, Henry & McAlister Law Firm at two o'clock—three hours earlier than normal for a Friday afternoon. His office was in a modern three-story building in downtown Atlanta. The firm specialized in corporate law, defending companies against lawsuits—some legitimate, some not. It made no difference to Cody whether the case was legit or not. The way he saw it, his job was to put on the best defense possible for his clients. It was up to the jury to do the rest. Sometimes it was difficult to separate the human factor from the equation, but he always seemed to manage. He had just finished a trial last week, and had spent the last few days tying up loose ends—and preparing for his much needed two-week vacation.

The case had worked its way through the court system for the last year and a half, and involved one of the firm's top clients, Branson & Sons Pharmaceuticals. A sixty-five-year-old woman was suing Branson & Sons for her husband's premature death. She claimed her husband had died of a sudden heart attack after taking a new blood pressure medicine recently put on the market by Branson & Sons. It had been a hard-fought trial with expert medical witnesses from both sides battling it out in front of the jury. Forbes, Henry & McAlister had poured a massive amount of resources into the case, and had been paid handsomely for their efforts by the big drug company. They had pulled out all the stops—hiring the best jury consultants and scouring the country for medical experts willing to dispute each and every claim made by the opposing side—for a sizable price, of course.

It was the kind of case that could make a young attorney's career.

The courts had been inundated in recent years with cases filed by personal injury lawyers on behalf of their grieving clients. They advertised almost nonstop with TV and radio commercials, newspaper ads, roadside billboards, and any other means available. Despite all the advertising to the contrary, their number one purpose in life was to fatten their own wallets—not help victims of accidents or bad medications. They asked for huge damages, most of which the lawyers would keep when all was said and done. Every ambulance chaser and malpractice attorney wanted his or her piece of the corporate pie. Cody looked at them the same way a snake looked at a rat—good for nothing, except food—and he loved to eat them alive in the courtroom.

The corporations took these lawsuits very seriously, because a successful outcome for a plaintiff would open the floodgates for other so-called *victims* around the country, and could cost the company billions in lost profits and legal costs.

Cody had spent the last year and a half preparing for the trial, which had gotten underway six weeks ago. It had gone on for close to a month, and after a four-day deliberation, the jury had come back with a verdict.

A major victory for Cody.

The jury cited insufficient evidence that the new blood pressure medicine had caused Mr. Wilby's unfortunate demise. The drug company executives were very pleased with Cody's efforts. After the customary celebratory handshakes and pats on the back, Cody had turned his attention to his upcoming vacation. He didn't have another case starting anytime soon, and the slowdown was much needed.

He accelerated and passed a beat-up green station wagon. Two kids had their arms stuck out the back windows and several worn-out suitcases were strapped to the roof rack. It looked like a scene straight out of *National Lam-*

poon's Vacation. It was the first Friday in May, and the sky was a deep blue with no clouds in sight. The temperature was a comfortable seventy-two degrees, a great day for a road trip. Cody rolled his window down and let his sandy blond hair blow in the wind. After months of anticipation, he was finally on his way.

He had been on the road for a little over an hour now, and the traffic was still heavy—evidently, he was not the only one who had left work early today. The beautiful spring weather had brought people out in force for the weekend. Dads and moms were scurrying home to pack up the kids and head to their favorite campground or amusement park or wherever families went to have fun these days. A few, like the green station wagon now in his rearview mirror, were already on their way.

The weather forecast was great for at least the next four days, and after a colder-than-normal Georgia winter, it seemed everyone was going to take advantage of an early summer weekend getaway.

Ten minutes later, he spotted the exit sign for I-985. He guided his bright red Toyota pickup onto the exit and headed northeast. His destination was the Great Smoky Mountains, and he wanted to get there in time for a good night's sleep. As he merged onto I-985, the congestion began to improve. Soon the rat race that was Atlanta would be behind him. He quietly promised himself he would not think about it for the next two weeks.

He glanced in his rearview mirror and saw the big city skyline fading behind him. A smile spread across his face as he pushed harder on the accelerator.

2

As Cody continued north toward the mountains, his thoughts turned to the mess his life had become.

His father had been killed in a car accident when Cody was just eight years old. Unable to cope with the loss of her husband and the responsibility of raising two kids on her own, his mother had fallen into a deep depression. In the year after the accident, she spiraled downward into a black abyss that Cody had not been able to fully understand at his young age. She lost her job and was struggling just to put food on the table. It finally became more than she could bear. One cloudy Saturday morning, she packed two suitcases, one for Cody and one for his eleven-year-old sister, Sally, and drove them fifteen miles down a narrow country road, not speaking a word. When they arrived at his grandparents' house, Cody assumed they were just being dropped off for a weekend visit, as had been the case many times in the past. He and his sister always loved spending time with their father's parents, so he thought nothing of being left there by his mother. She had waved goodbye to Cody and Sally as she drove away from the farmhouse, her old Chrysler leaving a cloud of dust hanging in the South Georgia air.

That was the last time Cody saw her.

Years later, when he was in high school, he asked his grandfather what had really happened to his mother. His grandfather had tried to brush him off, but Cody was a persistent teenager. Finally, he heard the cold, hard truth.

Four years after Cody's mother had abandoned him and his sister, a phone call had awakened his grandfather at two in the morning. It was the Las Vegas police department. They had found his mother dead of an apparent drug overdose in a back alley.

A few months later, a letter had arrived at the farm from one of his mother's close friends in Vegas, detailing the specifics around his mother's death. It described his mother as a warm and caring person, but also as someone battling personal demons that she could never shake. Her friend had promised Cody's mother that if anything bad ever happened, she would contact her children and tell them that she loved them and was sorry—for everything.

Cody's mother had gotten involved in the shady side of Sin City that is, for the most part, kept out of view of the high-rolling tourists that pour billions of dollars into the local economy every year. She had bounced from one minimum wage job to another before she started selling her body to keep the bills paid. She had shacked up with some loser in a low-income housing project and was soon hooked on heroin. After that, the prostitution became a way of life for her. More than a way of life—it became a necessity. The monster named *heroin* does not care what you have to do to feed it. It just wants to be fed. Period.

She had somehow gotten hooked up with a street pimp who took most of her money and beat her whenever he felt she had *stepped out of line*. She was far from one of the high-priced "escorts" often idealized in movies and on television—she had become a straight-up street whore. When she could no longer take the constant physical and mental abuse, she had taken the money from her last trick, bought enough heroin to do the job, and overdosed in the alley.

Cody would oftentimes find himself thinking about his mother, usually around Christmas or Mother's Day, or sometimes just out of the blue. He tried to remember the good times—the peanut butter and jelly sandwiches she used to make for him every afternoon after he returned from school, helping him with his homework, baking cookies for a class fundraiser. But no matter how hard he tried—and God knew he did try—he could never get the image of what his mother had been reduced to—the things she had done for money—out of his head.

She had died cold and alone, the antithesis of the loving mother she had once been. Cody was always sorry for that. She had made lots of mistakes, but she was still his mom, and he wished he could have at least been there to hold her hand when the end came.

His grandparents had done their best to provide for Cody and his sister. They owned a twenty-acre farm in Southern Georgia, and Cody had thrived there. He loved the open country and, for the most part, stayed out of trouble through his teenage years.

Herschel and Missy McAlister had been married for forty-five years when Cody and Sally came to live with them. They had a strong marriage, and Cody could tell they loved each other deeply. They were just beginning to enjoy their retirement years when Cody and his sister were abandoned.

Herschel had a meager retirement fund from the state Transportation Department after thirty years of service, but that was not enough to pay all the bills and feed two extra mouths they had not counted on being responsible for. He had taken a job at a local hardware store to supplement their income. Missy had stayed home with the kids, providing stability and a much needed familiar face after school each day.

The family grew most of their food in a garden, raised a

calf once a year for beef, and hunted wild game during the fall. This had helped lower the grocery expense, but still, they struggled. They were not as poor as some families in the area, but after the necessities were paid for, there was very little left for extras.

Cody had felt guilty about the whole situation. His grandparents were just about to enjoy their golden years together before they had been saddled with this unexpected and unplanned-for responsibility—more like a burden, at least from Cody's perspective.

He and his sister had both worked several odd jobs through high school, and that had helped take some of the pressure off Herschel. They had stayed out of any major trouble and tried to be as small a hindrance to their grandparents as possible. Of course, Herschel and Missy had never looked at the kids as a burden at all. They loved them as their own, and Cody had felt it. His grandparents were good people and came from the old school, where life was simpler and the most important things were God and family. They had done a good job of raising their two grandchildren, and Cody would be forever grateful for what they had done for them.

Cody had determined as a freshman in high school that he was going to make something of his life. There were not many opportunities for a young man just graduating high school in the small town where he grew up. You either went to work at the local lumber mill, joined the military, or went to college. He had set his sights on a job in the big city, which meant college. He had convinced himself he was destined for great things. Things you could not find in South Georgia.

With his grandparents' encouragement, he had devoted himself to his studies, hoping and praying for a scholarship. He knew that was his only hope of escaping a low-income job working at the mill.

Sally had gotten a scholarship to a local community college, but dropped out after her freshman year. She had met an investment banker on a summer trip to Colorado and was married six months later. She and her husband had been married now for fourteen years and lived in Denver. Sally played the dutiful housewife, and they had it all—a big house in the suburbs, three kids, and two dogs. Cody still talked to her on the phone once a week, normally on Sunday afternoon, but they rarely had a chance to see each other in person anymore.

Cody had gotten his much-anticipated scholarship, too. With a full ride to the University of Georgia, he earned his bachelor's degree in history and was then accepted into law school. There were no wild fraternity parties and late night keg stands for him. He knew this was his only shot and he was not, under any circumstances, going to blow it.

He was going far in life—there was no doubt about that.

He graduated law school with honors, passed the Bar, and after some looking, had landed the job with Forbes, Henry & McAlister. Back then it was just Forbes & Henry. Cody had made partner within four years, a remarkable achievement for a young lawyer. His work ethic and desire to climb the career ladder had impressed Mr. Forbes and Mr. Henry, prompting them to offer him a full partnership far ahead of schedule. Cody could have gotten away with calling his partners by their first names, but both men were in their early sixties and in deference to their seniority, he had always called them Mr. Henry and Mr. Forbes.

Cody was promoted to partner ahead of attorneys with more seniority, which had caused some hard feelings within the firm. But Cody didn't give a damn about anyone's hard feelings—he had jumped at the opportunity. It was everything he had worked for since he was in high school. Everything he had ever dreamed of. Now, after seven years at the firm, he was less sure. After making partner, he had thrown himself into his work even more. What seemed so great at the time had, ultimately, destroyed his marriage.

Amy had been his high school sweetheart, and they continued to date through college. She had gotten a job at a local car dealership as a receptionist after high school, and Cody had made the drive back home every two weeks while he was away at college. They were married as soon as he landed the job at Forbes & Henry. He helped her pack up her old car, and after family goodbyes were said, they headed toward Atlanta, certain they were about to set the world on fire.

For the first four years, things had gone well for the McAlister household. Amy had enrolled in night school six months after their marriage and earned her real estate license. She worked part-time at a local realty office Monday through Friday. They didn't need the extra income, but she enjoyed working, meeting new people, and making her own money.

She would always meet Cody at the door with a warm hug and kiss, no matter how late he had worked at the office. However, after he had made partner at the law firm, things slowly began to change. She was still working part-time, but Cody began to put in even longer hours at the office—extremely long hours. He routinely worked twelve to fourteen hours a day, five or six days a week. Add in the brutal commute time, and Cody was hardly ever home. He spent Sundays watching football in his recliner, too tired to do anything else. Amy usually went shopping with girlfriends on Sunday morning and would return just in time for a quick dinner and a shower before bed. Monday morning the circus started all over again.

Cody had known that Amy felt neglected, but what was he supposed to do? He was the primary breadwinner, and someone had to pay the mortgage on their house in Atlanta's Buckhead neighborhood. On top of the mortgage were the car payments. Amy insisted on driving a large, black SUV, even though they had no children. She claimed she needed it for her Sunday shopping trips with her girlfriends, but he knew she wanted it more for a status symbol. A *Look at me, I'm a lawyer's wife* sort of thing. Social class was everything in their neighborhood. Cody had opted for a Lexus. In a neighborhood peppered with doctors, lawyers, powerful politicians, and businessmen, appearances were important.

They took one vacation trip a year, usually in the summer. Normally they would take a cruise to the Bahamas or some other Caribbean destination. One year they had foregone the cruise ship for two weeks in Jackson Hole, WY. It was the new hot spot for America's well-to-do, which necessitated the McAlisters making an appearance. If nothing else, they could brag about it to their friends.

Cody and Amy had spent less and less time together as the marriage dragged on—even the vacations had turned sour the last couple of years. They spent most of the time fighting about hotel accommodations, dinner plans, or whatever other trivial problem arose, and neither of them felt refreshed when they returned to Atlanta. It had become more of a yearly chore than something to look forward to.

His responsibilities at the law firm had grown exponentially with his new stature, and he was often forced to be away for weeks at a time on business trips. This irritated Amy even more. She had accused him of having an affair, which he had vehemently denied. He knew she had not believed him, though. It became clear things were going south for the McAlisters' marriage.

Two years ago, after another long day at the office, Amy had met him in the living room with a look on her face that told Cody something was wrong. He could still remember every word they had spoken that evening.

"What's wrong?" he asked.

"It's over. This marriage is over! I can't live like this anymore, Cody!" she yelled. A single tear ran down her cheek.

"I don't have time for this now. Do you know what kind of day I've had?" Cody shot back.

"Dammit! I'm serious this time, Cody." Amy was sobbing and pacing around the living room with a look of determination on her face.

Shocked by the forcefulness of Amy's response, Cody tried to reason with her. "We can work it out, baby. Come here." He moved toward her with his arms open, intending to give her a consoling hug, but she pushed him back.

"No, we can't. Not this time. I'm sorry. Really . . . I am so sorry." She paused, the tears increasing in volume. "I went to see a divorce attorney today." She produced several sheets of folded paper from the back pocket of her blue jeans and thrust them into Cody's chest.

"Why, is there someone else?" he asked, astonished. There had been threats of divorce before, but nothing had ever gotten this far. But he knew Amy was dead serious this time.

"No," she shot back.

"Why, then?" His voice was beginning to crack.

"I'm tired, Cody . . . I'm tired of this mess we call a marriage. I'm tired of sitting in this lonely house until I fall asleep on the couch waiting for you to get home. I'm tired of always having to put a smile on my face for our friends, and your co-workers, and your bosses, and your country club buddies, when I'm dying inside. I can't live like this anymore! I just can't." Amy turned and walked into the kitchen.

"Fine, I'll be out of the house by next week!"

"To hell with you, Cody!" She spun and started walking back toward him. "Don't even try to make me feel guilty about this. You haven't been here for me in years. All you care about is your precious career and how much money you make!" Another pause. "And don't even get me started on Jessica."

"What are you talking about?" he asked.

"Don't pretend you don't know what I'm talking about. You know, Cody . . . your new assistant . . . the one with the tight ass and fake tits. Don't think I haven't seen how you look at her."

"You're crazy!"

"Oh, am I?"

"Yeah, you are. There's nothing going on between Jessica and me!" Although her accusation was untrue, Cody could not deny that he had been attracted to Jessica, at least on some level—but he had never crossed the line.

"Well, I wouldn't be able to tell. You're with her more hours of the day than you're with me. What am I supposed to think when you call and say you and Jessica have to '*work late on a project together*'?" Amy made quotation marks in the air with her fingers, a look of disgust on her face.

"If I were having an affair, don't you think I would come up with a better cover story than working late with Jessica?" He tried to reason with her, but to no avail.

"I don't know, Cody. I honestly don't." She looked down at the floor and ran her hand through her hair. "And really, to tell you the truth, I don't care anymore. If you're banging your assistant, I really don't give a shit. Honestly, I don't." Amy's tone was more subdued now, calmer, sad almost. "Do whatever you want to do. All I know is that I'm getting the hell out of this house and out of this marriage."

"Come on, Amy. Please don't leave, we can work this out. I promise I'll stop working so much, we can even go to counseling. I'll do whatever you want," Cody tried to bargain with her as she headed for the door. He grabbed at her arm and tried to stop her, but she pulled away, slamming the door on her way out. He could hear her sobbing as she walked off the porch, but it was no use going after her. He knew she had made her decision, and that it was final.

Nothing was going to make Amy stay—not the seven-figure salary, the fancy cars, or the luxury home. Nothing. She had decided it was over, and nothing was going to change her mind.

Cody wondered what all his hard work had been for. He had lost his wife, and all the money in the world was not going to bring her back.

He found out during the divorce proceedings that there was an affair—only he wasn't the one having it. Amy had been involved with the owner of the real estate agency where she worked, some middle-aged married guy, with lots of money and a bad mid-life crisis going on. He had said all the right things to her at a time when she felt neglected, even told her he would leave his wife if she left Cody, which, of course, he never did. He had broken it off with her only a month after she left Cody.

By the time Cody found out about the affair, it really didn't matter anymore. Too many things had been said in anger to ever repair their marriage. He was as done with the marriage as Amy was.

Fortunately, she had not asked for alimony but settled instead for a sizable, one-time cash payment, the house, and the black SUV. Cody had decided to cut his losses and make it as amicable as possible. At some point, before his career had gotten in the way, he had really loved her, and part of him still did—maybe always would—but that part of his life was over now.

Amy had sold the house for a nice profit, and the last Cody heard, she was living in Arizona with some guy she met on the Internet. He had not talked to her since the divorce was finalized.

At least there were no kids involved. No messy custody battle to deal with—he was thankful for that. They had tried to have children, but after several trips to the fertility clinic, Amy was told she would not be able to bear children. She had been devastated and had thrown herself into work and the social scene to try and get it out of her mind. She would never admit it, but Cody thought that somewhere deep down, that had something to do with her affair and the divorce.

He had moved into a modest two-bedroom, one-and-a-half-bath townhouse ten minutes from the office. It was small, but it was all he needed. At first, it was nice living the bachelor life again. No more dirty looks when he walked in late from the office. No more cold dinners left for him on the table. No more guilt trips about not spending enough time with Amy. It was liberating.

But after a couple of months, he began to really miss her.

The divorce had taken its toll, although at first, he didn't want to admit it. He found the townhouse an extremely lonely and depressing place. He longed for someone to scold him for working too late. So in order to avoid spending countless hours alone at home, he had thrown himself back into his work, putting in sixty to eighty hours a week at the office. Whisky became his only friend at night—something to drive away the sorrow and shadows.

As the months wore on, his drinking became worse. He often showed up to work with a stiff hangover. For the first several months, he was able to hide his new vice from his coworkers. But everything came to a head one morning when he missed a meeting with a billionaire client they had spent the better part of a year wooing away from a competing firm. The businessman was so incensed at the missed meeting, he stormed out of the building, taking with him any hope of gaining his business.

The other two partners were furious.

Cody had apologized profusely for the incident, fearing he would be fired on the spot—he probably should have been. But instead, Mr. Forbes, a short, pudgy man with red cheeks and a bad comb-over, pulled him into a small, private room and told him in no uncertain terms that he better get his act together or things were not going to end well for him at the firm.

After the severe scolding, Mr. Forbes had actually taken time to ask Cody what was going on. It turned out that what Cody thought had been so well hidden—his heavy drinking—had not really been hidden at all. Everyone in the office had noticed his change in behavior, none more than Mr. Forbes and Mr. Henry, who after all, had the most to lose if he went off the rails.

Cody confessed he had been struggling with getting his life back on track after the divorce and had turned to the bottle to take the edge off. Mr. Forbes shared that he had been through a similar experience several years ago and suggested that Cody go see a counselor. Cody thanked him for his help, but as soon as he walked out of the room, he dismissed the idea of seeing a counselor.

He was able to cut down on his drinking for a week or two, but soon the proverbial monkey on his back returned, and he was once again drinking heavily. He was on the verge of losing his career. If that happened, there would be nothing worth living for anymore. That thought scared the hell out of him, so finally, he sought outpatient treatment for the drinking and began seeing a therapist regularly.

The therapist had told him that he was working too hard, that he was trying to push his problems away with excessive work hours and alcohol. She had recommended he start spending fewer hours at the office and take up a hobby in his spare time. At first Cody had blown off her suggestions, but after a couple more months of wallowing in self-pity, he began to listen.

He forced himself to cut his work hours down to a more manageable fifty hours a week and had absolutely refused to come in on Saturday or Sunday, even during the Wilby trial.

The therapist had also recommended increased exercise, so at least four times a week he skipped lunch and headed straight downstairs to the ground floor of the Forbes, Henry & McAlister complex. The gym was a large room with thousands of dollars worth of exercise equipment put in three years ago, after Mr. Forbes's wife mentioned he was getting fat. Several of the employees had used it religiously for the first couple of months, but now Cody usually had the gym to himself.

He was five-eleven, and when he finished law school, he had weighed 185 pounds. By the time the divorce was final, he had ballooned to 240.

He was now down to 197 and felt much better. He had also grown a goatee, which made him look more like twenty-five than his actual age of thirty-two.

The Toyota Tacoma pickup he was now driving toward the Great Smoky Mountains National Park was also a post-divorce acquisition. He had traded the Lexus for it six months after Amy left. It had all the bells and whistles—a top-of-the-line, four-wheel-drive with a six-cylinder engine and off-road suspension package. He had not driven off-road in years, but the salesman had pointed it out, and at the time, it seemed like a good idea. He had opted for the six-speed manual transmission instead of the automatic. It could be a pain when driving in the stop-and-go Atlanta traffic but was a blast when he had the rare opportunity to drive in the country.

Cody had been on the road for around three hours when he drove into the small town of Franklin, North Carolina. He had driven non-stop from his office, and his bladder was about to burst. He hadn't had a chance to fill up the gas tank before he left, and the needle was now reading below a quarter of a tank.

He spotted a gas station ahead and pulled off the road.

He filled up the tank, impatient that the gas seemed to flow from the pump more slowly than usual, and then hurried in to pay the attendant. After a fast pit stop in the restroom, he headed back out to his truck. He wanted to get back on the road as quickly as possible.

He climbed back into the driver's seat and turned the ignition. The GPS unit came to life, and the digital readout told him he was still an hour and fifteen minutes away from his destination. The heavy traffic had slowed him down, and he was not happy about it.

Cody fastened his seat belt, eased out on the clutch, and pulled his truck back onto Highway 28.

Just a little bit farther, he told himself.

3

The sun was sinking on the horizon when Cody spotted a flashing marquee sign. At least seven or eight bulbs were burned out on the flashing arrow, but it was still serving its purpose. *Carolina Cafe* was printed in bold green lettering below the lights. The paint on the sign was beginning to peel, which added some rustic charm to the place.

Breakfast, which he had hurriedly prepared on his way out of the townhouse early that morning, had consisted of a toasted bagel with cream cheese. He had not eaten since then, and he was starving. A roadside burger joint seemed to be just what he needed. As if on cue, his stomach growled, reinforcing the notion. He had intended to finish his trip without stopping again, but the hunger pangs forced him to change his mind.

He down-shifted the pickup and pulled off the right side of the two-lane road into the gravel parking lot in front of the diner. He found an empty spot and parked. Opening the door, he stepped out and raised his hands above his head, stretching his back and legs, simultaneously drawing a deep breath of the cool mountain air into his nostrils. The temperature was probably between forty-five and fifty degrees now, and it felt wonderful. The air up in the mountains was refreshing and inviting, unlike the downtown air of Atlanta, which felt heavy and suffocating—too much concrete and asphalt.

The restaurant was small but inviting. A few shingles were missing and he could tell the place was old. A fresh coat of blue paint had been added to the wood siding in an attempt to make it more aesthetically pleasing. It was a true roadside dive—just the kind he loved. Cody envisioned a greasy, calorie-laden meal in his future.

He walked around to the side and opened the weather-worn, wooden door that led to the enclosed porch. There were a couple of locals sitting around, drinking coffee and talking over the latest goings on and world politics. This was typical for a small southern town. Every community had a place where the locals hung out and enjoyed the latest town gossip or commiserated about how the world was going to hell in a hand basket. Nothing made hard news easier to handle than a good cup of joe with a side of biscuits and gravy. In the South, if you wanted to find out what was going on, you did not go to the local newspaper—you went to the local diner.

Cody plopped down in a booth in front of one of the windows. He could feel the aching in his legs and back, caused by the hours behind the wheel. He looked out the window on his left, across the gravel parking lot and state highway. A small stream bordered the road on the other side, and beyond it, a farmer's field that stretched to the mountains rising in the background. The spring weather had turned the field a brilliant color of green, and the grass was growing nicely after being dormant during the winter.

He missed the country and wide open spaces. What he had thought would be an exciting adventure living in the big city had turned into a necessary evil. He had grown to hate the city. All the traffic, car horns, long commutes, and stale air had turned him firmly against it.

The country vista turned his thoughts back to his teenage years on his grandparents' farm. The place he could not wait to escape as a youngster now held a very special place in his heart.

He often longed to be back there.

His grandfather had died from lung cancer two years after he finished law school. Missy had lived on the farm for another year and a half after Herschel's death, but with both of the grandkids gone and no one around to help out, she had sold the farm and moved into a nearby retirement community. Cody had made the trip to Southern Georgia as often as he could to visit her, but once Herschel died, she seemed to lose the will to live. She passed away not even a year after moving to the facility. The doctor said she died from a lung infection, but Cody knew she had died of a broken heart.

"What can I get you to drink, sir?" the waitress said as she placed a menu on the table in front of him. The waitress was an attractive young woman, probably nineteen or twenty, and he could tell by her accent she had grown up in the area.

"Sweet tea, please," he responded, snapping back to reality.

"No problem, I'll have it right out," she responded in a southern drawl that made Cody smile. She gave him a nice smile in return and briskly returned to the kitchen.

Cody looked over the menu, almost drooling. He settled on the double bacon cheeseburger with a side of beer-battered onion rings. He had a momentary flash of guilt, but he had a long walk ahead of him the next day, and after a short internal argument, he convinced himself he really needed all the extra calories.

The waitress delivered the burger and onion rings fifteen minutes later. Steam rose from the plate, and he was careful not to burn his mouth as he took the first bite of the burger—he had just died and gone to heaven. As he continued to eat, his thoughts turned to the weeks ahead.

The plan was simple—two weeks of fly fishing for wild trout in the Smoky Mountains. It meant freedom, albeit temporary, from the rat race that was his life in Atlanta. Away from the cell phones, answering machines, and a full email inbox. Away from all the stress.

He was brimming with anticipation for the weeks ahead.

He had finally taken his therapist's advice and searched out a hobby for himself. He tried golf, tennis, and bicycling, none of which suited him. One day, while he was down in the finance department of the firm, two of the accountants, Derek and Justin, suggested he take up fly fishing. He was hesitant at first, but after a little urging, he had given it a try.

Growing up, Cody had often fished for largemouth bass in local farm ponds with Herschel. It was a way to get additional food for the family, but he had enjoyed it above all his other chores. Herschel called them bucket-mouth bass, and he and Cody had spent countless hours casting a line together and sharing stories.

After Cody went away to college, he spent very little time in the outdoors, and he had not been fishing for years before Derek and Justin had introduced him to fly fishing. They had convinced him to take a trip with them the previous summer to Southwestern Montana, and Yellowstone National Park. They spent a week fishing the waters in and around the park—legendary rivers with names like Gallatin, Madison, and Yellowstone. They also fished some of the smaller streams, like Slough and Soda Butte Creeks, which he enjoyed even more than the larger rivers. The peace he had found with an eighteen-inch rainbow trout on the end of his line was like nothing he had ever experienced before. All his worries and problems seemed to melt away when he was fishing.

He was hooked.

By the time he added up the cost of the airfare from Atlanta to Bozeman, lodging, guide fees, and other miscellaneous expenses, the trip had cost him just over three thousand dollars. But it was the best investment he had made in years.

Upon his return to Atlanta, he had thrown himself into his new hobby with gusto. He had spent more money than he should have on new equipment, including a rod and reel outfit, which cost him eight hundred dollars, new waders, wading shoes, a multi-pocketed fly vest, fly boxes, and various other pieces of equipment he found online that he just had to have. He had recently received a mailer from the online retailer where he bought all his gear. It was a promotion exclusively for their *Preferred Customers*. Cody had laughed when he read it. With as much money as he had spent in the last couple of months, he should have bought stock in the damn company.

He subscribed to several fly fishing magazines and ordered instructional DVDs that taught everything from basic casting skills to streamside entomology. He spent a couple of hours each weekend practicing his casting skills in the backyard of his townhouse. In reality, his *yard* was little more than a skinny patch of grass, barely thirty feet long. But after a few months of diligent practice, and a lot of patience, his casting had improved fourfold.

Cody had two bites of the burger left when the waitress returned.

"Need some more sweet tea, sir?"

"No thanks, I'm almost done. I would like a cup for the road, though," he replied.

"No problem, I'll have it right out."

He wolfed down the last of the burger and got up to pay his bill. The waitress met him at the cash register and handed him a straw and large foam cup full of some of the best sweet tea he had ever tasted. The total came to seven dollars and forty-five cents. He gave the waitress a ten.

"Keep the change."

"Thank you, sir. Come back soon." She smiled again as she closed the register drawer.

"You bet I will," Cody replied. He returned the waitress's smile, grabbed the cup of sweet tea, and headed for the door.

By the time he crawled back into his truck, the air had a damp coolness to it, so he turned the heater on and directed all the vents toward himself. Rays of sunlight were breaking through the trees as the sun moved lower on the horizon. It created an eerie beauty—long spikes of brilliant light, intermingling with dark shadows. Soon the light would lose the daily battle and fade away as the shadows overtook the small mountain community.

With a full stomach and his excitement growing, he pulled the truck back onto the two-lane country road and headed farther into the mountains.

4

Twenty-five minutes later, Cody turned left at a large, wooden sign that read *Mountain View Resort*. The last shreds of light were fading fast as he drove up the steep road leading to the lodge. The small resort was tucked tightly into the Great Smoky Mountains and was surrounded by small, curvy roads, rather than the super-highways he had learned to despise.

Cody had done some research before he left on his trip and found out that the area's main attraction was Fontana Lake. The lake was formed when a 480-foot dam had been completed in 1944 as part of the Tennessee Valley Authority projects. The dam had played an important part in America's war effort by sending power to Oak Ridge, Tennessee, where nuclear enrichment was taking place. The efforts at Oak Ridge, and various other locations around the country, had been pivotal in building the atomic bombs that ultimately ended the war.

The resort was not a place with flashing neon lights, big amusement parks, rows of door-to-door shops selling overpriced souvenirs to tourists, or twenty-four-hour wedding chapels. It was a place where you could really get away, catering to the person who wanted peace and quiet, not big attractions and the big crowds that accompany them.

He continued up the hill and soon had the lodge in sight. It was a large, two-story building, with natural rock siding on the outside. The front sported oversized windows and a huge walkout deck supported by large rock pillars.

Cody turned right, swinging the pickup into the parking lot that lay behind the building. He turned the truck off and stepped outside. After gathering his luggage, which consisted of a small suitcase and a large backpack containing all his camping and fishing gear, he began to make his way to the lodge entrance.

He struggled to make it through the double-glass doors with the luggage. He felt the exhaustion, caused by the hours on the road, coursing through his body. He also felt every bit of the weight in his backpack, which must have been at least fifty pounds, despite his purchase of only the latest, most lightweight camping *necessities*. He began to wonder if he had over-packed.

The automatic doors opened as he approached, and he stepped into the lodge's Great Room. He spotted the registration desk to his right, and he struggled over to the counter, dragging the backpack and suitcase.

The reservations clerk was a tall young man with a close-cropped haircut dressed in a white button-down shirt and burgundy tie. He looked like he was still in high school, perhaps earning money for an upcoming college semester. The plastic name tag pinned to his shirt told Cody his name was Mark.

"Good evening, sir, can I help you?" Mark asked as Cody rested his arms on the counter.

"Yeah, I have a reservation for tonight," Cody responded, yawning as the clerk began typing in the computer system.

"What's the name on the reservation, sir?" the clerk asked, continuing to stare at the computer screen.

"Cody McAlister."

"All right, just a second." More typing, then the phone rang, interrupting the clerk's work. "Excuse me, sir," he said as he picked up the phone.

Cody let his eyes wander around the room while Mark was on the phone. The Great Room was a large space with polished oak flooring that reflected the light from the large chandelier hanging from the center wooden beam. Several stone columns rose from the floor to the vaulted ceiling above. A large fireplace, with the same type of rockwork as the columns, sat on the end closest to the entrance. The rockwork continued up the entire chimney, all the way through the high ceiling. Several leather couches had been placed in a semi-circle in front of the fireplace, and a wooden table held copies of magazines and a rumpled newspaper. On the opposite end of the room, the wall was almost entirely glass, framing a spectacular view of the mountains. A set of double doors led onto the deck Cody had first observed a few minutes ago while driving up the hill. The sunset had turned the sky above the mountains a brilliant fire-orange color—that view in itself was worth the drive from Atlanta.

"Yes, sir, I'll have someone send up some extra towels and soap," Mark said into the phone before hanging up and turning his attention back to the computer screen.

"Okay, Mr. McAlister, I have you confirmed for a single king-bed lodge room, is that correct?"

"You got it." Cody handed his credit card to the clerk, who quickly ran it through the scanner and handed it back to him.

"Thank you, sir."

The cost of the room was around a hundred bucks a night, which was cheap by Atlanta standards. Mark tore the receipt off the machine and handed Cody a pen. He quickly signed the receipt and pushed it back across the counter toward the clerk, in a hurry to get settled in his room and just crash.

"All right, sir, you'll be in room 205, which is down the hall to your right. Checkout is at eleven in the morning. We offer a full-service restaurant at the end of the hall to your left. It closes at nine tonight but will open again for breakfast at seven in the morning."

The thought of food right now almost made Cody sick. The burger and onion rings he had eaten earlier were still sitting heavy in his stomach.

"Enjoy your stay, sir. Is there anything else I can help you with?"

"I need a ride across the lake to Eagle Creek in the morning," Cody said as he grabbed the room key card and map of the village Mark had put on the counter.

"All right, one moment please." Mark picked up the phone again. "Hey, Frank, it's Mark. I need to set up a shuttle to Eagle Creek in the morning, the name is Cody McAlister." Mark looked at Cody. "What time do you want the ride, Mr. McAlister?"

"I'll be down there at six-thirty in the morning, if that's all right," Cody replied. The sun would be coming up about that time, and he wanted to get started as early as possible.

"Frank, he said he'll be down there at six-thirty in the morning. Will there be someone there to give him a ride?" After a brief pause, Mark said, "Okay, thanks," and hung up the phone. He turned back toward Cody. "You're all set, sir. He said there will be someone down there in the morning waiting for you. Is there anything else you need tonight?"

"No, that should do it. Have a good night," Cody said as he picked up his luggage and began walking down the hall.

"You too," he heard Mark reply as he turned the corner.

Room 205 was five doors down on the right. He slid the card into the lock, turned the handle, and pushed open the door with his foot. He struggled to get the backpack and suitcase through the door, but he finally managed. After searching several seconds with his free hand, he found the light switch on the wall.

The bathroom was on the left, just inside the door. He walked farther into the room, where he found a large king-size bed with nightstands positioned by the headboard on either side. Beyond the bed sat a small table and recliner. The floor was covered with dark green carpet, and the walls were painted an off-white color. It was typical hotel fare, but it was clean, which was the important thing. Cody was a bit of a germaphobe.

He dumped his luggage on the near side of the bed, glad to be rid of the extra weight, then walked to the window and pulled the vertical blinds back. The last bit of daylight was silhouetting the mountaintops in the distance. He turned and emptied his pockets onto the small, round table in front of the window and then almost threw himself into the recliner that was sitting in the corner between the bed and the wall. Sinking back into the soft cushion, he let out a big sigh. He never wanted to get back up—but he knew he had to. He still had to shower and go through the packing list one more time. He definitely didn't want to get five miles into the mountains and realize that he had forgotten something he really needed. He took his shoes off and pulled the handle back on the recliner, stretching his legs out. He decided he would just rest his eyes for a few minutes. He thought about Katie and wished she would call.

His newfound hobby was also what had led him to meet Ms. Katie Ann Richardson. She ran the *Tried and True Fly Shop* with her brother, Collin. Cody had found them in the phone book and then drove over one Saturday morning. It was only a forty-five minute drive from his townhouse, so he had made frequent trips there over the last nine months.

The first time he had walked into the shop, Katie caught

his eye. She was young and attractive, with straight blonde hair that came down to the middle of her back. She had a slender frame, but filled out her blue jeans and tight-fitting blouse very well. She also shared his passion for fly fishing, which was refreshing for him since most of the women he knew were button-up business types.

Before he met Katie, Cody had not dated since the divorce. He had finally gotten up the nerve to ask her out one day while he was in the shop. She seemed a little hesitant at first, but had ultimately accepted.

They had been dating now for about six months, although it had not turned into anything serious yet. They had a standing dinner date for Friday nights, and occasionally they would meet for dinner and a movie at Cody's place during the week.

Katie was the kind of girl that Grandma Missy would have been proud of. She was a Georgia girl, born and bred. All of her immediate family lived within twenty-five miles of each other and remained a close-knit bunch. A woman of simple means, she seemed to have her priorities straight in life. He had especially liked the fact that on their first date she had not even asked what he did for a living. When it finally did come up, she simply replied, "That's nice," and moved on to another subject. It seemed she did not care about how much money he made, and right now, that was the kind of friend he needed.

She had come over to his townhouse on Christmas Day, and after they had exchanged gifts, they cooked Christmas dinner together. It was a simple affair, a small roasted turkey breast, some cornbread stuffing, sweet potatoes, and pecan pie for dessert. After dinner, they had curled up on the couch and watched *It's a Wonderful Life* together. After the movie, Katie had given him a hug and a quick kiss before heading over to her parents' house. It was not an extravagant Christmas by any stretch of the imagination—but it was the best one Cody had experienced in years.

Still, for all they had in common, neither one seemed ready to jump back into a serious relationship yet. Hell, after six months of dating, they still hadn't even had sex. She described herself as an *old-fashioned kind of girl* that did not just crawl into the sack with any man who crossed her path. Cody respected her for that. During one of their dinner conversations, she revealed that she had been widowed two years before at the young age of twenty-seven. Her late husband had been a captain in the Georgia National Guard and was killed in Afghanistan by a roadside bomb. Cody's heart went out to her when she had first opened up and told him. That explained why she seemed so distant at times, afraid of another serious commitment—afraid of getting her heart broken again. Still, the sharing of common tragedies between them—one bitter divorce and one tragic, untimely death—had led to some long talks and many hours of consoling one another. He did his best to support her and reassure her that it is possible to rebuild and move on after life deals you a shitty hand, but he also understood why she would be leery of jumping into another relationship.

Cody really liked Katie. Hell, maybe he was even beginning to fall in love. He just wasn't sure. The fact of the matter was that he was hesitant, too—maybe even more so than Katie. He had been hurt badly by the divorce and did not want to jump headlong into another long-term commitment just yet. Maybe they were an unconventional couple, but so what? He really enjoyed spending time with her, and he thought she felt the same about him.

Cody felt himself falling asleep. The urge to drift off and not move another muscle overpowered him, but then his cell phone rang, and his whole body jerked back into consciousness at once, his heart pounding from the rush of adrenaline. He had almost forgotten about his phone. It had not made a sound all day, a very rare occurrence in his life.

He struggled out of the recliner and walked over to the table where he had left his phone.

He was glad to see it was Katie calling, her picture displayed prominently in the center of the smartphone's screen. He slid his finger across the screen to accept the call, put the phone to his ear, and said, "Hello," trying not to sound too excited to be hearing from her.

"Hey, Cody, how's it going?" Katie said in an upbeat voice.

"Good . . . things are going good. I'm glad you called. It's good to hear from you."

"Did you have a good trip up?" she asked.

"Yeah, I did. It was a good trip . . . not too eventful."

The two chatted for a few minutes about mundane topics before Katie turned the conversation to a more serious topic. "Everything set for tomorrow? You didn't forget anything, did you?" she asked.

"I still have to go over my list and double check, but I think I have everything I need."

"Good. I hope you have a great vacation. Enjoy yourself, Cody . . . you deserve it. Please be careful, though."

Cody noticed a twinge of concern in her voice. "I will, don't worry. Everything will be fine, I promise," he replied, trying to put her at ease.

"Well, have a good time and catch lots of fish. Call me as soon as you get back."

"I will. Thanks for checking on me," he said in a voice meant to project confidence that he really knew what he was getting himself into.

"No problem. I'll talk to you next week." Katie sounded kind of sad that she would not be talking to him for a while, and that made him feel good inside.

"Sounds good. Talk to you later," Cody said with a slight smile on his face. He turned the phone off and grabbed the charger out of the top of his suitcase. He walked into the bathroom, plugged the charger into the power outlet over the sink, and then connected the smartphone.

He undressed and stepped into the shower. The air in the bathroom was chilly, so he adjusted the water temperature until it felt very warm on his skin. The water washed away any chills almost at once, and he loved feeling it flow over his body. This would be the last shower he would have for several days, so he lingered longer than normal, enjoying the steamy heat.

Feeling somewhat revived, he stepped out of the shower and grabbed a towel that was hanging on the nearby rack. He dressed in his pajamas, which consisted of cotton pants and a worn out T-shirt, then returned to the bedroom. He grabbed the television remote and turned it to a news channel, then sat down on the edge of the bed and pulled his backpack close to him.

The pack was a top-of-the-line model he had ordered online for about three hundred bucks. It boasted enough storage space for a week-long trip in the backcountry and had a lightweight internal frame, which made it a perfect choice for his upcoming trip. He pulled his list out of one of the side pockets and began reviewing it, trying to recall packing each item. He just wanted to do a final check over his list to make sure he had not missed anything critical—he did not have the time or energy to unpack and recheck every single item.

After reviewing the list, everything seemed in order. If he had forgotten something, he would just have to live without it. He had plenty of fire-making equipment and enough food to last a week, even though he would only be in the backcountry for four and a half days.

He finished getting ready for bed by brushing his teeth and locking the deadbolt on the door. The alarm clock sitting on the nightstand read ten o'clock—he had hoped to be asleep by now. He set the alarm for five in the morning and turned the television off. He pulled the covers up to his neck and allowed his head to sink down into the pillow. It was nice to finally relax—it had been a very long day. He closed his eyes and drifted off to sleep.

Tomorrow the adventure would begin.

5

Cody awoke to the insistent buzzing of the alarm clock Saturday morning. He felt a sudden urge to hit the snooze button but, instead, forced himself to turn the lamp atop the nightstand on. He reached over and turned the clock off, desperately trying to make the annoying buzzing stop.

He sat up and yawned deeply, stretching his arms above his head. After several seconds of hesitation, he swung his legs off the side of the bed and planted his feet on the carpeted floor. After a few more seconds, he put his hands on his knees and stood up, moving his head in a slow circle and rolling his shoulders to get the blood flowing. He had gotten a good night's sleep but still felt groggy.

He slowly made his way to the bathroom, shaved around his goatee, and brushed his teeth. After using the restroom and washing his hands, he went back to the bed, grabbed the remote, and turned on the television. After some brief channel surfing, he found *The Weather Channel*—he wanted to check the forecast one more time before he left.

The weather still looked good for most of the trip. The five-day forecast that was displayed on the screen said temperatures should be in the upper-seventies during the daytime, with lows in the mid to upper-forties. No rain was forecast until at least Wednesday. *Perfect*, Cody thought. He turned the TV off and got ready to leave.

He dressed in a green T-shirt and a pair of lightweight tan pants that sported large cargo pockets on the side of each leg. He made sure to put on two pairs of thick socks, which would provide extra protection for his feet during the hike. He put his hiking boots on and gathered the rest of his things before hauling the suitcase and backpack out the door.

He made his way out to the Great Room and then to the double glass doors that opened to the parking lot. He inhaled deeply as he stepped outside, drawing in a full breath of the cool mountain air as he walked to his truck. It was invigorating.

He opened the side door and threw his luggage into the back seat. He was glad he had spent the extra money for the extended cab model because it provided more room for his fishing gear, groceries, or whatever else he happened to be carrying. The morning air was chillier than he had expected, so he unzipped his suitcase, pulled out a long-sleeve, button-up shirt, and put it on over his T-shirt.

He shut the truck door and walked back inside the lodge. Mark was gone, and the man now working at the front desk was heavyset, with salt and pepper hair.

"Morning," Cody said as he walked up to the desk and put his room key on the counter.

"Good morning, sir. Checking out?" the clerk asked in a somewhat tired voice.

"Yep," Cody replied.

The clerk looked as though he had been there all night and was fighting to stay awake. He pushed a few buttons on the computer keyboard while squinting at the screen. Cody soon heard the printer come to life, and the clerk produced an invoice, which he slid across the counter.

"All right, sir, that's it. Thanks for staying with us."

"You bet. Thanks," Cody replied as he folded the paperwork and slid it into his front shirt pocket.

He turned from the counter and looked down at his watch—he still had some time to burn before he had to be at the marina. He noticed some pastries and a steaming coffee pot on a table in the center of the room. He walked over and grabbed a danish and a cup of coffee, then made his way to the leather sofa that sat in front of the rock fireplace. He picked up a copy of the morning newspaper that had been placed on the sofa and flipped through the pages while finishing his breakfast. The pastry was the kind that had cream cheese filling in the center—his favorite. He probably should have eaten a piece of fruit instead, but he reminded himself he would need the extra calories today. He finished his last sip of coffee, gave the clerk a quick wave goodbye, and walked out of the lodge toward his truck. As he drove out of the parking lot, he turned the heater on, trying to dispel the chilly morning air.

The marina was only a ten-minute drive from the resort, back across the same curvy road he had driven on his way into the village the night before. He could feel the excitement in the pit of his stomach as he drove toward the lake. He could not wait to start his fishing trip. He planned to stay on Eagle Creek until Wednesday and then spend the rest of his vacation visiting different areas of the Smokies, exploring new trout streams as he went.

Ten minutes later, he pulled his truck up to the permit station at the top of the hill above the marina. Katie had told him not to miss it when she had first helped him plan his trip months ago. He stepped out and walked over to the check-in station. General park rules were posted, along with a large map of the park. He pulled a blank permit out of the wooden box that was mounted on the left side of the sign and began to fill it out. He quickly put down his name, vehicle information, where he was going, and the dates he would be in the park. He looked on the map and located the campsite he was headed to. It was campsite ninety-seven, which Katie referred to as *The Walnuts*. He tore the carbon copy from the back of the form and stuck it in his pants pocket, then slid the original into the slot on the lock box. He grabbed one of the trail maps that were provided and walked back to the truck.

He drove down the steep road that led to the marina and found a parking space on the right side of the road. He backed his truck into the spot and turned the ignition off. He pulled his cell phone out of his pocket, turned it off, and put it in the glove box—he would not need it where he was going. To his delight, there was no cell coverage on Eagle Creek. It would be the first time he had been without the annoying little device at his fingertips for years.

Total solitude.

Cody opened the door and removed his backpack from behind the seat. He made sure that the rod case, which held his fly rod and reel, was securely strapped onto the side of the pack. He locked the truck and heaved the pack onto his back. He adjusted the shoulder straps and hip belts to allow most of the weight of the pack to rest on his hips, not his shoulders. It took him a minute to get his balance and get used to walking with the extra weight. He took a few steps, paused to make sure he still had his balance, and then continued slowly down the steep grade. The first hints of daylight were dancing across the sky, and he could see the lights of the marina shining in the pre-dawn darkness about forty yards away. As he drew closer, he could hear the small waves breaking on the shore, a stiff breeze rippling the surface of the lake. As he stepped onto the marina walkway, the smell of fish reached his nostrils. He was not sure if it was coming from the water or somewhere else, perhaps a nearby cleaning station. Wherever it was coming from, he hoped it was an omen of his future success.

He opened the glass door that led into the store section of the marina. An elderly man behind the counter looked up briefly from his newspaper and coffee before quickly moving his eyes back down to the paper.

"Morning," Cody said, trying to sound as friendly as possible.

"Here awful early, ain't ya?" the man said in a voice that told Cody he was a little irritated at having to be at work so early in the morning.

"Well, I wanted to get an early start," Cody replied as he walked to the counter.

"That's sure as hell right," the man said in a half-irritated, half-jovial voice. He folded the newspaper and set it down on the counter. His gray beard covered much of his lower face, but Cody could tell he had spent many years in the outdoors by his well-weathered forehead and cheeks. He looked to be in his mid-sixties and was a little on the chubby side. He made a slight groan as he got up from his chair. His name tag was now visible, and Cody could see his name was Jesse.

"Sorry," Cody said, trying to sound apologetic, although in reality, he was not sorry at all.

"That's all right, just a little cranky this morning. Where you headed?" Jesse asked.

"Eagle Creek."

"Gonna do some fishing?"

"Yep, fly fishing for trout. Have you heard anybody say how the fishing has been?" Cody asked.

"Well, there were a couple of guys that came out of there 'bout the middle of last week and said they had good luck. Caught several nice uns, too."

"Sounds good. How much do I owe you for the trip across?"

"Fifty bucks for a round-trip."

That was a little more than Cody had expected to pay, but he pulled his credit card from his wallet and pushed it across the counter. Too late to quibble about a few extra dollars now.

While Jesse was completing the credit card purchase, Cody looked around the room. There were racks and shelves full of fishing gear. There was a large corkboard on the right side of the counter, to which dozens of pictures of people holding fish had been pinned. He noticed several pictures of smiling anglers holding smallmouth bass or stringers full of walleye and crappie. On the opposite wall, a largemouth bass, a couple of large crappie, and a musky were mounted on pieces of driftwood. At the opposite end of the room, another glass door led to the long boat slip area.

Below the fish mounts there was a cooler full of soda cans and snacks. He walked over to the cooler and swung the door open. He grabbed a can of soda, and as he walked back toward the cash register, he picked up a candy bar from a nearby shelf. By the time he put the items on the counter, the credit card machine was printing out his receipt.

Jesse handed him the receipt for the boat ride and added up the total for the candy bar and soda. Cody pulled a five out of his wallet, plunked it down on the counter, then stuffed the change Jesse handed him into his pants pocket.

"Ready to go?" Jesse asked.

"Yeah, sure." Cody tried to suppress the excitement he was feeling inside. He did not want to come across as just another stupid tourist.

"Follow me," Jesse said as he walked out the glass door.

Cody followed Jesse onto the aluminum dock, which was long and narrow with boat slips on either side. They passed several bass boats and ski boats on their way down the dock before reaching a large, silver pontoon boat that had *Mountain View Resort* painted on the side in large green letters. As Cody stepped into the boat and found a seat, Jesse untied the dock lines and then went to his position behind the control panel.

After a few unsuccessful attempts, Jesse finally got the motor started and they began to pull away from the dock. Cody opened the soda and took a long drink. The air was crisp and fresh as it blew across his face, and he felt exhilarated to finally be underway.

After a couple of minutes, they had made it out of the cove where the marina floated and onto the main lake channel. The sky was light enough to see clearly now, and Cody could see up and down the channel. Large mountains, covered with the bright green color of the new spring leaves, surrounded the lake on both sides. The ripples that had been on the water when he first arrived had vanished, and the water was now dead calm. The rising sun painted an orange glow across the cloudless sky and reflected it to the water below.

It was the most beautiful sight Cody had ever seen.

Katie had told him that this part of the Smokies remained relatively untouched. The Great Smoky Mountains National Park owned the forest on one side of the lake, while the U.S. Forest Service owned most of the other. This prevented a mass of lakefront homes from popping up along the shore.

It was all Katie had described, and Cody was thrilled. This was not the first time he had been to the Smokies, but it was the first time he had come by himself. He had taken a couple of weekend fishing trips with Katie and her brother that the fly shop offered. They had fished the Davidson and Nantahala Rivers during those trips, but she had recommended Eagle Creek for true solitude. She and Collin had been coming up here since they were kids and, according to her, there was no place like it. The natural beauty of the area was enough in itself to justify the trip, but a few trout on the end of a fly rod was the cherry on top of the proverbial ice cream sundae.

Katie had been apprehensive when Cody first told her

of his plans to spend several days camping in the back-country alone. She had warned him that it was not the best trip for a novice angler to take by himself. The water currents could be strong at times, and surprise spring rainstorms often made the creek impassible. Fishing a smaller creek like this required climbing over large boulders; one slip could leave you with a broken leg—and miles from help. She had offered to go with him, and although he found this very tempting, Cody had decided to go alone and Katie, being her usual supportive self, had understood. That was another thing that he loved about her—she got him. With all his problems and baggage—she got him. He would have loved to spend a couple of weeks with her in the mountains and get to know each other better, but he needed time alone to clear his head after everything that had happened in his life, and Katie knew that.

The main lake channel was fairly narrow, and it only took about two minutes to cross, then they headed up the Eagle Creek arm of the lake. Cody turned around for the first time since they had left the dock and saw Jesse behind the driver's seat, looking doggedly straight ahead, his gray beard blowing in the wind. Cody gave him a slight smile. Jesse smiled back and nodded. "Lookin' for driftwood. Mess a boat motor up somethin' awful," he said.

Cody gave a nod in return, looked forward once more, and watched as the channel made several sharp turns and began to narrow even more as they moved closer to the mouth of the creek. A bald eagle flew out of a tree in front of them and swept low over the water, the white feathers on his head and tail shining in the early morning sunlight. Cody watched it fly off and light on a large pine tree above the water. After a few more minutes, he felt the boat begin to slow.

As they made the final turn, he could see Eagle Creek flowing into the lake. Cody estimated that it was probably about twenty or thirty yards wide at the mouth, and the water level appeared to be good for fishing. Unlike a lot of streams and rivers in the western states, which relied on snowmelt to sustain water levels, this area depended on rain, and lots of it. Fontana Lake received fifty to sixty inches of rain a year, and some of the higher elevations got even more than that.

Jesse aimed the front of the boat toward the bank and let the aluminum pontoons gently slide onto the mud and gravel. It was evident to Cody that this was not the first time Jesse had made this trip.

"All right, here you go. When do you want to be picked up?" Jesse asked as Cody stood up and hoisted his pack onto his back.

"Wednesday afternoon at three o'clock, if that's all right."

"Sounds good. Somebody'll be here waitin' for you," Jesse replied.

Cody took the last drink of the soda and tossed the can into the small trash bin that sat beside the driver's console.

"See ya later, an' you be careful," Jesse said.

"I will. Thanks for the ride over," Cody said as he stepped off the boat and onto the shore.

The two exchanged waves as Jesse shifted the boat into reverse and pulled away from shore. He turned the boat around and headed back toward the marina. Soon, he rounded the corner and was out of sight.

Cody stood alone on the shore.

6

Cody glanced down at his watch. It was almost seven o'clock. He drew in a deep breath and took a minute to look around and get his bearings. He pulled his worn-out baseball cap down on his forehead, put on his sunglasses, and began walking. He had done a quick distance calculation from the map at the check-in station and figured it was about five miles to the campsite from the lakeshore. If he took his time and rested when needed, he should be able to make it in about three hours.

He continued up the trail and soon came to a small footbridge that was laid across the creek. It was made of a single, large log that had been split to allow for a flat walking surface on the top side. There was a wooden railing, hewn out of a small tree, attached to the right side that provided some stability. As he stepped on the log he could feel it bounce slightly, and the handle wobbled when he grasped it. He took his first steps slowly and concentrated on maintaining his balance, which was more difficult with the heavy pack on his back. Halfway across, he almost fell into the flowing waters below but pulled hard on the handle, regained his balance, and kept going. Soon he was across to the other side and planted his feet on solid ground.

The trail was fairly level and he was making good time. He was handling the extra pounds on his back well, too. The mountain laurel and rhododendron bushes were in bloom, their white and pinkish colored flowers scattered among the bright green leaves of the forest. It was so refreshing for him to be up here, among the mountains and streams. To be really alone—away from work and his cell phone and all other modern *conveniences*.

This was a far cry from the concrete jungle he lived in. Even when he was by himself in his townhouse, he never really felt alone. He was always within instant contact, and his cellphone was rarely quiet, even on the weekend. The office could call at any minute and often did, having no respect for his private life. He sometimes felt like a lion at the zoo—confined to a glass and steel cage that people would walk right up to, peering and pointing, little kids taunting him by sticking out their tongues. The lion was powerless, trapped in a man-made enclosure, forced to suffer the daily humiliation of indifferent onlookers. It did not matter how many times the lion roared and charged the glass wall—the gawkers still came, day after day, week after week, month after month, year after year. They knew he was powerless to do anything about it. It was hard to let your mind clear in a situation like that.

But this place was different. Special. Cody had never felt so invigorated and alive as he did now, in the middle of the forest, walking and breathing in the fresh air. Right then and there, he decided he would find a local real estate agent once he returned. It wouldn't have to be anything major, just a small cabin that he could escape to on the weekends, and during summer vacations. He had to do it. The city was killing him. Slowly, something within him was dying. His sense of adventure and love for life were being smothered in the constant noise and insanity that was Atlanta. A smile spread across his face, and he was surprised at how quickly he had made a decision of that magnitude. Still, it was the best feeling he'd had in years, the most peaceful, which told him it was the right decision.

He walked for another forty-five minutes before he stopped at one of the many places where the trail crossed the creek. He decided to take a break. He leaned against the bank and released the clips that were holding his pack on. He slid his shoulders out of the straps and let out a sigh as he felt his muscles relax. He grabbed the water bottle that was clipped to the side of the pack and slowly made his way down to the stream. His leg muscles were already beginning to stiffen.

He filled the water bottle and reinstalled the cap and filter assembly. He had bought it before his trip because it had a built-in purification system that allowed you to drink safely out of almost any water source. Although the mountain stream looked pristine, he knew that clear water did not mean clean water, and he didn't want to take a chance of catching giardia or some other waterborne illness. The prospect of getting the trots five miles into the backcountry did not appeal to him. He took his first drink, and the mountain water, devoid of chlorine, tasted awesome. He sat down and continued to drink for a few minutes while he rested his legs.

The creek had narrowed and was now only about thirty feet wide. Cody looked upstream and noticed a deep pool of water—the kind of place big fish live. He watched for a few minutes and spotted a brown trout eating small insects from the surface. It was working with methodical precision, sucking one bug under and then circling back to its position before catching the next one that was heading toward it. The fish looked to be about eight to nine inches long, which was a good-size trout for this area. Cody had an almost irresistible urge to pull his fly rod out and try to catch it, but he restrained himself. He wanted to make it to the campsite in time to fish before dinner.

Watching the trout feed had only increased his excitement—if that was even possible—and he was anxious to get going again. He refilled his water bottle once more before strapping his backpack on and heading up the trail. Large pines, poplars, oaks, and maples lined the trail on both sides. The air felt warmer on his skin, and bright rays of sunlight were now penetrating the dense forest canopy, lighting the trail ahead of him.

Two and a half hours later, he saw a small wooden sign ahead, and he quickened his steps. It was campsite ninety-seven. Cody smiled, relieved to finally be at his destination. All the creek crossings had slowed him down—only two bridges existed on the entire trail. At the rest of the crossings, he had been forced to wade through the swift water, a difficult task even without the weight of the loaded pack on his back. He was not sure how many times he had crossed the creek—he only knew he had lost count at ten. It had been a longer and more grueling trip than he had anticipated, though he was in decent physical shape.

The campsite was to his left and slightly below the trail. The terrain sloped down gradually, through the campsite and toward the creek. He walked down into the level area and was relieved to see no other campers using the space. He had deliberately picked this time of year to come to the mountains. It was before Memorial Day weekend, when thousands of college students and families with school-age kids in tow would be flocking to the Smokies for their first taste of summer. The Great Smoky Mountains National Park was the most visited park in the country, and it got very crowded during the summer months.

Cody's back and leg muscles were killing him. He lowered the pack to the ground and grabbed his water bottle for a drink. Despite the cool temperatures, his shirt was soaked through with sweat. He sat down on the ground with his legs stretched out and leaned back on the pack, resting his entire body. He took a drink of water and closed his eyes, letting the cool breeze blow across his face. The sound of the creek rushing past just a few yards away bombarded his ears, lulling him into a state of complete relaxation. He almost allowed himself to doze off, but after several minutes, he struggled back to his feet, feeling somewhat rested.

He took a deep breath and stretched his arms out above his head, standing on his toes, to revive his tired body. A fire pit was located about fifteen feet in front of him, surrounded by large rocks. It contained several pieces of charred wood, left over from the last fisherman or hiker who had stayed here, he surmised. A large sawmill blade was leaning on the rocks, and Cody knew it must have been left behind from the logging industry that had thrived in this area prior to the creation of the national park. It looked to be fairly heavy, and he doubted that anyone would have taken the time to carry it up here from the lake. By its darkened and slightly rusted appearance, he could tell it had served hungry fishermen as a makeshift stovetop for many years.

He walked down to the creek, which was now only about twenty feet wide. The cold water spilling out of the mountains cooled the surrounding air, and he could feel a noticeable temperature difference next to the stream. The creek was now forming deep pools at regular intervals— perfect habitat for trout. He refilled his water bottle and splashed some of the cold water on his hot face. He admired the view once more, then turned and walked back to the campsite.

He worked for an hour, setting up his small tent, hanging the lightweight hammock he had brought along for evening relaxation, stringing a piece of cord between two trees to serve as a clothesline, and gathering enough firewood to get him through the night.

When he was finished, Cody stood back and admired his handiwork. He had not set up a campsite since his college days, and although it had taken him twice as long as it should have, he was proud of himself.

He lifted his backpack off the ground and walked over to the steel cable and pulley system that was hanging in the trees about ten yards behind his tent. It was used to raise food items off the ground—and out of reach of a hungry bear—at night and while you were away from camp. He hated to admit it, but he probably would not have known what it was for, except that Katie had told him to be sure and use it. He hoisted the pack fifteen feet off the ground and secured the cable to the side of the tree.

It was finally time to go fishing.

7

He walked down the trail with a spring in his step, even though almost every muscle in his body was still aching from the morning hike. Cody had been looking forward to this for so long, he felt like a seven-year-old on Christmas Eve. He was full of anticipation of the trout he was going to catch. His mind drifted back to his grandfather, who had often said, "Cody, don't count your chickens before they hatch."

He smiled at the memory, cautioning himself not to get overanxious at his expected fishing success. He was, after all, a relative newcomer to fly fishing, and he had a feeling that the wild, native trout that filled these waters had a lesson or two to teach him. He would, no doubt, be humbled a few times.

A sharp hunger pang shot through his abdomen. The cream cheese danish he had eaten for breakfast was the last solid food he had put in his stomach—and a single danish hardly counted as solid food. Remembering the candy bar he had bought at the marina, he reached into his pocket and pulled it out. It was squashed, having not fared so well during the long hike. Still, it was all he had at the moment, and he quickly tore open the wrapper and took a large bite. He continued eating as he walked down the trail, and soon his hunger subsided. He was already looking forward to a hot meal tonight by the campfire.

He stopped at a creek crossing, about a mile downstream from his camp. The trees were full and bright green, their large canopies blocking out a good portion of the sunlight on this clear day. Numerous small bushes were in bloom, and the ground was dotted with patches of brilliantly colored wildflowers. The creek made the air around him feel moisture-laden, like being in a rainforest.

He unzipped a pocket of the fishing vest he was wearing and pulled out one of his fly boxes. He had spent around two hundred dollars at Katie's store last week on flies alone. He had learned that fly fishing could be an expensive hobby, but he was glad he had found something that he enjoyed so much, so he didn't mind spending the money. He had stocked his boxes, four in all, with scores of flies that worked especially well on these smaller streams. The boxes contained Blue Winged Olives, Thunderheads, Royal Wulffs, Tennessee Wulffs, Palmers, and a multitude of other patterns, in different sizes and styles. He opened the lid and looked over the mass of fur and feathers. He debated which pattern to select with the same care he prepared a closing argument for the courtroom. He finally decided on a size sixteen Female Adams. It was a mix of grayish-white and brown-colored hackles up front, with gray and white hackle tips serving as the wings. The body was made from a gray synthetic fiber with a small yellow section at the rear imitating an egg sack. Pheasant feathers had been used to create the orange and black tail. He quickly tied it onto the end of his line and then applied a small amount of a special gel to the fly, which would help it float on top of the fast moving water.

He glanced down at his watch and thought of Katie. She had given it to him for Christmas last year, and he rarely took it off. It was a solid, stainless steel model made for scuba diving. He had never gone scuba diving in his entire life, and doubted he ever would, but the fact that Katie had given it to him made it special. It was just after twelve o'clock, which meant he still had plenty of afternoon fishing ahead of him. He saw a trout rise and take an insect in the pool just upstream. He crouched down and began to ease forward.

Cody moved with all the precision of a lion stalking its prey. Wild trout were easily spooked, and a sudden movement, or even a shadow moving across the surface of the water, could send them swimming for cover.

Just as he got within casting distance, he saw the trout rise again. A more beautiful sight he had never seen—the bright red stripe of the rainbow trout clearly visible as it smacked the surface of the water, engulfing another small insect.

Cody's heart began to race. He struggled to calm his nerves as he prepared to make his first cast. Just as he got the fly line into the air, the trout rose to the surface again. Cody had spent hours practicing in his small backyard but was now full of self-doubt and wondered if he would be able to weave the fly line through the narrow opening in the trees above his head.

He held his breath as he made several false casts, releasing a small amount of line each time. When he had enough line out to reach the upper end of the pool, he let the Female Adams land on the water about ten feet upstream of the rainbow. His heart was beating even faster now as the fly rode the current toward the feeding trout. He took special care not to let the fly drag unnaturally on the surface—that was a sure sign to any trout that the fly was not what it seemed to be.

He felt his palms begin to sweat as the fly got within two feet of the big rainbow. This was it. The moment of truth. He watched as the fish began to rise slowly from the stream bed, then in a flash, the trout hit his fly with a ferocity that surprised Cody. He jerked the rod tip upward, expecting the fish to head upstream fighting with all it had. Instead, he felt the line go slack and saw the fly get hung high in a tree about ten yards downstream.

"Shit!" Cody exclaimed, the frustration inside of him boiling over into a screamed expletive that no one else was around to hear. He had missed the fish. He had set the hook too soon, before the trout had taken it into its mouth. The result was a tangled mess in the tree instead of a fish on the end of his line. His zeal had gotten the best of him, and he was kicking himself inside.

He walked downstream to where the fly was hung and tugged on the line several times, trying to free the hook from the branches above. He heard a loud snap and was left holding the line in his hand, his fly still stuck in the tree, out of reach. He found a nearby moss-covered rock and took a seat while he tied on another Female Adams. He was happy he had purchased several flies of the same pattern. Even with all his backyard practice, he was still learning to cast, and with all the tree limbs overhanging Eagle Creek, he was bound to lose a few more flies.

After a few minutes, he was ready to fish again. He advanced upstream once more and was surprised to see the trout he had just missed still rising and taking insects from the surface. He moved the rod upward and lifted the fly line into the air. As he cast, he could hear Katie's voice in his head.

Ten and two o'clock, Cody. Don't move your wrist so much. Cast with your forearm . . . let the rod do most of the work.

He could feel the rod bending as it worked to propel the fly line forward. With one final push, the line streaked through the air, and Cody dropped the rod tip, allowing the line to land softly on the water's surface. The fly hit its mark, landing upstream of the trout, and Cody watched as it drifted close to the big rainbow. Suddenly, the water below the fly exploded, and he saw the distinctive red stripe flash as the fish jumped out of the water. This time he waited a split second to make sure the fish had taken the fly into its mouth, and then he lifted the rod tip quickly to set the hook. This time he was not disappointed—he felt the weight of the fish on the end of the line as it began to fight. It made a quick dash upstream, headed for deeper water, and Cody let some of the fly line slide through his fingertips so his line would not break. The rainbow leapt from the water and into the air, trying to rid itself of the hook.

As the fish began to tire, Cody started pulling the fly line in with his left hand, bringing the trout closer to him. The fish jumped two more times as Cody moved upstream into the pool and tried to steer the fish toward the shore. A few seconds later, he was able to pull the rainbow onto a large rock near the creek bank.

"Yes!" Cody exclaimed as he pounced on the trout with his left hand, making sure it had no chance to escape back into the water. Once he knew the situation was under control, he relaxed a little. The whole event from start to finish had taken less than a minute, but it was the most fun he had experienced in a long time.

It was amazing how such a small fish could upset a man so.

Cody opened the top of the creel that hung on his side and slid the trout inside. He knew some fly fishermen thought it almost a sin to keep a trout for food, but he did not share that opinion. He usually released the fish he caught to fight another day, and on the rare occasion he did keep some to eat, he never took more than he would use.

He was anxious to try a wild mountain trout. It would be a first for him. Katie had told him that a trout born and raised in a mountain stream instead of in a hatchery was some of the finest dinner fare around and would rival the best meals served in Atlanta's ritziest restaurants.

He intended to find out firsthand tonight.

Another deep pool lay ahead and he moved forward, again careful not to spook the fish. He began casting and managed to place the dry fly near the head of the hole. The swift current carried it uneventfully back to Cody. He pulled in the slack and cast once more, again aiming for the bubbling water at the opposite end of the pool. He watched the fly drift toward him for a second time, and Cody saw a shadow streak out from under a large boulder on the left side of the creek. The trout shattered the calm of the water, and he set the hook for a second time in a matter of minutes. The fish fought hard and jumped a couple of times, trying to throw the hook. The constant pulling and shaking of the fish on the end of the line created a vibration in the graphite rod, which was transferred through the cork handle, and directly into Cody's palm. He loved it. He soon had the fish pulled over to the shore. It was another beautiful rainbow, about nine inches in length. He quickly unhooked it and put it in the creel with the other. He was ecstatic. He had only been fishing for fifteen or twenty minutes and already had two nice trout for dinner. The limit was five per day, but he would only keep what he could eat, which was three or four at most.

Cody fished for another hour with no more keepers. He had missed several and caught three more that were under the minimum size limit of seven inches set by the Park Service. He continued upstream and soon came to another deep, dark hole with a beautiful, small waterfall spilling into it at the head, which created a foaming white mass that churned like a huge washing machine. He stopped for several seconds and admired the awesome beauty of this place tucked so far back in the mountains—a world away from all the hardships and disappointments of his *real* life.

Cody pulled his cap down tight against his forehead and adjusted the sunglasses on his face. He made long forward casts of the line, trying to reach the upper-end of the hole. His first attempt landed short, just missing a low-hanging tree limb. As the fly floated back toward him, he was ready for another violent strike at any second, but it never came. He tried again, pushing his fly rod to the limit, and this time, his fly landed just shy of the foaming whitewater.

Three seconds later, another trout struck his fly, and Cody set the hook with the precision of an experienced angler. He was getting better. The trout surged toward the creek bottom and pulled hard. There were no acrobatic jumps, just hard, steady pressure with intermittent forceful runs upstream, peeling line from the reel. The reel made a high-pitched screaming sound as the fish continued to pull out line at an impressive pace. Just when Cody thought he had won, that the fish was worn out, it made another hard run and dove deep back into the pool of water. He had not been able to get a good look at the fish, but the deep bend in his rod told him it was a nice one.

After about a two-minute fight, Cody moved farther up into the pool, sensing the fish had almost been conquered. It made one final surge, then surfaced, exhausted. He could now see it was a beautiful brown trout, about eleven or twelve inches long. The colors on this native fish were spectacular, much deeper and brighter than those seen on hatchery fish. The back and sides were brown in color, transitioning to almost yellow on the belly. Profuse black and red spots, encircled with a light bluish ring, ran the entire length of the fish.

After such a great fight, Cody could not bring himself to put this fish in his creel—Katie said the smaller ones were better to eat, anyway. He carefully placed it back in the water, while supporting the underside of the fish with his right hand. Katie had taught him to cradle a fish that had fought hard before releasing it. It allowed the fish to regain some strength before swimming away into the current. After a few seconds, the trout started to move in his hand, and he knew it was ready to go. He watched as it kicked its tail and returned to the shadowy depths of the pool.

Cody straightened up, let out a big breath, and smiled. This was why he had come to these mountains. This one experience had just made his entire trip. His hands were still shaking from all the excitement, so he sat down on a nearby rock to regain his composure. After a few minutes, he got up and was ready to fish again—he still needed at least one more trout for dinner tonight.

Two hours later, he had three nice-sized trout in his creel, which was plenty for him. He saw his campsite just upstream on his right. He looked down at his watch, surprised to see it was already four o'clock. He could have fished longer, but his stomach was starting to growl, and he was anxious to cook his dinner and then relax around the campfire. He climbed out of the creek and walked back to his campsite.

After cleaning and prepping the fish for dinner, he removed his soaking wet clothes and changed into a pair of jogging pants and a long-sleeved pullover shirt. The warm cotton felt good on his chilled flesh. Dry socks and a pair of tennis shoes completed his camp wardrobe.

He thought about what to have with the fish and decided on some instant mashed potatoes and mixed vegetables. Most of the food he had brought along with him was either dehydrated or vacuum packed so it would not need refrigeration. He took out a pot to boil some water on his small propane camp stove. While cooking on a campfire was more traditional, Katie had suggested he buy one of the small stoves made especially for backpacking. They were small, lightweight, and allowed you to cook your meal more quickly. Plus, if you had a stove, you could still cook your meal if rain had moved through and soaked all the firewood.

When the water came to a boil, he poured in the instant

potatoes and vegetables. He stirred them a few minutes and then set them aside.

He coated the trout in a mixture of flour and cornmeal, along with some special spices that Katie had added. He placed a small frying pan on the stove burner and added a spoonful of bacon grease he had brought from his own kitchen. Shortening was okay for some things, but nothing could beat bacon grease for real flavor. Once the grease was hot enough, he placed the three trout in the pan. The pan came alive with the popping and hissing sounds of fresh meat hitting the hot oil. Soon, wonderful smells were wafting through the forest, and Cody could feel his belly growl. He had not eaten much all day, despite all the work he had done, and the tempting aroma from the food only intensified his hunger pangs. After cooking the trout for about two or three minutes on each side, he scooped them out of the pan with a spatula and placed them on his plate, along with the vegetables and mashed potatoes.

As he took his first bite, he was amazed at how good everything tasted. Even the instant mashed potatoes tasted great. Cody realized that more than likely he was experiencing what old-timers had known for years—everything tastes better in the backcountry. The fish was white, flaky, and flavorful. He had eaten fish at many five-star restaurants during his career as an attorney, but none had ever tasted so good. He savored every bite. This was not the kind of meal you rushed through.

Before he knew it, Cody had finished the entire meal. All the mashed potatoes, vegetables, and the three trout were gone. His stomach felt like it was about to pop. He leaned back and let out a sigh of pure contentment. After he had recovered enough from the large meal, he got up from the small campstool and cleaned up. Then he returned the small propane stove, dishes, and utensils to his pack.

After his chores were done, Cody decided to try to build a fire. It had been years since he had built a campfire, and he wondered if he still had the knack. He went to his pack and retrieved a cigarette lighter. Then he arranged some of the small kindling he had gathered earlier into a teepee shape in the center of the fire ring. He placed a few dry leaves in the center of the teepee, then struck the lighter and touched the flame to the leaves. He blew a couple of breaths across the growing fire, and soon the kindling was ablaze. He placed a few pieces of larger wood onto the fire and then returned to his campstool. As the flames began to lick at the dry wood, he stretched out his hands and warmed them. Daylight was fast retreating, and the warmth provided by the fire helped to drive away the chill in the air—like being wrapped in a heavy wool blanket snuggled next to his grandmother as a child. He missed being a kid on his grandparents' farm—so many good memories. And so good to feel totally safe and protected. As the fire flickered, it cast dancing shadows on the surrounding forest—just like the fireplace in Grandma Missy's house.

Cody reached into his pack and retrieved a large cigar. It was one of the vices that he had not managed to give up yet—the booze had been hard enough. The cigar was a top-of-the-line Cuban, and he ran his nose down the length of it, taking in the sweet tobacco aroma. Don, one of his lawyer friends from Miami, had given them to him. The two had been roommates in college, and he was one of the few classmates Cody still stayed in touch with. Cody would ship him fresh Georgia peaches every year and, on occasion, some homemade jellies and jams—Don loved them. In exchange he would ship Cody a box of Cubans from time to time. Cody never asked how or where Don acquired them—he figured it was probably better left unsaid.

He lit the cigar and took several deep draws from it. He knew it was bad for him, but he rarely smoked. And what was life without a vice or two, anyway? Dull and boring, that's what. He loved the smell of the tobacco more than anything. He drew the smoke into his mouth for a few seconds and then exhaled. It was too strong for him to pull into his lungs. He had tried that one time and thought he was going to cough his guts out.

As he looked into the fire and enjoyed his cigar, he reflected on the day's journey. It had been long and hard, but well worth it. The complications of his everyday life had not crossed his mind once, and his soul felt refreshed already. By the time the fire was starting to die down, he had finished the cigar. He flipped what was left of it into the fire pit and stood up to stretch. His eyelids felt heavy and he decided to call it a day. He carried the backpack to the pulley system and raised it high into the air for the night. Then he made his way to the tent, unrolled his sleeping bag, and tucked himself in. He allowed the relaxation to flow through his body, and before he knew it, he was drifting off to sleep.

Tomorrow would be another adventure—one hopefully filled with lots of big trout.

8

At eight o'clock Monday morning, Katie Richardson sat at a corner booth of Cook's Country Diner. It was one of her favorite places to eat. She loved the fact that this place served real food—none of that fu-fu, granola shit they served at the coffee house across the street. She was a bacon and eggs kind of girl, and she often stopped in to have breakfast at Cook's on her way to work. The fly shop she and Collin owned was located just a half-mile down the road.

The interior of the diner made her feel like she had walked straight into an episode of *Happy Days*. It was decorated in classic fifties style, with a chrome-trimmed bar along the back wall. Chrome stools with red cushions were pushed up to the counter. Behind the bar were the typical diner accoutrements—two large coffee makers, an ice cream cooler filled with everything from vanilla to Katie's favorite, peanut butter and chocolate, and a stainless steel milkshake machine that was on its last leg after decades of use. A checkerboard pattern of white and black tiles covered the entire floor, and an old-fashioned jukebox that played vinyl 45s sat in the far corner. Gladys Knight's soulful voice was echoing throughout the eatery—Katie could not remember the name of the song, but she was humming along anyway.

Behind the bar, Judy and Carlie were busy pouring coffee and grabbing the trays of food that Harold slid through the open window connecting the kitchen and dining areas. Each time he completed a customer's order, he would tap a silver bell and announce, "Order up!" Harold was an older black gentleman who had worked at Cook's for twenty-five years. He always greeted Katie with a wink and a smile whenever she walked through the door. He was a consummate ladies' man, and Katie always played along with his innocent flirting by giving him a wink in return.

Katie was sitting opposite the bar in a booth with thick red cushions and a black, chrome-lined table that matched the bar's design. She stared out the large picture window that overlooked Highway 78 and then turned her gaze back to the front door, two booths down from her, watching it with anticipation.

Today she was meeting her best friend, Tiffany Colson, for breakfast. It was sort of a standing date between the two of them—every Monday morning right here at Cook's. It helped get the week started off on the right foot, they told each other. Tiffany worked a couple of miles from the diner as a dental hygienist. Katie had known her since the seventh grade, when Tiffany's parents had moved to Georgia from Texas. On Tiffany's second day of school, she was sitting in the lunch room at a table all alone. Sarah Farnswarth and Rebecca Johnson—of the *too cool for school crowd*—were whispering and pointing in Tiffany's direction. Tiffany had tried to ignore them and keep her head down, eating her food in silence. When Sarah flung a french fry across the table and hit Tiffany square in the forehead, a chorus of giggles and whispers had ensued. Katie saw what was going on from her seat across the room and got up, yelling at Sarah and Rebecca to stop it. She hurled a few curse words—words that she would not have dared let her mother hear come out of her mouth—their way, too. Then she went over and sat down across from Tiffany. They had been best friends ever since.

Katie smiled and gave a slight wave when she saw Tiffany come through the door. An old-fashioned steel bell hanging above the front door announced her arrival to the rest of the patrons. Several turned to see who had just entered, then went back to their meals. Heads always turned when Tiffany walked by—she was absolutely stunning, with long auburn hair and emerald-green eyes. She looked more like someone on the cover of a modeling magazine than a dental hygienist.

Katie remembered that the guys in high school had been crazy about Tiffany, but she had not reciprocated. There had been the occasional boyfriend, but never anything too serious. Even after she finished her dental hygienist degree, she had not settled down. She said she enjoyed the single life, although Katie knew she was anything but wild. She was a lot like Katie—humble, down-to-earth, and she enjoyed a movie and pizza at home on Friday night more than hitting the clubs around Atlanta.

Tiffany approached the table and Katie stood and gave her a hug. "How have you been, Tiff? Have a good weekend?" Katie released her embrace and scooted back into the booth.

"Yeah, had a great weekend. Didn't do much, just hung around the house and watched TV. Bet I slept till eleven yesterday morning. Charlie finally jumped on the bed and licked my face until I rolled over and got up." Tiffany laughed and the thought of it made Katie smile. Charlie was a mutt Tiffany had rescued from a local animal shelter when he was just a puppy. "How 'bout you?" Tiffany asked.

"It was pretty good. Didn't do much either. I went in and worked at the shop until around noon on Saturday, and then went home and cleaned the house. Just hung around yesterday and vegged." Katie looked up at Judy, who was approaching with a coffee pot in her hand.

"Mornin', girls," Judy said as she set two coffee mugs on the table.

Katie picked her mug up and held it for Judy to fill. "Thanks, Judy," she said as she took her first sip. The coffee was so hot it almost burnt her lips. It was good, though, and she felt the heat run down the back of her throat, warming her body as it went. "Coffee's good this morning."

"Just made a fresh pot when I seen you come in a little bit ago. I know how you like your coffee . . . hot and black. Just like your men, right?" Judy smiled and nodded over her right shoulder.

Katie almost spit out the coffee in her mouth trying not to laugh. "So you know about Harold and me, huh?" she said with a sly smile that feigned secrecy.

"Oh yeah, the whole diner's been talkin' bout it. Harold can't keep a secret, you should know that, darlin'!"

Katie leaned her head around Judy and caught Harold's eye as he stuck his head through the food window behind the bar. "Harold, you promised that was just between the two of us!"

"Sorry, sweetie. Gotta keep my reputation up!" Harold smiled and winked as he pulled his head back through the window.

Katie laughed and returned his smile with one of her own. He was such a nice man. Just joking around with him made it worth stopping at the diner. Katie looked at Tiffany and then back up at Judy. Both looked like they were about to burst with laughter. "Stop it, girls. A lady has her secrets, you know," she said in a mysterious tone that made all three give in to the laughter that was building inside them.

"Whatcha girls havin' to eat this morning?" Judy asked as she pulled her receipt pad from the front pocket of her apron and a pen from over her right ear.

Katie, starving, was the first to respond. "I'll have two eggs, scrambled with cheese, bacon, whole wheat toast, and grits. Oh, and don't forget the butter for the grits."

"I hate you," Tiffany said as she cut her eyes at Katie to show her disapproval. "I'll just have a bowl of oatmeal and some toast. Oh, and Judy, hold the butter on mine, please," she said with emphasis, again looking at Katie. Tiffany was always complaining that she had to work out constantly just to keep her weight down, while Katie could eat whatever she wanted.

"All right, girls, I'll put this in and it should be out in a few minutes. Let me know if you need anything else." Judy spun around and headed back behind the counter. Katie heard her yell the order to Harold before she started refilling the coffee cups of the customers sitting at the counter.

"So how have you been, Katie?" Tiffany asked as she raised her coffee cup to her lips.

"Okay, I guess. Trying to stay busy. Had a few guide trips down at the shop last week, so I got a chance to get some fishing in."

"That sounds fun. You always were the tomboy. I remember back in high school how you used to hang right with the boys, no matter what the sport was—deer hunting, fishing, whatever. Remember that old Chevy truck you fixed up and would race down Main Street on Friday nights? What was it you called that old heap? Storm? Thunder?"

"Lightning. Yeah . . . fun times. Remember that jackass Steve Lyons?"

"How could I forget? His family had more money than the rest of the county combined, and he never let anyone forget it," Tiffany replied.

"This one time, during senior year, his parents bought him a brand new Dodge pickup . . . V8 engine, 350 horsepower . . . I mean, this thing was sweet, right down to the chrome wheels. Well, he had been talking trash all week at school about how he could beat anything else on the street. By Friday, I'd had enough. I caught up with him in town at a red light. I pulled up along the driver's side of his pickup and rolled down my window. I asked him if he was ready to put his money where his mouth was, and I think I also insulted his manhood or something. Anyway, he was pissed by then and cussed me out pretty good. I revved my engine and waited for the light to turn green. When it did, me and old Lightning took off like a bat out of hell. I looked in my rearview mirror and saw poor Steve and his precious truck jerking down the road like somebody having an epileptic seizure. The truck had a manual transmission, and I guess he was still learning to drive a stick-shift. He had popped the clutch too fast and just jerked and lurched his way through the intersection. There were plenty of kids standing around on the street that saw it go down, and they teased him something awful. He never brought up the topic of his expensive truck again at school or anywhere else, at least not to me." Katie finished the story with a devilish grin and another drink of coffee.

"That's awesome!" Tiffany said, laughing. "I never heard that one. Wonder whatever happened to old Steve?"

"Last I heard, he was working at his dad's dealership detailing cars. Guess he tried college for a while, but his folks got tired of paying to support his frat parties when all they got in return were failing grades. He played Mr. Big in high school, but I knew he would never amount to much."

By this time Judy had returned with their food and set it down in front of them. "Let me know if you two need anything else. Enjoy."

"Thanks, Judy," they both said in unison.

Katie was the first to dig in, taking a large bite of the

scrambled eggs. They were so good, but she tried not to let it show on her face. She didn't want to rub in the fact that Tiffany was eating oatmeal and toast.

"So really, Katie, how have you been doing?" Tiffany said as she put a small amount of sugar in her oatmeal and stirred it with a spoon. Her look told Katie to cut the bullshit and come clean.

"Oh, that?" Katie said, her voice taking a more serious tone.

"Yeah, that . . . I know what today is. It can't be easy for you. Talk to me, please? I'm your best friend, for goodness sake. But I feel like when it comes to this, you just shut me out," Tiffany said, a worried look on her face.

"Okay, I guess." Katie paused and took another drink of coffee. "I try not to think about it much. Most of the time, it's just easier not to talk about it. Just trying to move on with my life, the best I can, you know?" She paused again and looked out the window. "But dammit . . . I miss him so much sometimes."

The question Tiffany had asked took Katie back in time two years. She had been washing dishes in her kitchen on a beautiful spring day when she looked out the window and saw the sight she never wanted to see—prayed she would never see—two men from the Georgia National Guard walking up to her front door in their dress uniforms. Katie knew it could mean only one thing, and she had almost fainted. She grabbed the edge of the sink to steady herself and tried to catch her breath. Her head was swimming, and she immediately broke out in a cold sweat. By the time the doorbell rang, she was barely hanging on. She managed to get herself to the door and opened it to see the two men standing on her porch with sadness and regret in their eyes. "Nooo! Nooooo! Nooooooo!" she had screamed at the top of her lungs. "Go away . . . go away now! I don't want to hear it! No! Get the hell off my porch!"

"Ma'am, we regret to inform you that your husband, Captain Eric Richardson—" Those were the last words Katie remembered. She had just gone into shock after that. The neighbors across the street had seen what was happening and called her mother. A doctor had called in a prescription for a sedative, so she spent the next couple of days in a drug-induced stupor.

Once the funeral was over and things settled down a bit, she was told the full story of what had happened to Eric. He had been in command of a convoy team moving supplies to a remote base. He was in the lead vehicle, which had not surprised Katie at all—Eric always led from the front. When his Humvee was hit by the IED, it had thrown Eric's vehicle twenty feet into the air. Everyone in the truck had died.

The drugs the doctor had prescribed had initially numbed her mind to the reality of what had happened, but in time, she was forced to come to terms with the loss of her husband. The one she wanted to spend the rest of her life with. The one she had intended to have children with. The one she would share a home with—they had planned on building a house in the country once he returned from his deployment. All those dreams had died with Eric in a fireball along a dusty, barren road in Afghanistan.

Katie took some comfort in the fact that he had not died alone. She thought that would be almost the worst thing that could happen to someone. To die alone, with no one there to comfort you or hold your hand as you drew your last breath. Eric had died with his men. He had loved every one of them. She often heard him speak of how great they were and how much responsibility he felt to get them all home safely. She knew if Eric had survived, he would have felt tremendous guilt about the loss of his men. He would have wanted to die with them. She didn't understand it, but she had come to accept it.

At first, she had withdrawn from everyone around

her—from all the family and friends that she so desperately needed at the time. Most people didn't understand. They would look at her with sad eyes, not knowing what to say, and then just turn away. She felt like she was alone in the world, without any support. She had allowed only her mother and Tiffany to see her in the two months that followed Eric's death. Most days she had not even gotten out of bed, spending all of her waking hours crying herself back to sleep.

Finally, her mother had come to her one morning and, in a not-so-subtle tone, let her know it was time to get up and get moving again. With her mother and Tiffany's help, she had begun to recover, slowly letting people back into her life. It was hard at first, but something that had to be done. She could not lie in bed the rest of her life and cry about what could have been. Still, there was one secret that she had kept to herself through the whole ordeal. The one area she had never allowed anyone into—one secret she had kept just for herself and Eric—until today. Today she was going to tell Tiffany and remove the last barrier to her recovery.

Katie turned her gaze away from the window and back to her plate when she heard Tiffany offering words of encouragement. That was one of the things Katie loved about her. Ever since that first day in the lunchroom, they had been there for each other, no matter what. She knew Eric's death had been incredibly tough on Tiffany, too, but she had stuck by her—like a real friend is supposed to.

Tiffany was almost halfway finished with her oatmeal when Katie looked up from her food and said, "Tiff, I need to tell you something."

Tiffany looked up and met Katie's eyes. "Okay, shoot," she said.

Katie took a deep breath, followed by a sip of the hot coffee, before continuing. "You remember that Eric was killed only one week after returning to Afghanistan from his two weeks of R&R leave?"

"Sure, I do. You two were so happy during his leave."

Tears started to well in Katie's eyes.

"Sorry, Katie, I didn't mean to upset you." Tiffany put her hand across the table to comfort her.

"No, it's fine. I'm just still emotional about the whole thing, I guess."

"Well, I think anyone would understand that. You've been through a lot . . . more than most people ever go through in their entire lives."

Katie gave a half-hearted smile and, after a moment, continued. "There is something about the weeks after Eric's death that I never shared with anyone—you and Mom included. I couldn't bring myself to tell anyone. It was just too painful."

"It's okay . . . you know you can tell me anything. I'll always be here for you," Tiffany said as she gave Katie's hand a comforting squeeze.

Katie looked down into her coffee cup, sadness and tension in her voice. "A week after Eric's funeral . . . I found out I was pregnant."

"What?" Tiffany asked, stunned.

Katie could hear the shock in Tiffany's voice. "Yeah, I had a feeling for a few days that I was, but I wasn't sure. So one night while you and Mom were still staying at the house with me, I waited until both of you were asleep and I sneaked out of the house. I walked to the convenience store down the street and bought a pregnancy test. It was positive. I was so happy . . . it was like God was giving me a gift from Eric. A piece of him that would remain with me forever, you know? I kept it a secret because I was in shock, and I just didn't know what to do. I still wasn't thinking straight, and I didn't know how people would react. I was afraid some people would start rumors that it wasn't Eric's baby. It was, of course. No doubt about that—Eric was the only man I had ever been with, and I would have never cheated on him. Not in a million years."

"Of course, I know that," Tiffany replied. "I still don't understand why you didn't tell me. You know I would have believed you, been there for you."

"Yeah, I know you would have. I was just scared, Tiff, that's all. It's not that I didn't trust you . . . please understand that."

"Sure, I understand. So what happened?"

"Well, after you and Mom left, I made an appointment with the doctor. I needed to be sure that this was real, needed a doctor to tell me I was pregnant. I was almost positive I was, so I had stopped taking the sedatives immediately after I took the pregnancy test because I was afraid they would hurt the baby. But I still needed confirmation. After the blood test came back at the doctor's office, he walks in and says, 'Congratulations, Mrs. Richardson, you are, indeed, pregnant.' I broke down right there in his office. I just sobbed and sobbed and couldn't stop. The poor doctor wasn't sure what to think. I finally calmed down enough to tell him what had been going on. He was so nice and told me if there was anything he could do to help me to just let him know. I left his office excited, scared, and sad. Excited for the new life that was growing inside me, scared of the new responsibility that lay ahead of me as a single mother . . . and sad that Eric wasn't going to be there to experience the awesome journey with me."

By this time, tears were pouring down Katie's face, and she looked up to see Tiffany's eyes welling up too. Tiffany pulled two napkins from the silver dispenser on the table and handed one to Katie before using the other one to dab her own eyes.

"Thanks," Katie said. "So anyway, everything was fine for the first several weeks. I was starting to get excited about the baby and planning for the nursery. I knew I wasn't going to be able to keep it a secret much longer because I would start to show in a few more weeks. And besides that, I was dying to tell you guys. Then one night I was lying in bed watching TV when I started cramping really bad."

"Oh no," Tiffany interrupted.

"I went into the bathroom and I was bleeding. That scared the shit out of me, so I drove myself to the emergency room. The whole way to the hospital I was begging, pleading with God to save the baby. Anyway, I made it to the emergency room and walked to the nurse's station. By that time, I was almost doubled over, the cramps were so bad. I told them what was going on, and they took me back immediately. My doctor was out of town, so another doctor, someone I had never met, came in to examine me and do an ultrasound. He completed his tests and told me matter-of-factly that there was nothing they could do, that I had lost the baby. The guy was so cold. It didn't seem to bother him at all, and that just made it a thousand times worse. No one I trusted and loved even knew I was pregnant, and the doctor acted like he didn't give a shit. That pissed me off, but mostly it made me feel alone and scared. I knew he probably saw this kind of thing all the time, but he could have at least shown a little sympathy."

Tears were now flowing freely down both Tiffany and Katie's faces, streaking their make-up. Neither of them said anything for a minute or two, they just let the tears fall. Katie turned her head and looked out the window again. People were walking and driving and shopping and just carrying on with their lives, not knowing the pain she was feeling. At that moment, the world outside Cook's Diner—the one just beyond the panes of glass lining the wall—felt cold and distant. A shadow in the darkest cave of the earth. An iceberg floating in the farthest reaches of the sea. Visible, but not within reach.

It scared her.

After a couple of minutes, Katie regained her composure and continued, "The next day, after everything was finished at the hospital, I drove myself home and then lay in the bed, crying for a week. That was the time that I wouldn't even let you and Mom come over. You guys just thought I was still dealing with Eric's death, and I let you keep thinking that. I was all alone. It was my own fault for not telling you and Mom, but I sure as hell wasn't going to say anything after the miscarriage. I was afraid people would think I was just making up a story to get more attention. I know it's stupid, but that's the way I felt . . . in addition to being a failure. I mean, I couldn't even carry Eric's baby without failing."

"You know that's not the truth, though, right?"

"Yeah, I know. I was just in a very bad place then. I thought it was my fault . . . something I had done . . . or not done. Then I was mad at God. Still am a little, I guess. I didn't understand why He would let me get pregnant, take Eric from me, and then take the baby, too. To me, it just seemed cruel. I just couldn't bring myself to understand, and frankly, I still don't. You see all the people in the world who don't deserve children, who mistreat them or are drug addicts or whatever, and it makes you wonder why they get to have kids and God took mine. It would have been more humane to never have gotten pregnant than to get pregnant and miscarry.

"But over the next several months, I slowly came to realize there was nothing I could do to bring either the baby or Eric back. They were both gone forever. I still kept it to myself . . . it was just too painful to tell anyone. I buried it deep down in the most inner part of myself, afraid to let anyone see my pain and vulnerability. I tried to forget the whole ordeal, but that didn't work." She paused and took a deep breath. "But now, I'm ready to move on. And I knew I had to tell you if I was ever going to be able to move forward with my life."

"I don't know what to say, Katie." Tiffany wiped the tears from her eyes before she continued. "Except that I am so, so sorry. I wish you would have come to me earlier so I could have been there for you, like I always have been." She continued to wipe tears from her eyes.

"I know. You've always been my closest friend, and I don't know what I would do without you."

"Same here," Tiffany responded. "Have you told your mother yet?"

Katie sighed. "No, not yet. I will . . . someday. When the time is right, I'll tell her. Not now, though. I'm just glad I finally told you. I feel like such a weight has been lifted off my shoulders."

"How about Cody? Does he know?"

"No. I haven't had the courage to tell anyone until just a few minutes ago, when I told you," Katie replied.

"You should tell him. I know he'll understand. He's been through a lot, too. You two could help each other work through things." Tiffany paused and looked at Katie, rubbing her hand. "He really cares for you, Katie. I can see it in his eyes when he's with you."

"I know he does, and I care a lot about him, too. I'm just not sure if I'm ready to open myself up like that again."

"You will. When it's time . . . you will," Tiffany said.

Katie looked up and saw Judy heading back to the table with their check in her hand. Katie quickly rubbed her eyes with her shirt sleeve, but she doubted it did much good. She could tell Judy knew something was up, but like a well-experienced waitress, knew when to keep her distance.

"I'll take that, Judy. Thank you." Tiffany took the check from Judy's hands.

"Thanks, girls, and come back soon," Judy said as she turned and left the table, but not before giving both of them a sympathetic smile.

"You don't need to do that, I was going to get your breakfast today. You got the last one, remember?" Katie protested as Tiffany pulled her credit card out of her wallet.

"Nonsense. You can get the next one . . . and the one after that . . . and the one after that."

Katie laughed. "Thanks, Tiff . . . for everything."

"I'm always here for you, and don't you forget that. You ever need to talk, just give me a call, day or night."

"Thank you, Tiff. That means the world to me."

Trying to lighten the mood, Tiffany asked, "What is Cody up to this week?"

A smile came across Katie's face. "He's actually up in Western North Carolina, doing some fly fishing in the Smokies."

"That's cool. When is he supposed to be back?"

"Couple of weeks. He's camping up in the park until Wednesday, then he's going to drive around and fish some of the larger rivers, I think. I have to admit, I was a little worried about him hiking and fishing in the mountains by himself. I even offered to go with him, but he insisted he wanted to do it alone."

"Well, I'm sure he'll be fine. What do you say we get out of here?" Tiffany asked.

They both slid out of the booth and headed toward the cash register. After paying for the meal, they walked outside and gave each other a goodbye hug.

Katie walked to her car and opened the driver's door. She paused before climbing behind the wheel and watched as Tiffany backed out of her parking spot, then turned right onto Highway 78. It was a beautiful spring day in Georgia—mild temperatures and a slight breeze. Katie felt like her life was back on track. She looked into the deep blue sky and felt the wind on her cheeks. Everything was going to be okay. She smiled and drew a deep breath into her lungs.

Then overwhelming anxiety slammed into her like a lightning bolt. She was overcome with a feeling that something was terribly wrong—or about to be. Her stomach twisted into a knot, and her heart began to race. She needed to get away. She hurriedly sat down in the driver's seat, but before closing the door, she glanced back at the clear cobalt sky once more.

And somehow she knew—without a doubt, she knew.

Storm clouds were coming.

9

Monday afternoon was warm and peaceful on Eagle Creek. Cody was resting in his hammock with his head propped up on a small pillow. The pillow was made for backpacking, and it was not nearly as comfortable as the pillow he slept on back in Atlanta, but it would do. The hammock was not especially roomy, either, but like the pillow, it would do when you were miles away from civilization.

When the sun had risen this morning and awakened him in the tent, he had decided to spend most of the day resting. Over the last couple of days, he had learned that fishing could be hard work. His muscles ached, and he was just plain tired. So he stayed in his sleeping bag for an extra hour, enjoying the relaxation.

Yesterday had been another excellent day of fishing. He had walked down the trail a couple of miles and fished back upstream toward his campsite. He had probably caught twenty to thirty fish, but he stopped counting after fifteen or so. A lot of the fish were not keepers, as was to be expected on a small mountain stream, but he caught several nice ones and had kept four of them for dinner. After stuffing himself for the second day in a row, he had crawled into his sleeping bag and passed out.

It was now two o'clock in the afternoon, and Cody was fighting off the urge to nod off again. He had fallen asleep in the hammock a couple of times already, sleeping for twenty or thirty minutes at a time. He turned the page of the Dean Koontz paperback he was reading. He really wanted to finish the chapter, but his eyelids felt like they were made out of lead. A warm breeze blew across his face, and he decided to stop fighting the drowsiness he so desperately wanted to give in to. He nodded off again, the paperback resting on his chest.

When he awoke ninety minutes later, Cody stretched his arms above his head and let out a big yawn. He looked at his watch and was surprised he had slept for so long. He still had to make dinner and plan out tomorrow's fishing trip, so he decided he'd better get up and get moving. Tuesday would be his last full day of fishing on Eagle Creek. He was due back at the lakeshore on Wednesday at three o'clock in the afternoon to catch his ride back with Jesse.

He rolled out of the hammock, stretched his back out for a few seconds, and then walked over to the wire harness that held his pack in the air. Once he had lowered the pack, he removed the remaining packages of food and tried to decide what to have for dinner. There would be no fish tonight, so he would have to improvise.

After a few minutes, he decided on a package of dehydrated spaghetti and meatballs and a couple of rolls that had been squashed almost beyond recognition by something heavy in his pack. It wasn't much, but it would do for tonight. He had not eaten lunch after a late breakfast, and his stomach was beginning to rumble.

He walked over to the fire ring and set up his small stove, then grabbed a pot and went down to the creek to fill it with water. He put the pot on the small flame and allowed the water to boil for a few minutes in order to kill any waterborne bacteria. Then he poured it into the bag of spaghetti and meatballs and resealed the package to rehydrate the food. After a few minutes, he grabbed a fork and ate the meal right out of the package. It filled the hole in his gut, but that was about the extent of it. It was good—but not great.

After dinner, he decided another fire was in order and gathered some wood from the pile he had accumulated over the past three days. He had a nice-sized fire going in no time and sat close to enjoy the warmth it provided. He reached into his backpack and retrieved the trail map he had gotten at the check-in station Saturday morning.

He spread it out on the ground next to the fire and began to study it. He found his current location, campsite ninety-seven, tracing the line that designated the trail with his index finger. Upstream from the campsite, the trail followed Eagle Creek for a couple more miles before leaving the creek and veering off to the northwest, making a sharp climb up the mountain and then intersecting the Appalachian Trail along the Tennessee and North Carolina border. So far he had fished only downstream of his campsite. He decided for his final day, he would venture above the campsite and see what the fishing was like farther upstream. With the terrain becoming steeper, as it appeared on the map, the change in elevation should offer plenty of deep pools of water for big fish to hide. He doubted this section of the creek received much fishing pressure. Heck, he had been here almost three full days and hadn't seen another soul.

After finalizing his plans for the next day, Cody returned the map to the backpack and withdrew one of the Cubans from another pocket. He lit the cigar, leaned back against a giant oak, and relaxed. He took a deep pull from the fat cigar and let the tobacco smoke linger in his mouth a few seconds before exhaling.

Twilight was now upon Eagle Creek, and darkness was not far behind. He took another pull from the cigar and stared at the cherry glowing brilliantly at the end. His thoughts drifted to Katie. He missed her. He loved being up in the mountains—he had finally found the solitude he had been so desperately seeking—but he could not deny that he missed her. He would love for her to be here with him now. In this moment, he regretted discouraging her coming with him. He wished he could hear her voice, even if just on the phone. When he got back to his cell phone on Wednesday, he would call her first thing.

What did this longing for her mean?

He wasn't sure. He was still hesitant to open up again after being so badly wounded by the divorce—he guessed most people would be. He would focus on his and Katie's relationship once he got out of the mountains and returned to Atlanta. But right now, he needed this time to just let his soul heal, time away from everything but nature.

For now, there was more fishing to be done, and he focused his mind on the next day's trip upstream. He dreamed of a twenty-inch brown trout. Although unlikely, anything was possible.

And possibilities were what dreams were made of.

10

Cody awoke Tuesday morning just as streaks of daylight were beginning to permeate the forest canopy, casting shadows inside the tent. He rolled onto his side once, then twice, trying to stretch his legs within the confines of the sleeping bag. For a moment, he thought he was back in his apartment with the familiar city sounds of Atlanta and the smell of his coffee maker that was set to brew automatically at five o'clock every morning. As he opened his eyes, reality was a welcome intrusion.

Sitting up, he yawned and stretched his arms high over his head. This was his last full day on Eagle Creek, and he did not want to lose a minute of it by being lazy and sleeping in. This would be his last chance for a hot breakfast as well. Tomorrow he would rise early and pack for the return trip. He planned to fish some more on his way back to the lake, so he would just eat a granola bar or something quick on his hike out in order to save time.

Cody pulled on the sweatpants and long-sleeved shirt he had been wearing while hanging out at camp. They were slightly damp from the humid night air and chilled his skin as he slipped them on. After three days without a shower, they were starting to get a funk about them, too. He unzipped the tent and crawled out, lowered his pack, and collected everything he needed for breakfast. He decided dehydrated bacon and eggs were on the menu. Yum. As much as he loved being in the mountains, he was looking forward to a nice steak tomorrow night once he returned to civilization.

Breakfast was ready in less than fifteen minutes. Cody slowly sipped a cup of instant coffee as he ate.

After breakfast, he gathered together the things he would need for the fishing trip and packed a lunch for himself, which consisted of some tuna, a pack of cheese and peanut butter crackers, and a Snickers candy bar.

He had noticed several cream-colored insects flying near the water yesterday and began searching through his fly cases to see if he had anything that would mimic the insects. Fly fishermen called this process *matching the hatch*. It was a critical skill to have, especially when fish were finicky and feeding on a specific type of insect. Sometimes they were not finicky and would eat almost anything you tied on the end of your line, but often they were very selective.

After looking over his fly collection for a couple of minutes, he decided on a size sixteen Pale Morning Dun. Its light cream body, combined with the bluish hackles and wings, were the closest match in his fly case to the insects he had seen. Confident in his selection, he deftly tied the new fly onto the end of his line.

The preparations complete, he walked over once more to the tent to ensure it was zipped up. He wasn't worried about thieves—he still had not seen another person up here—but he wanted to keep insects out of his sleeping area. The tent secured, he walked up to the trail and then paused to look back, feeling a sense of pride. In three short days he had turned what had been just a clearing in the woods to a functioning residence. There was his tent, the clothesline he had hung between two trees, his hammock swinging in the breeze, his cooking area, and other small things scattered around the camp. He thought the place looked downright homey. Pleased with what he had accomplished, he turned and started following the trail upstream.

As Cody walked along the trail, he noticed the forest felt alive with activity. He stopped to listen for a moment, and the wilderness seemed to explode into an orchestra of natural sounds. The birds were singing, a squirrel was barking in a nearby hickory tree, the wind was rustling the brilliant green leaves of the trees, and in the background, the sound of Eagle Creek dancing down the mountain melded all the sounds together. There was something about the mountains and streams that got in a man's blood, and once it was present, there was no satisfying it apart from giving in and indulging yourself wholeheartedly. Cody didn't—and he probably never would—fully understand it. But that was just fine with him, because he felt a jubilance just being here that was almost unexplainable.

He had traveled up the trail a few hundred yards from his camp when he came to another spot where the trail crossed the creek. This seemed like a good place to start, so he slowly waded into the water and prepared his fly rod to begin fishing. The sides of the creek were overgrown with tree branches and rhododendron bushes, making it apparent that not too many people ventured this far up the creek to fish.

As he moved into the first deep pool, the water slowly rose until he was waist deep. The fierce cold almost took his breath away when it reached his groin. His respirations were coming fast and furious as his body tried to compensate for the sudden temperature change. He took a few deep breaths as his lower extremities became acclimated to the water. Katie had told him that the mountain waters ran cold all year, even during the hot summer months, and he definitely believed her.

He began fishing but became frustrated by the tight

casting space caused by the thick vegetation which had overgrown the creek. His line got stuck in tree limbs multiple times during the first half-hour of fishing, but soon he figured out a better way to cast within the tight quarters. He let out about a rod-length of line and, while holding the rod in his right hand, pulled the line tight with his left until the rod tip bent slightly. Then he released the fly in his left hand. The fly shot forward, like an arrow from a bow, and traveled underneath the low hanging limbs. After several times of trying this technique, he became rather good at it and was soon expertly placing the fly into the tight spots.

Cody didn't even get a strike in the first couple of holes, but when he waded into the third and lobbed his fly to the head of the pool, a fish swam out from under a rock and sucked the fly under the water. He set the hook and let out a small shout of satisfaction. He allowed the fish to play itself out on the end of the line and had it landed in less than a minute. It was only about five inches in length, hardly a trophy, but when Cody realized what he had caught, he could hardly contain his excitement. It was a native brook trout. Katie had told him all about these fish, which were usually found at the higher elevations of mountain streams, but he had never actually seen one. The locals called them speckled trout or simply *specks*. There had been efforts over the past several years to save this sub-species of brook trout that lived within the Smokies. They were the only true native trout in the mountains. The rainbow and brown trout that dominated most of the streams were both brought into the mountains years ago in an effort to increase fishing opportunities for anglers.

The *speck* was an absolutely beautiful fish, sporting a fire red belly and fins. The leading edges of the fins were painted a bright white, which made the redness on the fish's underside even more impressive. The red changed to a golden color, then green, then almost black as it moved up the side of the fish to its back. The sides were mottled with brilliant red spots encircled by blue halos, and along its back was an intricate design which resembled a maze. Cody turned the fish over in his hands, admiring its beauty, before placing it gently back in the water and watching it swim back to the rock from which it had ambushed the fly.

He fished another couple of hours, catching several more brook trout and a few rainbows. Only three had been large enough to legally keep, but he had decided to release all his fish today. He intended to fish all day, and he doubted he would feel like cooking a big dinner once he got back to camp. He would just opt for another quick meal of dehydrated spaghetti and meatballs, instead. It wasn't great food by any stretch of the imagination, but it was quick, hot, and filling.

At around noon, Cody found a large, moss-covered boulder on the left side of the creek and removed his fishing vest. It had been an awesome morning on the water, and he hadn't thought about food once, but now his stomach started to growl. He removed his lunch and water bottle from the large compartment on the back of the vest. He ate slowly, sitting on the boulder and enjoying the scenery—a far cry from the stress-filled business lunches he was accustomed to. He dreaded going back to Atlanta.

After he finished lunch, he rolled onto his back, stretched out his legs on the rock, and stared into the sky. A thin layer of cirrus clouds now painted the sky milky-white. It had been perfect weather over the last several days, with crystal-clear, blue skies, warm temperatures, and light winds. Cody knew a layer of cirrus clouds could indicate an approaching frontal system, but he was not worried. The weather forecast he had checked prior to leaving the lodge on Saturday indicated no rain until at least Wednesday, and this type of cloud usually indicated the system was still twenty-four to forty-eight hours away. By then he would be back in a cozy hotel room.

The thick moss on the rock's surface padded his back, and he contemplated staying there all afternoon and enjoying a nice long nap. He decided to keep fishing instead. He could sleep once the trip was over.

Cody looked upstream and headed to the next hole. He made a few casts before hanging the fly in a nearby tree. As he turned around to get the fly loose, he almost pissed himself. A large black bear was standing along the shore just downstream.

Cody froze.

What am I supposed to do? Stay still? Scream? Run? I can't remember. Shit! Think, Cody, think.

The bear swung its large head toward its left shoulder, then the right, and then let out a low, guttural growl.

What does that mean? I don't know. I'm screwed. No gun. No bear spray. Nothing to defend myself—

By this time, Cody was in a full-blown panic. His breathing had become rapid and shallow. Beads of sweat popped out on his forehead, and his hands were almost dripping with the salty liquid. His mouth became dry as he struggled to swallow. He tried to remember what he should do in a situation like this but couldn't. He cursed himself again for not being prepared—but it was too late now.

He wondered if the bear had been stalking him, or if their paths had just happened to cross by chance. Maybe it had smelled his lunch or was just protecting a cub? But he didn't see a cub anywhere. Whatever the reason, it didn't matter now—he and the bear were here in this place, at this particular time together—a mere fifteen or twenty yards apart. Nothing was going to change that unless he acted—and acted fast. He had to figure a way out of this.

As the bear shook its head again, Cody found himself looking directly into its eyes. *Dammit, don't do that! You are not supposed to look them in the eyes. They see it as a challenge or something.* He quickly dropped his gaze and focused on some large rocks in the stream just to the left of the bear. He tried to clear the cobwebs in his mind by talking himself through the problem. *Get it together, Cody . . . you better calm down and figure this out real quick, or this is not going to end well for you.*

The bear looked huge, probably pushing three hundred and fifty pounds. It was standing its ground, but not advancing toward him either, which he took as a good sign.

Rocks! I'm supposed to bang rocks together! He remembered reading somewhere that if confronted by a bear, you should bang rocks or pans or anything that would make a loud noise together. And wave your arms in order to appear larger, speak loudly, and of course, avoid eye contact. *Well, I've already screwed that one up.*

He began to lower his body, careful not to make any sudden movements, while at the same time keeping his eyes on the bear. After gently placing his fly rod on the boulder he was standing on, he submerged his hands into the water to grab a couple of large rocks.

The bear made another head-shaking movement, accompanied by the same low growling sound.

Cody froze. After a few seconds, he decided it was safe to move again and quickly found two rocks, each about the size of a softball, under the water. As he began to pull them up, the one in his right hand became stuck as the other rocks around it shifted. In that split-second, he allowed his concentration to shift. He moved his eyes down to the water instead of looking forward toward the bear—just for a second—but a second was all it took. When he looked back up, the bear was charging him.

"Shit! Noooo! Stop!" he screamed. He was still crouched down, so he tried to quickly lift himself back up. The bear was making large strides, and the water was splashing around violently with each step the beast made toward Cody.

Cody managed to stand up, but he didn't know what else to do except try to run. He began to turn his body away from the bear, quickly scanning the area, hoping to find a weapon or something—anything—that would help him survive. It was hopeless, though. There was no time. Just as he completed the turn, positioning his back to the bear, he felt the impact.

He was suddenly thrown forward, the blow to his back causing a violent whipping motion of his head. The breath was immediately knocked out of him, and he found himself face down in the same pool of water where, just a minute ago, he had been trying to catch a fish. He felt one of the bear's huge front paws pressing firmly into the small of his back, trapping him under the water.

It's trying to drown me! Oh no! I'm going to die . . . I can't die here. Not now. No!

Cody felt his lungs begin to burn with an ever-growing intensity. He was struggling not to give in to the urge to open his mouth and take a breath. That would mean certain death. He tried to remain calm, but the panic was surging through him like a white-hot bolt of electricity. He was trapped, pinned solidly against the stream bed. The weight of the bear on his back felt like a truck had rolled on top of him. He dug frantically with his hand, searching for anything that would allow him to gain some leverage. The fire in his lungs increased. This was it. He couldn't take another second. The periphery of his vision began to blacken.

Then, in a flash, he saw Katie's face in his mind's eye. Why, he didn't know. It was just there . . . and then gone.

I'm not going to give in and just die. Get your ass out of this water, Cody!

Now!

Suddenly, the bear shifted its paw to the right side of his back, and Cody took the opportunity to roll quickly to his left. He burst through the water's surface, inhaling air like a jet engine, the burning in his lungs almost unbearable. His heart was racing so fast it felt like the next beat would tear it from his chest.

He was now face to face with the bear again. It took a swipe at his left thigh, and Cody felt the claws cut deep into his flesh. He watched as his blood began to stream into the water, turning it a light crimson color. He screamed.

The bear thrust forward and hit him in the chest this time, knocking Cody's feet out from under him and sending him flying backward into the water once more. He quickly regained his footing, determined the bear would not pin him underwater for a second time. He stepped toward the shoreline on his right, frantically grabbing at clumps of grass and tree limbs, trying to pull himself out of the water, but they just broke off in his hands. Then he felt the bear's mouth clamp down on his left arm, just below the shoulder.

"Aagghhh! No . . . stop! Please! STOP! HELP!" he screamed, although he knew that no one was coming to help him. "Please God, help me!"

His cries for help only seemed to encourage the bear in its relentless attack. His body began to thrash wildly through the air, causing every muscle and tendon to strain under the pressure. Cody thought for sure that his limbs were about to be ripped off. The bear released its grip on his shoulder, dropping him back into the water, but quickly grabbed him again near the small of his back. Then Cody felt himself being carried downstream. As his body was flung about, he could feel his flesh tearing with every stride the bear made, but he was helpless to stop it.

Things were beginning to blur, and he was afraid he was going to pass out. He could not let that happen. He had to stay conscious—that was his only chance of survival. He felt the bear turn sharply to the right, and soon it was dragging him through the forest. His head smacked against a tree, and he momentarily blacked out. When he came to, he cupped his arms around his head to protect it from the tree limbs that were rushing by. Everything was a blur. His mouth was flooded with the coppery taste of his own blood. He spit and saw a large amount of the red liquid fall to the ground.

Without warning, the bear stopped and flung Cody away. Cody sailed through the air and smacked into a large tree. He was sure he felt his back break. He slumped to the forest floor and curled into the fetal position, trying to protect himself from the onslaught that he knew was sure to come.

Within seconds, the bear was atop him again. Clawing, biting, trying to get at Cody's face and head, which he still had wrapped tightly with his arms. He could feel every rake of the claws and bite of the teeth. He screamed in pain constantly, but the bear kept up its attack.

Play dead! Play dead! The thought came to Cody in a rush, from somewhere within the recesses of his subconscious mind. *Something he had heard as a kid from his grandfather, perhaps?* Instantly, he allowed his body to go limp, tried to slow his breathing, and stopped screaming. He bit his bottom lip to keep the screams from involuntarily escaping his mouth. He kept his arms around his face and head, unwilling to cede that modest protection to the beast.

Within an excruciatingly long minute, the ferocity of the attack slowed, and Cody could hear the bear's breathing calm. Its hot, putrid breath assaulted Cody's nostrils and he almost vomited. He managed to keep his stomach contents down and then noticed that the bear had stopped clawing and biting him. Now, it was using its wet nose and large head to push Cody along the ground.

Keep your eyes closed. No sign of life.

The bear kept nudging him, intermittently making grunting sounds, trying to solicit some sign of life out of him, but Cody kept silent. He could feel each breath the bear took against his skin. After a couple of minutes, Cody heard the bear begin to walk off.

Don't do anything, stay still!

He remained in his limp, fetal position for several more minutes, until he was sure the bear was gone. The attack was over, but he remained silent, afraid the bear was still close enough to hear him and would come back to finish the job. He was bleeding profusely, but at least he had survived—for now, anyway.

Thank you, God. Thank you.

It felt like an eternity since he had first seen the bear, but in reality, the whole encounter couldn't have lasted more than five minutes. He began to whimper and cry with pain.

Then everything went black.

11

Darkness. Complete and utter darkness.
Cody's world was shrouded in black; not even a sliver of light reached his eyes.

I'm dead. I must be . . . I have to be. Where is the white light I'm supposed to move toward?

Suddenly, all of his nerves came alive at once, as if jolted from a long sleep, and an intense rush of agonizing pain flowed through his body. He screamed out, his voice echoing off the trees in the forest.

Damn, I hurt. I should have died . . . at least the pain would be over.

It was the most intense pain he had ever felt. He was lying motionless on his back. His lower back felt like someone had beaten him with a baseball bat. He remembered getting flung against the tree during the attack and believing his back had been broken. His head was swimming, and his memory hazy, so it was amazing he could remember anything at all. If his back really had been broken and he was paralyzed . . . well, that would not be good news at all. He hesitated, part of him not wanting to find out, but he finally made himself try to wiggle his toes. They worked. He let out a sigh of relief. He may have cracked a few vertebrate, but his spinal cord was intact, for which he was very grateful.

He was still blind, the blackness surrounding him, smothering him. He gingerly moved his right hand up to his eyes.

Please God, don't let my eyes be gone.

He was afraid to touch his face. Afraid of what he would find—or to put it more accurately—what he would find missing. Nevertheless, he had to see if he could clear his vision. Once his fingertips touched his eyelids, he was relieved to find his eyeballs were still intact. His left eye, however, was forced shut by an intense amount of swelling. Since there was nothing he could do about that, he moved on to his right eye. There was a small amount of swelling around it, but nothing like the severity of the left eye. He rubbed it slightly, being careful not to cause more damage. It was crusted over with a substance that Cody could only surmise was dried blood. He rubbed it a little more vigorously and the eyelid sprang open.

Good. I can still see.

It was pitch dark, with the exception of the little bit of moonlight that was streaking through the forest canopy. Cody didn't know how long he had been unconscious.

He tried to bring his left arm near his face to look at his watch, but his shoulder was so sore he could only manage to lift it a few inches. He brought his right hand, which seemed to be in fairly good condition, up to his face in order to assess the damage. He was having difficulty breathing through his nose, and the crooked shape he felt with his fingers told him it was broken. He blew his nose sharply, trying to clear it. A large clot of blood flew out and splattered on the ground beside him. *That hurt like hell.* Then fresh blood began to flow freely. He tilted his head back and pinched his nostrils together to try and stop the bleeding. That was when he felt the top of his scalp fall backward. Hesitating, he reached toward the top of his head, hoping that what he thought had just happened was only a figment of his imagination. But once his hand reached the top of his head, the worst was proven true. The bear had made such a large laceration in his scalp that the first five or six inches of skin and hair were peeled back and now rested on the back of his head. He felt a sudden sickness in his stomach and rolled onto his side just in time to vomit.

Once he finished emptying what little was left in his stomach, he steeled himself and grabbed the piece of scalp, then pulled it forward, back into place. He looked around for something to clean the wound, but the only water he had was what was left in his water bottle and that was in the back of his fishing vest. He had no idea where that was now. "Dammit," he whispered. He felt around his legs for anything he could use. Every inch he moved sent rivers of pain flowing through his body. Even something as simple as drawing a breath brought intense discomfort. He finally noticed that his right pant leg was torn from his ankle to just above his knee. He bent forward, grabbed the fabric, and was able to rip a section free, but he had only one good hand to help secure the bandage. His left arm still lay limp on the ground next to him.

He looked around, trying to construct some kind of plan. Then he saw a large pine tree standing about ten feet behind him. He began dragging himself along the ground, using his right forearm and elbow for leverage. Every inch he moved brought labored breathing and grunts of pain. He had to bite his lower lip, just as he had during the attack, to keep from screaming. Once he reached the tree, he managed to rest his head against the trunk. He then twisted the piece of torn clothing into a rope and placed it on top of his scalp. He used the tree to hold the fabric against the right side of his face, while he wrapped the other end around the left, before tying the makeshift bandage under his chin. The journey of only ten feet to the tree had left him feeling completely drained. He slumped to the fallen pine needles carpeting the ground.

He felt very thirsty too, but with his water bottle gone, he was out of luck. He could hear the creek flowing in the distance, although he was not sure in which direction or how far away it was, and he wasn't about to go dragging himself through the forest in the middle of the night without knowing precisely where he was going. The way his luck had been running, he would crawl straight into the bear's den.

His left leg felt like it was broken just below the knee. He couldn't be sure in the dark, he felt no bone protruding, but it was swollen and bent at an unnatural angle. He would take a closer look at it in the morning.

He proceeded to check the rest of his body for injuries as best he could. Everything else seemed to be intact, but he must have bled profusely—his clothes were covered in blood. He was weak, nauseous, and felt like he was on the verge of passing out again. He hurried the inspection of his body, checking for anything major before he lost consciousness again. He found no wounds that were still bleeding heavily, most had clotted, and the others were just seeping a small amount of blood.

His whole body was tender and sore, so when he pressed on his abdomen to check for possible internal injuries, it didn't tell him anything. His mouth felt like cotton, but he managed to cough up a little saliva and spit into his palm. Shifting his hand out from the tree branches, he let the faint moonlight strike his palm. He saw no bright red or frothy blood. That was a good sign. It meant, more likely than not, his lungs were okay. Of course, he could have missed something. It was dark and he was barely hanging on to reality, but the rest would have to wait until morning.

He pulled himself around to the backside of the tree and curled into a fetal position. If the bear came back, he wanted to be hidden as much as possible. He knew that thought was a delusion—the bear would have no trouble finding him if it wanted to. *Hell, it could probably smell me a good half-mile away.* There was nothing he could do about that, though. The only thing he could do now was try to get some rest and, as his grandmother used to tell him, hopefully things would look better in the morning.

If he made it to the morning.

12

Jesse pushed the throttle of the pontoon boat forward as he turned left, out of the cove where the marina was located, and began to cross the main channel of Fontana Lake. He glanced down at his watch. He was early for the three o'clock pickup on Eagle Creek, but things had been slow at the marina, as they usually were during the middle of the week, and he had left early. He usually tried to arrive at least a few minutes early anyway. Ninety percent of the time, the people he was supposed to meet would be waiting for him and, in many cases, would have been waiting for quite a while. The fact was, after spending several days in the backcountry, most people were ready to get back to civilization and take a hot shower.

He really couldn't complain about getting an hour away from work and taking a boat ride across the lake. It was hardly what most people would consider rough duty. He enjoyed being on the water, but he loved the mountains surrounding the lake even more. Their simple yet complex beauty never ceased to amaze him. He was not what people would call a philosopher by any stretch of the imagination, and he wasn't a regular churchgoer either, but being on this lake, surrounded by the mountains and everything they contained, always made him feel closer to God.

Fifteen minutes later, he pulled the boat onto the shore at the mouth of Eagle Creek. He stepped out and tied the bow line to a large rock on shore to prevent the boat from drifting away while he waited. He returned to the back of the boat and picked up his fishing rod. He baited the hook with a minnow and cast it out the back of the boat. If he caught something, great. If not, that was okay, too.

Jessie really wasn't supposed to be fishing while he was on the job, but he didn't see any harm in it. He still had at least thirty minutes to wait for Mr. McAlister, and the way he looked at it, he might as well have some fun in the interim. He never was one to waste an opportunity to fish. He set the rod down and stretched out on the bench seat that ran along the left side of the boat. Then he pulled his hat down over his eyes and waited for either Mr. McAlister or a smallmouth bass to show up. Either way, he was sure that one or the other would wake him up in a few minutes.

After a short nap, he was awakened by the sound of an approaching boat. He rose from his seat and saw a couple of fishermen stop the boat on a long point a hundred yards away. He gave a friendly wave and then got up to check his fishing pole. Nothing.

He looked down at his watch and was surprised to see that it was three o'clock already. He reeled in his line and placed the pole back behind the driver's seat. Scanning the shore, Jesse saw no sign of Mr. McAlister—or anyone else, for that matter. It was unusual for there not to be at least one group of campers down at the mouth of the creek, especially at this time of year. It was a popular spot, but today the campsite stood empty.

Jesse sat back down in his seat behind the steering wheel and waited.

Thirty minutes later, he was growing frustrated and impatient. He needed to be back at the marina by four o'clock for a scheduled boat rental. It was not unusual for clients to not show up. Often they would come out a day or two early and catch a ride with a local fisherman or walk the Lakeshore Trail back to Fontana Dam, where they could catch a ride from a passing motorist. That option meant several more miles of walking, but it sometimes happened.

What pissed Jesse off the most was that folks seldom called to cancel their pickup. To him, it was just common courtesy, but today's generation often did not think of the inconvenience to others—they just did what they wanted and to hell with everyone else. It was one of the many things wrong with modern society in general. At least, that was the way he saw it.

He stepped on the bank and untied the rope, then started the outboard motor and began pulling the boat away from shore. If he hurried, he would be back at the marina on time, with a few minutes to spare.

Twenty minutes later, he pulled the pontoon into the boat slip at the marina and secured it to the dock. As he made his way toward the building, he saw two people approaching from the parking lot. He unlocked the door and welcomed them inside.

By the time he finished filling out the boat rental paperwork and the two customers were on their way, Jesse had completely forgotten about the camper who failed to show for his scheduled pickup.

13

Cody awoke to the warmth of the sun on his face. He was still under the pine tree he had crawled to the previous night, although, at some point, he had shifted from the fetal position and was now lying flat on his back. The soreness felt ten times worse than it had before he had passed out. He could barely manage to move at all, and what movement was possible caused shooting pains throughout his body.

He looked down at his legs. The right one was in fairly decent shape, although the pant leg had been removed and was now tied around his head, holding his scalp in place. His left leg was much worse. He had checked it during the night and could not tell if it was broken. He pulled at the fabric around it and managed to rip it loose. Now, he could tell it was definitely broken. The swelling below his knee had increased and was now two or three times the normal size. The unnatural shape his leg exhibited removed all doubt that it was a severe break. The skin around the break had turned a deep purple and was extremely sore to the touch. If the bone had broken the skin, the risk of infection would increase. He examined the area carefully and saw no sign of protruding bone, which was one of the few things he had going for him at the moment.

His left shoulder still felt horrible. He hoped it was just dislocated, but feared it was shattered. He wasn't sure. He could find a couple of trees growing close together, jam his forearm between them, and try to set it. He had seen this done on a movie once, but things in movies seldom played out as well in real life. He wasn't sure he could perform the procedure correctly and didn't even want to consider the horrible pain that would accompany it—especially if he didn't succeed. So instead, he decided to use the pant leg he had just torn off to make a sling. Maybe that would suffice for a while.

He looked for something he could use to rip the fabric into smaller sections. He spotted a sharp piece of wood protruding about six inches from the tree trunk, where a limb had broken off. He picked up the piece of fabric and forced it onto the broken limb, then, using his right arm and his body weight to pull the fabric toward the ground, he managed to tear what used to be one leg on a sixty-dollar pair of fishing pants into two separate pieces. Using his right hand, he tied two ends together and tightened the knot by using his teeth to hold the fabric while at the same time pulling with his one good hand. He tied the loose ends together and tightened a second knot in the same manner. When he was finished, he had crafted a circle from the fabric, which he slipped over his head and then placed his left arm into the cradle of cloth. He used his right hand to reach behind his neck and adjust the sling to the position that offered the most comfort. His left shoulder still hurt something awful, but at least the sling took the weight of his arm and provided some minor relief.

He was disheartened to find that his watch had been torn off during the attack. He would have to improvise. He looked into the sky, the bit he could see through the mass of tree limbs above him, and estimated from the sun's angle that it was mid-afternoon, maybe three or four o'clock, which meant he had been out for at least twelve hours. He didn't know for sure, but that was his best estimate. If it was three o'clock, he had now missed his pickup at the lakeshore, which meant someone would be looking for him soon. He didn't think he could survive very long in the wilderness with the injuries he had sustained.

To make matters worse, he had no equipment to help him survive the ordeal. No way to signal someone, no way to start a fire—no way to do anything other than lie here and wait to die. And he refused to do that. Not yet, anyway. He still had fight in him, and as long as he had the will to live deep in his soul, he was determined not to give up.

He remembered that there was a small survival and first aid kit along with the water bottle in the back of his fishing vest, but that had been torn off in the attack, and he had no idea where it had ended up. The trauma had left his mind a cobweb of hazy memories. He decided that, for the time being, finding the vest would be his single focus—a simple goal to keep him going and give him a reason to keep breathing.

He needed to find the vest.

Just a few days ago, he had been a member of modern society. Driving his truck, eating microwave meals, talking on his phone, and doing all the other things people in the twenty-first century took for granted. Need something to drink? No problem, just turn on the faucet and clean, treated water flows at your command. Hungry? Just grab your smartphone and order dinner online—you don't even have to get off the couch. They will even deliver it to you. And now he had, for all practical purposes, been thrown back in time several hundred years. It was amazing how fast someone could be reduced to struggling for life's essentials—food, water, shelter, and basic medical care. He couldn't help but see the irony in the situation, and probably would have even laughed a little if it hadn't felt as if swords were piercing his side with each breath.

He had come to the mountains to escape all the conveniences of modern society, and he had accomplished that, for sure. But the solitude he had so longed for, and found, might very well end up being his death sentence. He never intended to be in this situation—but no one ever does, he supposed. What he wouldn't give now to be able to take a drink from a water fountain or order a pizza online.

Stay focused, Cody. Where is that vest?

He needed to get his bearings before he thought about anything else, though. He managed to pull himself into a seated position, with his back resting against the tree trunk. Straight ahead, he spotted the break in the forest canopy where Eagle Creek ran. It looked to be about one hundred and fifty yards away. He was surprised the bear had carried him that far from the creek, but everything had been a blur during the attack, and right now he was just glad the bear had stopped when it did.

Behind him, the terrain rose sharply toward the trail, which looked to be about three hundred yards up the mountain. Getting to the trail in his current condition was out of the question. To his left and right the ground was fairly level, but the nearest trail crossing, where he had begun fishing yesterday, had to be several hundred yards downstream. The realization that his current position would make it difficult to get help hit him at once. He was too far below the trail to be seen by a passerby, and close enough to the stream that the noise from the rushing water could drown out any cries for help he could muster, even if he was lucky enough to see someone else. This place was hardly what you would call a beehive of activity.

After taking stock of his surroundings, he began to scan the forest floor, looking for the vest. The bear could have carried it far away, in which case he would not be able to see it—let alone travel that distance in his current condition. He continued looking until his eyesight began to blur.

Nothing.

His vest was a sage green color, which didn't exactly stand out in the woods and, to make matters worse, his depth perception was screwed up because he was working with only one usable eye. After staring at the carpet of dried leaves, bushes, and fallen limbs until his vision began to blur again, he closed his eye in disgust and laid his head back against the tree. It was useless—he didn't see anything that remotely resembled the vest.

Dammit! I'm wasting time.

Then he realized the absurdity of that thought. What else did he have to do?

Nothing. Absolutely nothing.

His job right now was to make it out of this alive, and the contents in the back of that vest could mean the difference between life and death.

After letting his eyesight rest for several minutes, he started his search again, with a new determination to succeed.

Scanning the area in front of him again, he carefully examined each clump of leaves, each tree trunk, each rock, every area where something seemed even slightly out of place, desperately hoping to catch a glimpse of what may be his only way out of this mess.

Nothing.

More searching.

Still nothing.

Feeling totally defeated, he was about to give up when something caught his eye. It appeared to be a small piece of green fabric sticking above a fallen log about forty-five yards off to his right. A sense of excitement ran through him, and he felt as if he had won a victory in his current struggle—albeit a very small one.

He was not sure that what he was looking at was, in

fact, the vest. The object was on the opposite side of the fallen tree, which made a small target to begin with. After staring intently at the object, his vision blurred and his eye began to water, making him doubt if what he was seeing was real. Maybe his mind was playing tricks on him. Sort of like the guy in cheesy old movies who wanders through the desert, dying of thirst. Just before he collapses, he spots an oasis, but when he travels to it, he always finds he has been fooled by a mirage.

But this was no scene in a movie, and the consequences of being wrong would be disastrous, if not deadly. If he spent hours trying to drag himself to this small piece of fabric and it turned out to be a leaf or piece of trash, he would have expended a lot of energy for nothing, and it could cost him his life.

He had to make the right decision.

He shut his right eye once more, letting it rest for several minutes. He hoped the blackness would ease the strain and give him a clear picture of the object once he refocused, at least for a few seconds. When he opened his right eye and looked at the object once more, he was as certain as he could be that it was indeed the vest. Now he had to make a decision.

In normal circumstances, forty-five yards was nothing. It could be covered in a matter of seconds by a healthy adult. However, in his current situation, it would take hours and use valuable energy he needed to stay alive. But he had to try.

He gingerly pushed away from the tree trunk and rolled onto his right side. His left side was useless now, with the broken leg and injured shoulder. It was going to hurt like hell to drag himself along the ground, but he had no other option.

Act or die, Cody. Your choice.

With the right side of his body against the ground, he moved his elbow forward, enough to gain a small amount of leverage, and pulled himself forward about eight inches. Rivers of pain swept through his body, igniting his nerve endings until he felt like he was on fire. He screamed with everything that he was able to summon from his tortured body. His heart rate and breathing accelerated. Beads of sweat began popping out on his forehead, then on the back of his neck. He slumped back to the ground, trying to catch his breath. When he felt ready to move again, he used his elbow and forearm to pull his body another eight inches. He repeated the process over and over, finally able to move himself about three feet before collapsing again.

He was in agony, but he willed himself to continue moving. He knew that giving up would be the easiest option—but not the right one. He had never been a quitter, and he wasn't going to start now.

The methodically slow movement continued for the next three hours. Even though the terrain was relatively flat, his injuries made even the smallest of elevation changes almost impossible to negotiate. He tried to take the straightest path possible, but occasionally had to detour around a large tree or rock, which slowed his progress even more. The process left Cody feeling drained and helpless. He looked back at the tree, where he had slept last night. It was only about twenty yards away—he had covered less than half the distance to the vest.

He checked his target again. He could still see only two or three inches of fabric sticking over the top of the log. The good news was it didn't look any less like what he thought it was, but the bad news was that it didn't look any more like the vest either. He decided to keep going and hope for the best, but it was getting late and dark shadows began to encroach on the forest. He would have enough light to see for maybe another hour, but that didn't really matter because he had no more energy in his tank to continue any farther.

There was a large pine, a mixture of dark and light green

colors, located about ten feet to his right, and he decided to use it for shelter overnight. It took him several minutes to move the last ten feet, and once he was under the tree's canopy, he had to rest again before pulling himself into a seated position against the trunk. His right side was numb from the hours of crawling along the ground, and he was glad to be sitting up for a change.

Small victories, Cody.

The outer edges of the limbs hung so low they were almost touching the ground, but close to the trunk he had a foot of clearance above his head. He would be hidden to any predators outside, and he was thankful for that.

Small victories.

His mouth was incredibly dry and he longed for just a small drink of water. He had not had anything to eat or drink since before the bear attack. Food he could live without for a considerable amount of time, but he knew he would need to find water soon. He knew that the human body could only survive for a few days without water. Of course, there were always exceptions, but his situation was not ideal to begin with, and he doubted he would make it much past three days if he couldn't find water. He began to wonder if he had made a mistake by trying to retrieve the vest instead of heading straight to the creek, where he knew there was water. But it had taken him all afternoon to cover just twenty yards. He had estimated the creek to be one hundred and fifty yards away. At that pace, he would be dead before he reached the creek's waters anyway.

You made the right decision, Cody.

He was determined not to second-guess himself. In a survival situation, it did no good. He decided that when faced with a decision from here on out, he would carefully weigh the facts and his options, make a decision—and then stick to it. If he made the wrong decision, it could easily cost him his life, but so could a correct decision that was constantly reevaluated, resulting in self-doubt and re-adjustment. That would lead to inaction, and ultimately death, just as sure as making the wrong decision would. It was a waste of time, and right now the clock was working against him. Every hour he was away from the medical treatment he needed was an hour closer to his death.

About that, he had no doubt.

14

Katie tapped the fingers of her right hand rhythmically on the glass countertop of the Tried and True Fly Shop. She rested her chin in the palm of her left hand as she stared into the case containing new fly reels.

She was worried.

She had expected Cody to call yesterday afternoon after he returned from Eagle Creek, but he hadn't. Last night had been a fitful attempt at sleep because she had gotten up to check her cell phone every few minutes. Exhaustion had finally forced her to sleep around three o'clock in the morning, but her alarm woke her at six.

She had showered, dressed, made an egg-white and cheese omelet for breakfast, and then driven to the shop for the eight o'clock opening. It was nine-thirty now, and her anxiety was growing. The strange feeling in the pit of her stomach that had first occurred as she was leaving Cook's Diner on Monday was back with a vengeance. The fact was, it had never really left her. She could not explain why she felt like she did—she just had a feeling something was wrong.

Terribly wrong.

She didn't want to be the over-protective, obsessive girlfriend and send out the cavalry, only to find that he just hadn't picked up the phone and called. That would be embarrassing, not only for Cody, but for her as well.

"Excuse me, Miss."

Snapping out of her daze, Katie raised her head to see a man who appeared to be in his early fifties, with salt-and-pepper hair, standing only two feet from her on the opposite side of the counter. She hadn't even heard him open the door and walk in. "Oh, sorry 'bout that. I must have been daydreaming," Katie said, trying to cover her obvious surprise as best she could. "How can I help you?"

"Just looking for a new fly rod," he replied.

"Oh, okay. Well, we carry a lot of different options, depending on the brand and price range you're looking for." Katie began walking to the area of the store where the fly rods were kept. "Any idea what you're looking for or how much you want to spend?"

The man rubbed his double-chin as if in deep thought. "I just want a good all-around rod for a couple hundred bucks or so," he replied.

Katie showed him several different models they carried in his price range. He picked one of them up, making false casts to get a feel for the action, placed it back in the rack, and then repeated the process with another rod. This went on for about ten minutes, and Katie was growing impatient. *Just make a damn decision, man,* she thought. She knew she was not being very friendly to her only customer of the morning. She hadn't even introduced herself or asked his name, but the ever-tightening knot in the pit of her stomach made it difficult to concentrate, and she just wanted this guy to leave so she could decide what to do about Cody.

After another five minutes of testing the merchandise, the man rubbed his fat chin again, then declared, "I'll think it over and maybe come back later."

Great. "Oh, okay. No problem, come again anytime." Katie turned toward the door, hoping the stranger would be close behind.

After the man had left the store, she locked the door behind him and flipped the sign on the door to CLOSED. She placed her hand on her forehead and began to pace behind the counter. She wasn't sure what to do, but she had to do something. She didn't know if anyone else even knew where Cody had gone—what if she had been the only person he told? If that was the case, and something had gone wrong during the trip, she could not sit back and do nothing.

She searched the phone number for Mountain View Resort on her cell phone and dialed. After three rings someone picked up.

"Mountain View Resort, my name is Mark, how may I help you?" the voice on the other end of the line said in a rapid, rehearsed tone.

"Hi . . . uh . . . hi, my name is Katie Richardson, and I was calling to see if I could get some information about a friend of mine who was staying at your resort," Katie said in a nervous, almost halting cadence.

"What kind of information are you looking for, ma'am?" the clerk replied.

"Well, he came up to the mountains last Friday night to do some backpacking on Eagle Creek, and he was supposed to be out yesterday afternoon, but I haven't heard from him, so I just wanted to check with you and see if you could give me any information." Katie noticed her palms were beginning to sweat.

"What's your friend's name, ma'am?" Mark asked, sounding a little perturbed, like he had just been awakened from a nap.

"Cody McAlister," she replied in the friendliest tone she could manage, hoping to get on the clerk's good side.

"Do you know when he checked in?"

"It was this past Friday. He was supposed to check out the next morning and catch a ride across the lake to Eagle

Creek."

"Oh, yeah! I remember him now. Nice guy. Came in here Friday night about eight o'clock or so, I think. Looked really tired. As I remember, he went straight to his room and must have gone to bed. I didn't see or hear from him again before my shift ended. I got off at midnight, so I wasn't here when he would have checked out on Saturday morning." Mark was sounding less irritated.

"Is there any way you can find out if he actually checked out on time and went to the marina for the ride over to Eagle Creek?" Katie asked.

"Hold on a second and I'll check our system."

"Thanks," Katie replied, sighing as she spoke, which betrayed the anxiety she was trying to hold inside. She heard Mark typing on the other end of the line.

"Yes, ma'am, the computer shows he checked out at five-forty Saturday morning."

"What about the ride across the lake? Is there any way to know if he was actually dropped off at the trailhead?"

"Give me a minute and I'll call down to the marina and see if anyone remembers dropping him off."

"Thanks." Katie barely got the word out before the clerk put her on hold. A country music station was playing in her ear now. She continued to tap her nails on the glass countertop. It was a habit she found herself doing anytime she was nervous. She had done it as long as she could remember, even as a small child. After about five minutes on hold, she was growing impatient and considered hanging up and calling back. She took a deep breath and decided to wait a couple more minutes. Finally, she heard the receiver on the other end pick back up.

"Okay, I called down to the marina and talked to Jesse. He did remember him, and said that he dropped him off as scheduled on Saturday morning," Mark said.

Something in his tone made Katie think he was holding something back. "And?" she asked.

"And what?"

"And did Jesse or whatever his name is pick him up on Wednesday?" Katie was becoming frightened, her voice rising in agitation at the clerk.

"Well . . . no," Mark replied in a subdued tone, which further indicated to Katie something was wrong.

"What do you mean, no?" she asked. "Why didn't he go back and pick him up?"

"Well, that's the thing . . . he did go back, ma'am, but he said Cody never showed up. He said he waited more than thirty minutes past the scheduled pickup time, but your friend never showed, so Jesse returned to the marina. He said he thought he had just gotten another ride out." Mark spoke in a halting cadence that indicated to Katie he wasn't entirely comfortable with Jesse's explanation either.

"What do you mean, he never showed up? Did Jesse report him missing to the authorities or anything?" Katie was trying to hold it together, but her anxiety was mounting.

"Well . . . I . . . I—"

Katie could tell that she had definitely rattled Mark now, but she didn't let up. "Why wouldn't he report Cody missing to anyone?"

"I . . . I'm not sure, ma'am, why he didn't—"

Mark was stumbling over his words badly now, but Katie didn't let him catch his breath. Interrupting, she said, "Are you kidding me, Mark? Let me get this straight: a guy drives up from Atlanta and hires you to take him across the lake and then pick him up at a specific day and time, and you guys don't even bother to call anyone when he doesn't show up? Unbelievable!"

"Look, ma'am, I'm sorry, but things like this happen all the time up here. Hikers change their plans, come out a few days early and find a ride with someone else. I'm sure everything is fine."

By now Katie was having none of his explanations. "I don't care if it happens all the time, Cody didn't change his plans or find a ride with someone else. He wouldn't do that!"

"Well, I'm sorry, ma'am—"

Katie hung up and then threw the phone down on the countertop. She put her right hand to her forehead, pulling her blonde hair back. She began to pace, wondering what to do next. Finally, she decided to call the National Park Service and see if they had any information. She picked up her phone off the counter and searched for the number. The search resulted in at least ten different phone numbers, but she dialed the one that was labeled *Backcountry Office*, assuming they would be the ones that handled the camping permits and perhaps be able to help her.

"Great Smoky Mountains National Park Backcountry Office, this is Janice, how may I help you?"

Katie explained the situation to Janice. She was talking in rapid-fire sentences, barely taking time to breathe.

"Did the people at the resort report him missing already?" Janice asked.

"No, they didn't. They said hikers change their plans all the time and fail to show for their scheduled pickup. Pissed me off. I think they should have at least called someone."

"Yes, absolutely," Janice replied. "Let me get some information from you, and we'll see what we can find out."

"Thank you," Katie said and let out another long sigh.

After giving Janice her name, address, phone number, and a physical description of Cody, Katie waited silently on the phone. Janice had a soothing voice, like that of a grandma, and Katie guessed she was in her late sixties or early seventies. Katie assumed Janice was a part-time volunteer who answered phones at the Park Service in her free time to give her something to do. Whatever the reason she was on the other end of the line, Katie was glad she was there. Her presence, though physically separated by a couple of hundred miles, made the knot in the bottom of Katie's stomach loosen just a bit. Even the smallest amount of optimism was welcome now.

"Do you know which campsite he was planning to use?"

"It should have been campsite ninety-seven," Katie replied. She could hear Janice typing on a computer keyboard.

"Do you know if he obtained a backcountry permit before he left?" she asked.

"He should have. I told him where the registration box was at the marina, but I can't be one hundred percent certain that he filled it out. This is his first solo backpacking trip, so he may have forgotten."

"And you said he should have been back yesterday afternoon, correct?"

"Yes, around three o'clock."

"Okay, so he is around nineteen hours overdue. I'll go ahead and call the ranger that works that area and let him know what's going on. Is the number you gave me a good contact number for today?"

"Yes, that's my cell. I have it on me all the time. Please, call right away if you find anything." Katie knew her anxiety must be evident to Janice.

"I will, ma'am. Don't worry yourself too much. I'm sure everything is fine, but we will get someone to check it out just to make sure," Janice said in the grandmotherly tone that Katie had come to love over the duration of the short phone conversation.

Katie put her phone back in her pants pocket. She didn't know what to do next, but felt somewhat better for at least taking the step of calling the Park Service. She walked back to the front door and stared outside, trying to gather her thoughts so she could decide on her next move.

Just then, her cell phone rang. She dug in her pocket

for the phone, her heart racing, desperately hoping it was Cody calling. She looked at the screen, and disappointment flooded through her when she saw it was her brother, Collin. He usually worked the afternoon shift, but always called about this time of day to make sure Katie had made it to the store okay. He had always been protective of his little sister, but he had become even more so following Eric's death. Sometimes it annoyed her, but most of the time she found it sweet.

"How's everything going this morning?" he asked.

"Everything at the store is fine, but—"

"What's wrong?" Collin asked, interrupting Katie mid-sentence. He could always tell when something was bothering her.

After hesitating a few seconds, Katie said, "Cody's missing."

"What do you mean, he's missing?"

Katie could hear the confusion and concern in his voice. Collin had always liked Cody, ever since the first day he had walked into the fly shop, so she knew his concern was genuine. Katie explained what she had found out from the resort.

"That's bullshit. Sounds like someone trying to cover their ass to me," Collin replied.

"Yeah, that's what I thought, too. And I know he wouldn't have just changed his plans at the spur of the moment and not told anyone. Even if he did decide to come out early and get a ride with someone else, he would have let the resort know he no longer needed the pickup. He would have called me too, I know he would have. That's just the type of person he is."

"Have you called anyone else?"

"Yeah, I called the Backcountry Office at the park and reported him missing. The lady said she would contact the ranger that worked the Eagle Creek area and see if he could find out anything. I know something is wrong. I've had a bad feeling about this trip ever since he told me he was going. I didn't want to scare him or, even worse, have him think I was just being paranoid, so I kept quiet. I even offered to go with him. I knew he shouldn't have gone up there alone. It's my fault, I should have insisted—"

"All right, stop right there," Collin said. "It's not your fault. You couldn't have known something was going to happen.

"Yeah, but—"

"But nothing. It's not your fault . . . period," Collin replied, this time in a more forceful tone.

"You're right, I know it's not my fault, but I feel like I need to be doing more right now, like time is slipping away. I can't explain why I feel that way, I just do. I think I need to go up there."

"Okay, Katie, that's fine. But let's not get ahead of ourselves here and expect the worst," Collin said. "He's probably fine. Maybe he got delayed by a rainstorm that made the creek crossings impassable."

"Yeah, you're probably right. But still, I would feel better if I were up there . . . at least I could make sure someone was really searching for him." Katie appreciated Collin's attempt to be optimistic about the situation, but she knew deep down that everything was not all right. She didn't know how she knew this—she just did. She had learned long ago not to question her intuition, because more often than not, it was correct.

There were a thousand logical reasons that Cody had not shown up, but right now Katie was not buying any of them. He had not simply been delayed by a rain-swollen stream, or broken equipment, or even a bad case of the stomach flu—something was very wrong, and his life was in danger. She just knew it. The sooner she could get others to realize this, the faster help would get to him. The first step in making that happen was to drive up to the mountains as soon as possible and make sure a search was undertaken, even if she had to do it by herself.

"Okay, tell you what," Collin said, "I'll go ahead and come to the shop so you can leave. Give me about thirty minutes or so to get ready."

"Thank you, Collin."

"No problem. Love you, sis."

"Love you too," Katie replied.

Katie pulled the chair they kept behind the counter to her and sat down. Slumped over with her head in her hands, she thought about Cody and worried about what could have happened to him.

Why am I so worried about him?

She had known him for less than a year, and their relationship had not gotten too serious. Maybe there was something deeper between the two of them that she had failed to notice—or had refused to allow herself to admit. The loss of Eric in the war and then the baby afterward had been almost more than she could bear, and she hadn't wanted to jump headfirst into another serious relationship after losing them.

But now, sitting alone in the fly shop, she forced herself to face her true feelings for Cody. *I must love him, at least on some level. Why else would I be this worried about him when he's been missing for less than a day?*

She picked up her phone again and checked to see if she had any missed calls or text messages. Nothing. Just the same as it had been for the last hundred times she had checked since yesterday afternoon. She scrolled through her contacts list and tapped her finger on Tiffany's picture.

"Hi, Tiff," Katie said. "How's it going?"

"Pretty good, not too busy today at the office. What's up?" Tiffany asked.

"I was just calling to see if you were interested in a little road trip?"

"Road trip? Where we going?" Tiffany sounded puzzled.

"North Carolina," Katie replied, trying to hide her obvious nervousness.

"North Carolina? Why, is something wrong?"

"Cody didn't show up yesterday where he had arranged to be picked up. I've called everyone I can think of, and no one knows where he is. I've been a nervous wreck since last night, waiting on him to call. I tried to get him to take someone with him, told him it's not really safe to go by himself, but he wouldn't—"

"I'm sure everything is fine," Tiffany interrupted.

"No offense, but I'm getting really tired of people telling me everything is fine. I just have a really bad feeling something's wrong." It was more than just a bad feeling, she *knew* something was wrong, but she didn't want to come across as some wacko. "I can't just sit here on my hands and wait for another death notification to come knocking on my door. So I'm going to drive up there and make sure the authorities have started a search, that they're taking this seriously."

"Look, I'm sorry if I made you mad . . . I was just trying to help," Tiffany said.

"No, it's fine. I'm sorry. I shouldn't have snapped. I'm just really worried, that's all. So do you want to drive up with me? We can get a room at the resort until we figure out what is going on."

"Sure. I mean, why the hell not, right? It's supposed to be a slow day today and tomorrow, I'll just tell Dr. Martin that I'm taking a couple of days off. I have a few vacation days in the bank anyway. Samantha can cover my patients while I'm gone. I'm sure she wouldn't mind, either. I'm pretty sure the good doctor is banging her behind his wife's back, so they would probably like the office to themselves for a while." Tiffany laughed.

A smile came across Katie's face too—the first one she could remember since yesterday. "Thanks, Tiff. You always make me smile."

"That's what I'm here for. You driving or you want me to?"

"We'll take my 4Runner. We may need the four-wheel drive up in the mountains. Collin is coming over in a few minutes to take over at the store, and then I'm heading home to pack a bag. How long will it take you to get ready?" Katie asked.

"By the time I get out of here, run by my house, drop Charlie off at the kennel, then over to your place," Tiffany paused as she mentally calculated, "probably 'bout an hour and a half."

"Sounds good," Katie said, "and Tiff . . . thanks. I really mean it. You're always there for me."

"Always will be, girl. You'd do the same for me. And please, try not to worry too much. We'll find him safe and sound . . . I'm sure of it."

I can't lose someone else. "I hope so," Katie replied. "I hope so."

15

U.S. Park Ranger Jackson Hart sat beside his dining room table, his right leg propped up in one of the wobbly chairs that surrounded the table, his left resting on the hardwood oak flooring that ran throughout the house. Small mahogany wood shavings were drifting lazily off the carving he was working on to the floor below. A small pile had accumulated between his legs.

He had enjoyed carving ever since he was a child. Back then, he mainly just whittled down sticks or created simple designs with his pocketknife. As he had gotten older, though, he had found that carving provided much needed stress relief, and he had begun to devote more time to it over the past several years, gradually increasing the difficulty of the designs and figures he created. He was currently working on an Indian chief that stood eight inches tall. His collection of specially designed carving knives and picks were spread meticulously on the flannel cloth that covered the old wooden tabletop. He turned the chief over in his hand, then raised it to his mouth and blew the excess shavings off. They floated downward to join the others on the pile. The detailed headdress had been causing him a headache over the past couple of days. It was about eighty percent finished, and Jackson hoped to complete it by the end of the day.

Today was his day off. It was not unusual for him to have days off during the week—in fact, it was uncommon for him to have a weekend off. Weekends were the busiest time in the park, and that meant he was usually out hiking trails, checking fishing licenses, or responding to minor medical situations.

He had worked late last night trying to gather information on some suspected poachers. At three in the morning, he had called it quits and headed home with nothing to show for his hours of lying chest down on the cold forest floor, concealed under a tree. That was the life of a park ranger, though—sometimes exciting and rewarding, other times the long hours and disappointing results could lead to deep frustration.

Deep down, though, he loved his job. It was what he had wanted to be ever since he was a child and his parents had taken him to Yellowstone. While there, he had attended a youth program taught by one of the rangers, and he was hooked. In college, he had gotten a degree in wildlife biology with a minor in criminal justice. Before he had even graduated, he had applied and been accepted into the ranger training program.

After he completed the program, which included some intense law enforcement training, he had been stationed at Rocky Mountain National Park in Colorado. He loved it out there, but after four years he had decided it was time for a change, and when a position opened at the Great Smoky Mountains National Park, he had applied for a transfer. It would be five years this October since he had arrived at his current post. For the first two years, he had been stationed at park headquarters, near Gatlinburg, Tennessee, but since then, he had been stationed here, at the Twentymile Creek Ranger Station. Located between Fontana Lake and the Tennessee border, just off North Carolina Highway 28, it was much quieter than headquarters, and he enjoyed the solitude.

He lived in the simple wood-frame house that had been built in the nineteen-forties to serve as housing for the assigned ranger. It was a nondescript dwelling, with clapboard siding and a covered front porch that creaked when you walked over it. The white exterior paint was peeling in places, and he had intended to repaint the house two years ago, but so far had not gotten around to it. The inside was as simple as the outside, with a small kitchen and dining area just inside the front door. The kitchen countertops were covered with a pastel yellow and flower-patterned laminate straight out of the seventies. The living room was just beyond the kitchen, and contained a rock fireplace on the north wall. The living room always gave Jackson a cramped feeling, so he didn't spend much time in there, except during the winter, when he would start a fire on cold nights and relax in the worn-out leather recliner that he had inherited with the house.

Winter was the loneliest time at Twentymile. The closest large city was Knoxville, Tennessee, which was about an hour and a half away. Once the weather turned cold, the number of park visitors diminished, too, so Jackson spent a lot of the sunlight-starved days alone, doing odd jobs around the property. At night he fixed himself dinner, usually something in the microwave, and either watched a movie or worked on his latest carving project.

Beyond the living room and down a short hallway lay the rest of the house. The first door on the right led to a bathroom that was large enough for only a small tub, toilet, and sink. Three small bedrooms, two off the left side of the hallway and one on the right, past the bathroom, completed his modest accommodations.

The largest of the rooms, the last one on the left, served as his bedroom. He slept on a worn-out double mattress that sat atop a wire bed frame. He still had one heavy blanket on top of the mattress for the cool spring nights.

During the winter, he had to use two. But during the summer, he stripped both of them off and just slept under a thin cotton sheet. The house was old and drafty—cold in the winter and hot in the summer. He really didn't need the other two bedrooms, as he had no other family living with him, but he had turned the one directly across from his room into a small office.

As he continued to work on a feather in the Indian's headdress, crafting the lines with intricate detail, his small knife slipped off the end of the wood and straight into his thumb below. "Dammit!" he yelled.

He put his thumb into his mouth and applied pressure with his back molars, trying to stanch the blood flow. Just as he was getting out of his chair and heading to the kitchen sink, the telephone rang. He turned the cold water on and stuck his thumb underneath, watching the red liquid stream down his hand and into the drain. With his right hand, he grabbed the roll of paper towels that was sitting on the counter and pulled several from the roll. He wrapped his thumb and applied pressure with his free hand. "Shit, that hurt." He opened several drawers, looking for a bandage.

The phone was still ringing.

In the third drawer, he finally found a box of adhesive bandages and set them on the counter.

Ring.

He tore the top of the box open and pulled out a bandage, tore the wrapper with his teeth, and somehow managed to get it quickly applied to his injured thumb with only his right hand.

Ring.

"I'm coming . . . hold on!" he shouted at the phone. He walked over and dropped the bloody paper towel and bandage wrapper in the garbage can.

Ring.

"Hello?" he shouted into the receiver.

Taken aback, Janice said in a soft voice, "Jackson, this is Janice at the Backcountry Office, is everything okay?"

Realizing how angry he must have sounded, Jackson said, "Yeah, sorry about that, Janice. I cut my thumb just before you called and was trying to get it bandaged before I answered the phone." He paused and a grimace came across his face. His thumb was still throbbing. It felt like the blade had gone all the way to the bone. "What's up?"

"I just got a call from a lady in Georgia, who said her friend hiked into Eagle Creek last Saturday to do some fishing and was supposed to return yesterday afternoon, but he never showed for his pickup at the lake. She sounded really worried. I told her everything was probably fine, but I knew she wouldn't let it rest until I called a ranger to check it out."

"He's less than a day late and she was worried about him, huh?" Jackson asked.

"Yep, sounded really upset to me."

"Well, if she calls back, tell her that he probably just stayed an extra day or hiked out a different way. Hikers do this kind of thing all the time."

"I know, Jackson, but would you mind to go check it out? She just sounded so worried, poor thing. She said her friend didn't have a lot of experience backpacking, either."

Janice obviously didn't know how to take a hint. "It's my day off, Janice. Anybody else who could do it?"

"No, I already checked. No other ranger is in the area today. Sorry."

"Well . . . what the hell. I just sliced my thumb open good, so I don't guess I'll be doing any more carving to-day, anyway. I've got a couple of things to take care of here, and then I'll head on over and check on him. What's his name?"

"She said his name was Cody McAlister. And thanks, Jackson. I owe you one."

He grabbed a pen from the counter and wrote the name

on his palm. "Don't you forget it, either. How about another one of your famous apple pies the next time I'm over there?"

"You got it. Just let me know you're coming and I'll have one ready for you," she said.

"Will do. I'll radio in to dispatch once I'm on the road. Shouldn't be more than thirty minutes or so. If I find anything, I'll call it in and then you can let his friend know."

Jackson hung up and walked back to his bedroom, where he changed into his uniform and grabbed his backpack out of the closet. He unzipped the pack and checked inside to ensure he had all the essentials for an overnight stay in the woods, should it be necessary—a lightweight hammock for sleeping, some first-aid supplies, all-weather lighter, flashlight, water filter, a change of socks and underwear, and a few other essential items. He walked back into the kitchen and opened the cupboard, pulled out an MRE and a couple of Clif Bars, then shoved the food into his pack. Next, he went into the living room, where his .45 caliber Glock semi-automatic pistol sat on a small end table next to the recliner. He clipped the gun onto the leather belt around his waist, grabbed his jacket, and headed for the door.

As he stepped outside onto the porch, a cool breeze swept down the creek valley. He pulled the baseball cap that bore the National Park Service emblem on the front down over his forehead and put his arms through the sleeves of his jacket.

Twentymile Creek ran behind his house on its way to the confluence with Cheoah Lake, which lay just on the other side of Highway 28. Jackson could hear the sounds of tumbling water and leaves rustling in the breeze. After a cold, gray winter with its howling winds, the delicate sounds of spring were a welcome change. Jackson looked to the sky and noticed that a thick cloud cover had descended over the mountains. Strong cold fronts regularly pushed through the area in spring, often bringing heavy rains and strong winds. He had missed the weather forecast this morning and wondered if a front was on the way.

The small barn and corral lay about thirty yards upstream from the main house. His paint horse, Nickel, and an ornery pack mule he had named Diablo, which was Spanish for Devil, were kept there. The Park Service had furnished the animals, which were used for extended treks in the backcountry. Nickel neighed as she saw Jackson approaching. "Just a minute, girl, I'm coming!" he shouted out.

Once he reached the corral, he went to the food bin, scooped oats for Nickel and Diablo, and filled their water barrels with fresh water from the hose that hung on the side of the barn. He stroked each one on the mane and said, "Be back in a little bit. Got to go check on something."

He left the two animals to their food and walked toward his Chevy Suburban that bore the distinctive green stripe and logo of the National Park Service. A minute later he was heading down the rocky driveway toward Highway 28. Once he reached the highway, he called dispatch on his radio and told them he was headed to Eagle Creek. As he accelerated, he looked across Cheoah Lake on his right. The narrow lake had a pronounced ripple on the surface, from the wind, which had increased in intensity throughout the day. He tuned the radio to a classic rock station as the Suburban cut through the mountain air.

Thirty-five minutes later, Jackson pulled up in front of the backcountry permit station just above Fontana Lake. As he exited the vehicle and walked toward the station, he pulled the key to the lockbox from his front pocket. He gathered all the permits, then returned to the truck and spread them out on the passenger seat, looking for one with the name Cody McAlister.

After a minute or so, he found what he was looking for.

He unfolded it and held it close to the driver's window so he could read it. The permit itself was a straightforward document that required the permittee to provide his or her name, address, vehicle description and tag number, and the dates and locations of their stay. Jackson saw that Mr. McAlister had filled the permit out as required, listing an Atlanta address and his itinerary. He had planned to hike to campsite ninety-seven on Saturday and return on Wednesday. It was a simple plan and should have been no problem for an experienced hiker. But Jackson knew nothing about Mr. McAlister, other than the information on the permit and what Janice had told him. The fact that he wasn't an experienced hiker complicated things. Jackson had seen it before. Rookies often came into the mountains unprepared, and then suffered the consequences. The mountains were beautiful, but they could kill, too. They demanded respect.

Jackson drove down the hill that led to the marina and boat ramp, looking for the red Toyota Tacoma pickup Mr. McAlister had listed on the permit. He found the truck about halfway down the ramp and pulled to a stop in front of it. He reached behind him and lifted his backpack into the passenger seat, then retrieved his flashlight from the pack's main compartment and stepped out of the Suburban. Mr. McAlister's Toyota was backed into the parking spot, so Jackson had to walk around the side of the truck to check the license plate. He compared the number on the permit to the plate and confirmed it was a match. This was definitely Mr. McAlister's vehicle.

He checked the doors, but they were all locked. He shined the flashlight into the truck's interior. The truck was clean and looked almost brand new. A small suitcase sat in the backseat. Jackson ran his hand through his hair. Everything seemed in order, no signs of forced entry or foul play.

He returned to his Suburban and found a parking spot.

He grabbed his pack off the seat and locked the doors before heading toward the marina. The aluminum walkway that connected the marina to the shore bounced slightly with each stride he took. He opened the front door and saw Jesse sitting behind the counter, eating a sandwich.

"Hey, Jesse."

Jesse put the sandwich down and hurriedly swallowed the large bite in his mouth. "Hi, Jack. How's it going?"

Jackson preferred to be called by his full name, but a lot of his friends shortened it to Jack, and he always just let it slide. "You know anything about this missing hiker?" he asked.

"No, I sure don't. Supposed to pick him up on Wednesday, but he never showed. I didn't really think anything of it, thought he had gotten a ride out with someone else. Guess his old lady called up here today, raising hell about why we didn't notify anyone, but you know as good as me, Jack, that this shit happens all the time."

Jackson stifled a laugh. "Yeah, I know. Well, she must have contacted us right after she talked to you guys . . . got a call about an hour ago. I'm gonna go check it out. Boat ready?"

"Yep, she's down at the end of the dock, all fueled up and ready to go. Took care of her myself, just this morning."

"Thanks, Jesse, I appreciate that." Jackson started toward the door that led to the boat slips.

"Look, I . . . I'm sure sorry if I've caused a problem with this whole deal and everything. I honestly didn't think nothin' was wrong."

Jackson stopped and looked back toward the counter. He could see the concern on his friend's face. Jackson liked Jesse. Sure, he could be a little cantankerous sometimes, but when Jackson had first arrived at the Twentymile duty station, Jesse had offered to show him around the area and give him a tour of Fontana Lake. They had even spent a few days on the water together, catching smallmouth bass and crappie. "I know you didn't. Don't worry about it. I'm sure everything is fine. I'm just going to run over to Eagle Creek and have a quick look. Take care of yourself, Jesse."

"Yeah . . . you do the same, Jack."

The hesitancy in Jesse's voice betrayed the anxiety he was feeling, and Jackson actually felt a little sorry for him. He knew Jesse was rough around the edges, but inside he was a good-hearted person, and if something had happened to Mr. McAlister, Jesse would likely never forgive himself.

Jackson pushed the door open and walked onto the pier. His hiking boots made a hollow clanging sound on the aluminum walkway as he made his way to the last slip on the right. A gentle breeze was blowing off the lake, and he lifted his head to take in the fresh air. He had loved being on the water ever since he was a kid.

He reached the Park Service boat and threw his pack inside before untying the dock lines. The boat was an older model Boston Whaler, painted white with a distinctive green stripe down the side, just like his Suburban. White lettering, in the center of the stripe, read *National Park Service*. It was nothing fancy, a far cry from the newer, larger models he had seen at other parks, but he liked it and always enjoyed taking it for a spin. He climbed aboard and took his position behind the wheel. There was a bench seat a few feet behind the console, but Jackson liked to drive standing up. He buckled his life jacket, started the engine, and backed away from the dock.

As he pulled away from the marina, he increased the throttle and the boat lurched forward, racing across the lake's surface. By the time he reached the main channel, he was going full-speed, about fifty-five miles an hour. The wind, funneled by the mountains on both sides of the lake, had created rolling, white-capped waves on the surface. The big, powerful boat rode high in the water, across the crests of the waves. Jackson constantly worked the steering wheel, keeping the boat moving straight ahead across the water. He never lifted off the throttle—instead, he smiled and enjoyed the rough ride. His jet-black hair was whipping back and forth in the wind, and the spray from the lake was hitting him in the face, running down his square chin, before dropping onto his jacket. He felt invigorated. Alive.

He loved it.

The clouds had thickened throughout the day, and it looked like rough weather would be moving in sooner rather than later. He hoped any bad weather would hold off, at least until he had located Mr. McAlister.

Most importantly, though, he hoped this search would turn out better than his last.

16

By Thursday morning, Cody didn't think he could move another inch. His whole body was stiff, and his muscles and joints hurt more than he could ever remember. He had not slept well under the pine tree, either. The frequent shifting on the cold ground, combined with his injuries, had caused flashes of pain to wake him numerous times during the night.

He felt the need to urinate for the first time since the attack. He rolled gingerly onto his right side and unzipped his pants. His urine was a dark orange color, almost brown, with a strong smell of ammonia, and it burned slightly as it left his body. He knew this meant the dehydration was worsening. He had to find some water today.

He zipped his pants and rolled onto his back. The pain he felt in this simple movement reinforced his belief that at least a couple of vertebrae were cracked. He hoped it was just a minor fracture. If it was a severe break, any additional movement could paralyze him for the rest of his life—which, by the way things were looking, could be just a matter of days. He really had no choice one way or the other; he had to keep moving. All he could do was hope that his back held together long enough for him to reach the vest and be rescued.

He used his right elbow and right leg to inch himself toward the tree trunk and into a sitting position, slightly alleviating the pressure on his back. Although he didn't feel like moving at all, he knew he needed to continue his slow crawl toward the fishing vest—or at least what he hoped was the fishing vest. After taking several minutes to rest, he rolled onto his right side and scooted from beneath the tree's canopy. He scanned the horizon to try to get a fix on the vest's location. After a minute or two he relocated it, about twenty-five yards ahead and slightly to his right.

Once again he began to move, slowly and deliberately, using his right forearm and leg to propel himself along the ground. It was grueling travel. For every foot he moved, Cody could feel the energy leave his body and transfer to the cold ground beneath him. After only a few feet, beads of sweat had broken out on his forehead, and he was becoming short of breath. He rested for several minutes and then moved a few feet more. The process was the same as yesterday, but the pace was much slower. His body was weakening—and fast.

Still, he continued on. One move at a time. Right arm forward, right knee forward. Pull with his arm, push with his foot. Rest. Repeat the process. Again.

And again.

By noon he was completely exhausted. He looked back toward the big pine to see how much progress he had made. A flood of despair hit him. He had moved only ten yards.

How could I have gone only ten yards?

The realization that he was barely making progress depressed him to the core.

I can't go on.

He collapsed in a slump of defeat.

I have to go on.

He did not want to give up. Could not give up. He still felt the candle of hope burning deep inside him, however dim—at least it was still burning.

Flickering.

But he didn't know how much more he could take. His pain was getting worse, not better, and his thirst was now reaching an almost unbearable level.

He lifted his head to survey his surroundings. He spotted a clump of grass about five feet to his left. His tongue and mouth were dry and burning. He wanted a drop of water—just a single drop—and he would be happy again. He squirmed toward the grass, reached out, and plucked a handful from the ground. He had never eaten grass before, so he didn't know what to expect. He hoped it would contain at least a little bit of moisture that would quench his thirst.

Holding it by the small root ball on the bottom, he slowly moved the grass toward his mouth and took a bite. Much to his disappointment, it contained no perceivable moisture. If felt dry and scratchy in his mouth. Bitterness flooded his taste buds. He wanted to spit it out on the ground, but something told him to keep chewing. If it had any moisture or nutrients at all, it would be better than nothing. So he continued to chew until he could manage to swallow the first bite. It tasted terrible.

For some reason, the experience brought to his mind the picture of Christ on the cross, when he had requested water and the Roman soldier gave him vinegar instead. He didn't know why the picture had flashed in his mind. Perhaps he had heard the story in Sunday school as a child. Missy and Herschel had taken him and his sister to church every Sunday. But Cody had not set foot in a church in years. He wasn't even sure he still believed in God. But at this moment, he needed something to believe in—something to keep him going.

So for the first time in years, he prayed.

Dear God . . . please help me . . . I need help . . . to get out of this alive . . . Amen.

It wasn't much of a prayer; he doubted Missy and Herschel, or his Sunday school teacher, or God Himself, for that matter, would be impressed—but it was the best he could manage right then.

He took another bite of the bitter grass and forced it down. When he had finished, he dusted the dirt off the roots and ate those, too. When they were gone, he thought about grabbing another handful but didn't think he could stomach it. Instead, he raised his head and continued on.

The several minutes of rest he had taken to eat the grass had given him a small boost of energy, and he felt like he was beginning to make progress again. So he kept going.

17

By the time Ranger Jackson Hart reached campsite nine-ty-seven, it was almost four o'clock in the afternoon. He stopped on the trail and stared into the camping area, searching for anything amiss. What he saw was a normal looking campsite. Nothing unusual at all.

"Mr. McAlister!" Jackson stood silent for a moment, waiting for a response.

Nothing.

"Mr. McAlister, are you okay?" he yelled again. "I'm Ranger Hart with the Park Service. I'm just here to check on you."

After waiting in silence for a moment, he made his way down into the campsite and approached the tent, his right hand moving instinctively onto the Glock that was strapped around his leg. "Cody, this is Ranger Hart. Are you in there, sir?"

Experience had taught Jackson to always be cautious when walking into an unknown situation. He never knew what would be waiting for him. Usually it was nothing dangerous, but he always hoped for the best and expected the worst. The mountains had been known to draw not only nature lovers and fishermen, but also criminals trying to hide out from the authorities. Being a park ranger was not all fun and games.

It could be dangerous work.

As he drew closer to the tent, Jackson's mind flashed back to six years before, when he had lost Scott in Rocky Mountain National Park. The two had been friends since the training academy. Scott had stopped a car near Bear Lake for a burnt-out tail light. As he approached the driver's side window, the occupant shoved a .357 Magnum revolver out the window and pulled the trigger. The slug caught Scott in the forehead and blew the back of his head out. His body was discovered lying in the road a few minutes later by some tourists who called for help. But there was nothing that could be done. Scott had been dead before he even hit the asphalt—he never had a chance.

The perpetrators had gotten away, but were eventually caught a few days later in Northern New Mexico, while trying to hold up a convenience store. They were just a couple of crazy college drop-outs who had murdered an elderly lady in Florida, stolen her car, and decided to go on a cross-country crime spree. They had also killed a liquor store clerk in Arkansas, who refused to hand over the cash when they attempted to rob him, prior to meeting up with Scott in Colorado. They would have killed the clerk in New Mexico, too, if an off-duty cop hadn't walked into the store and interrupted the robbery. After some legal wrangling between the various jurisdictions, both of the young men had been tried in Florida, where their crimes began, and were sentenced to death.

The experience had shaken Jackson badly. Every time he had driven the road up to Bear Lake and passed the spot where Scott was gunned down, he had been forced to relive the incident. When he had requested the transfer to the Great Smoky Mountains, Jackson had told himself he just needed a change of scenery. But deep down, he knew he had to get away from that single spot in the road.

"Cody, you in there?" Jackson asked again as he reached

the tent. He waited a few seconds and when he heard no response, he reached down and disconnected the straps that held the protective rainfly in place, throwing the right side upward and exposing the vestibule. He now had a clear view into the tent itself. It looked to be empty, but he hunched over so he could get a better look through the mesh door.

His hand remained on the Glock.

He unzipped the door and leaned inside, hoping to find a clue as to what had happened to Mr. McAlister. Nothing struck him as suspicious. There was a sleeping bag sitting atop a self-inflating pad and a paperback novel lying next to it. Jogging pants and a pair of socks were thrown haphazardly into the opposite corner.

Satisfied nothing untoward had happened in the tent, he began to examine the campsite itself. He looked for any obvious signs of trouble: blood stains on the ground, suicide note taped to a tree, anything that might point him toward the missing man. He found nothing—with the exception of Mr. McAlister's backpack suspended high in the trees from the cable and pulley system. He walked over and lowered the pack to the ground. After a quick examination, he determined there was nothing of evidentiary value contained within it and zipped it closed before returning it to its perch in the trees.

He walked over to the fire ring where he noticed a small pile of coals. He placed his hand near them first, and when he felt no heat, he picked up one of the coals. It was stone cold. That told Jackson that no fire had been built for at least a day or two.

Next, he followed the well-worn path that ran from the camping area to Eagle Creek. Maybe Mr. McAlister had fallen and hit his head while gathering water. Once he reached the stream, Jackson looked across to the opposite bank and scanned the water's surface, both upstream and down, looking for any sign of Mr. McAlister. He yelled out once more and waited a few seconds, listening, but once again, received no reply. On his way back to the campsite he scanned the dense foliage on both sides of the path, but that, too, yielded no results.

No sign of the missing fisherman could be found. That was unusual. Normally Jackson could find at least a small clue. Something. Anything. But not this time.

Empty-handed, he decided to return to the main trail and walk upstream toward the next creek crossing. As he walked along, he scanned the trail and the immediate area surrounding it. Sometimes fishermen or hikers would leave a sign in the trail as to which way they were traveling: an arrow formed out of a couple of broken sticks or some rocks piled together. He saw nothing.

A few minutes later, he reached the area where the trail crossed the creek. He stopped just shy of the water and knelt down, resting his weight on the balls of his feet. He picked up a small, flat stone and skipped it across the surface to the other shore. He watched as it made one . . . two . . . three jumps before landing on the other side.

Where are you, Cody McAlister?

He considered going back to the campsite and hanging around for another hour or so to see if the elusive fisherman would appear. Perhaps he had just decided to stay an extra day and was out fishing. But it was already four-thirty in the afternoon, and daylight, choked out by the thick tree canopy above, would begin to fade over the next couple of hours. With the heavy cloud cover today, darkness would come even earlier than usual. Jackson wanted to be back to the boat he had left docked at the mouth of Eagle Creek before the light faded away completely, if at all possible. Wading across all of those creek crossings in the dark was a good way to get your leg broken.

Well, maybe I'll go back to the campsite and wait at least thirty minutes, Jackson thought.

He placed his hands on the tops of his knees and, with

a slight rocking motion, pushed himself back into a standing position. Just as he was about to turn and head back toward the campsite, something in the water caught his eye. About halfway across the stream, something florescent was being tossed around by the current, waving back and forth like a slithering snake.

What is that? Wait . . . is that a . . . fly line?

He waded out into the stream, the cold water rushing around his feet and ankles. Once he reached the object, he realized it was more than just a fly line—it was a reel and part of a rod, too. He reached down and lifted it off the stream bed. About six or seven feet of the line had been stripped from the reel. He tried the reel and the operation was still smooth, which meant it hadn't been in the water very long, or else the water would have begun to deteriorate the spindle grease, and sediment would have gotten into the moving parts, creating a rough feeling when he turned the handle. The reel was attached to a broken graphite fly rod, which had been snapped just above the cork handle, creating a jagged point on the end.

The line was still thrashing about in the water, dancing with the flowing rhythm and moving carefree with every undulation. He stared at it for a second, and then reeled the line in. He walked back to shore and took his backpack off, then shoved the reel and piece of rod into the pack.

The discovery of the rod and reel troubled Jackson. It wasn't uncommon for fishermen to break their rods. It was easy to lose your balance in the stream and fall onto the narrow piece of graphite, snapping it in two. But if that had happened, the fisherman would not have left the reel and line attached. A good fly line and reel could run several hundred bucks. Why would someone just leave all that money sitting at the bottom of the creek? It made no sense. Unless the rod had been broken farther upstream, and then been washed away from its owner by the swift current. He continued to play out the scenario in his mind.

But wouldn't the owner have seen the reel in the creek as he hiked out?

Of course he would.

The only way back to the campsite was along this trail, and whoever had lost the reel would have had to walk right past it while crossing the creek.

So why hadn't they picked it up?

The only explanation Jackson could come up with— the only one that made any sense, anyway—was that the owner had not returned via the trail. Which, in turn, meant that if it was Mr. McAlister's rod—and Jackson had a growing suspicion that it was—he could be injured somewhere upstream and unable to make his way back out.

Jackson could be wrong, of course. There was always the possibility that whoever had broken the rod just had not had time to make it out yet. But that seemed unlikely. Why stay on the creek if you had no fishing gear? Or the whole thing could just be a big coincidence—but he doubted it. The idea that Mr. McAlister might be injured was not certain by any means, but it was the best theory he could come up with. That being the case, he had to check it out.

He pulled the backpack onto his shoulders and then reached down to grab the two-way radio he always kept on his left hip.

It wasn't there.

"Shit!" Jackson yelled.

He had a habit of taking his radio off while driving because he didn't like the way the seat belt made it press into his side. He must have left it in the truck back at the marina. Now he would have to wait until he returned to the lake and use the boat's radio to call headquarters and report what he had found.

Forgetting the radio was a stupid, rookie mistake.

As he started walking down the trail, back toward Fontana Lake, he silently cursed himself for his own carelessness. Who knew if the extra time it would now take to get the official search started would be the difference in Mr. McAlister living or dying?

This search had to end well. It just had to.

18

By five o'clock, Cody had managed to crawl the remaining fifteen yards to the fishing vest. And although he could barely move when he reached his arm over the fallen log to grab for the vest—that single action alone filled him with such a sense of overpowering joy that he didn't care if it ever ended.

He had made it.

He embraced the tree and began to sob. What few tears his dehydrated body could muster rolled down his cheek and onto the soft moss covering the wood.

He had endured every painful inch of his journey across the cold forest floor. Stuck it out long enough to make it to this decaying log he had been staring at for the last day and a half. The fallen tree he had regarded with such great hope and promise, as if it held some magical power that would rescue him.

Heal him.

There were thousands of logs just like this one lying dead in the mountains, but this particular one was special. This was the one that would save him. And he had finally reached it. Willed himself to it. He had pushed himself so hard to reach this goal. At times, it had seemed impossible—but he had endured. One foot at a time, crawling across the ground, he had persevered and forced himself to continue. Even when he wanted to give up and just lie down and die, he had kept going—and now he had made it.

And now everything was going to be okay. It had to be okay. Soon he would be back in his own house, sleeping in his own bed. He was going to get the water he needed, patch his wounds with the first aid kit, and build a signal fire so the searchers could find him.

Surely they were searching for him by now.

He pulled the vest over the top of the log and spread it out in front of his legs. His one good leg now looked like it had been run through a cheese grater. It was so scratched and bloodied from crawling all day that the sight of it startled him. He hadn't realized it was in such bad shape until now. His left leg was still broken, bruised, and useless, just as it was when he started on the journey, but now the swelling was even worse than before. The area around the break, just below his left knee, was now almost the size of a volleyball. He didn't see how it could get much worse without his skin rupturing.

The fishing vest was in pretty rough shape, too. It had been pulled from his body by the bear and was torn in several places. He frantically unzipped the large pocket on the back of the vest and shoved his arm in. He found the first aid kit, quickly removed it and tossed it aside, then reached his hand back into the pocket for the water bottle.

It was there.

His throat was on fire, and he felt his heart leap in anticipation of the cool water. He pulled the bottle out of the vest and opened the nozzle that would allow the life-saving water to flow out. He turned the bottle up, tilted his head back, and squeezed, ready to take a long drink. The first few drops hit his tongue, then—nothing. He shook the bottle violently and squeezed again.

It was dry.

Something must be wrong. It should have plenty of water inside. Maybe the nozzle had malfunctioned. He turned the bottle in his hand to examine it, and then he saw the two large holes in the side. There were two additional holes opposite those. Teeth marks. The bear must have bitten the bottle when it ripped the vest off of his back. The realization that the water was gone sent rivers of despair through his bruised and broken body. He began to sob. "No . . . No . . . Nooooo!" he cried. The screams just made his throat burn more. The few drops he had gotten from the bottle had done little to quench his thirst.

When he had first looked at the fly vest, he had failed to notice that the lower half was wet from the water that had leaked from the bottle. Now he saw it and quickly grabbed the fabric and thrust it into his mouth. He sucked, trying to draw what little moisture remained into his mouth.

He was desperate now.

After he had sucked one area dry, he moved on to another. This went on for several minutes before he had exhausted the supply and the vest was once again almost bone dry. For all the effort, he had gotten maybe a tablespoon of water, counting the few drops he had gotten from the bottle.

Hardly worth the day-and-a-half journey, crawling like an animal on the forest floor.

He had made the wrong decision. He should have tried to make it to the creek. Maybe he would have made it, maybe not, but at least he knew there was water there. Now he was in a hopeless situation, and every cell in him just wanted to die and end this misery. He tried to keep crying—forcing the anger and pain to flow out of him— but he was so dehydrated that his tears soon dried up.

He picked up the first aid and survival kit, hoping there would be something inside he could use. He spilled its contents on the dry leaves and took an inventory. A small tube of antibiotic ointment, a few adhesive bandages, two doses of Tylenol, anti-diarrhea medication, antihistamine, some moleskin for foot blisters, a small stick of fire starting material, a book of waterproof matches, a hook with some attached fishing line, a pocketknife, and a small emergency blanket now lay in front of him.

He tore open one of the packages of Tylenol and popped the two tablets in his mouth. He tried to produce enough saliva to make them slide down his throat. When that failed, he crushed them between his teeth and managed to swallow most of the powder. The bitter taste of the pills made him want to retch, but he took a deep breath and managed to keep it down.

He looked around him and spotted another large pine tree, similar to the one he had spent the previous night under, off to his right. Daylight had begun to fade and he needed to find shelter soon. He shoved the contents of the first aid kit back in the plastic case and then tossed it and the ruined water bottle back in the fly vest.

The tree was only about ten feet away, but dragging the vest behind him slowed his progress even further, and it took him almost twenty minutes to cover the short distance. When he finally pulled himself under the boughs of the big evergreen, he collapsed with exhaustion. He lay there for a few minutes, catching his breath.

After he had recovered enough to move into a sitting position against the tree, he collected the fire starting stick, matches, and pocketknife. He hoped a fire would make him feel better, at least for a while. After a few minutes, he had gathered a small stockpile of twigs and dry pine needles, which were available in abundance under the tree.

He cleared out a place in front of him, exposing the soil, and placed a handful of the dry needles in the center of it. He broke a few of the larger sticks into smaller pieces and placed them on top. He cut off a small piece of the fire starting material, which was a stick of compressed wood fibers covered with a waxy substance, and placed that at the bottom of the needles. He had little strength left in his damaged arm, but he managed to place the matchbook in his left hand and hold it steady enough to strike the match against the book with his right. It took three attempts before the head of the match burst into flames, but when it did, he quickly moved it to the pile of material. A small flame spread over the needles and then grew until it had engulfed the sticks on top. He began adding more twigs and needles as the fire grew. It was not large by any means, but just having some light to drive away the encroaching darkness was a boost to his spirits.

He squeezed some of the antibiotic ointment from the tube and applied it to his scratched and bleeding legs. He doubted it would help much, but maybe it would relieve the constant stinging sensation he had felt all day.

He returned all the materials he had taken from the kit then placed everything back in the fishing vest, with the exception of the emergency blanket and pocketknife. A damp chill had filled the air as the sunlight dimmed, so he opened the blanket and spread it over himself. He put the knife in the front pocket of his pants.

There, lying on his side under a cloudy and threatening Smoky Mountain sky, he stared into the small fire burning in front of him and tried to find a reason to go on.

To keep pushing himself.

His quest for water had been fruitless and emotionally devastating. If he wasn't found soon, he would die out here—maybe under this very tree. He knew he could not travel much farther, certainly not all the way to the stream, where gallons of water flowed by every second.

He broke a few more branches and placed them on the flame.

One more night, Cody . . . just one more night. They will come tomorrow. They have to . . . they just have to.

19

By the time Jackson reached his boat at the mouth of Eagle Creek, it was almost six-thirty. A heavy, gray blanket of clouds hung above Fontana Lake as far as he could see. The wind whipped around his body and chilled him. He pulled his lightweight jacket from the backpack and put it on. What had been a strong breeze when he had crossed the lake earlier in the day had turned into a steady wind. Small waves were now breaking against the shore. He knew this meant waves on the main channel, where the wind blew between the mountains unabated, would be far worse. It would be a bumpy, jarring ride back to the marina.

He had pushed himself on the walk back, stopping only a couple of times to catch his breath. He dropped his backpack on the bottom of the boat and walked behind the driver's console, where the radio was located. He flipped the power switch and turned the dial to channel ten. He waited a few seconds for his breathing to calm before transmitting because he didn't want to sound panicked over the airwaves.

He depressed the transmit button on the side of the microphone and said, "Headquarters, this is Ranger Hart." After a few seconds with no reply, he tried again. "Headquarters, this is Ranger Hart. Come in, please."

After more silence, the microphone finally crackled back at him, "Ranger Hart, this is Headquarters . . . go ahead."

He recognized the voice on the other end. It belonged to Sarah, a single, twenty-four-year-old with a smoking-hot body, brown hair, and beautiful hazel eyes. He was eight years older than she was, but that didn't discourage him at all. They had even gone out for dinner a couple of times, when he was stationed at headquarters a few years ago, but nothing serious ever came of it. She was a looker, though, and he always made sure to swing by the dispatch office any time he was at headquarters to say hello.

"I'm currently at the mouth of Eagle Creek. The Back-country Office got a call this morning from a lady who said her friend had come up here on a camping trip and hadn't returned. Janice thought it was probably just a mis-communication between the two parties, so she called me and asked if I would come check it out before we sent the cavalry in looking for this guy." He paused to catch his breath, his heart still racing from the hike out. "Anyway, I walked up to campsite ninety-seven and found his tent and other belongings, but I couldn't locate him . . . over."

There was a pause before Sarah returned to the radio. "Headquarters copies . . . I'll let Bobby know what's go-ing on so he can start coordinating the search and rescue operation."

Shit. Bobby's there . . . I thought he was on vacation this week. "Okay, sounds good. If Bobby needs to contact me, I'll be at my residence gathering a few things for the search," he said, trying to hide the irritation that had sud-denly arisen in him at the mention of Bobby's name.

"Copy, that. Headquarters out," Sarah replied.

Some girls have it all, Jackson thought. *Even her voice is sexy.*

He reached down and turned the ignition. Bluish smoke

filled the air, carrying with it the smell of two-cycle engine oil, as the old outboard sputtered to life. He jumped back onshore and released the dock line, then pushed off from the rocky bank with one foot as he simultaneously climbed back aboard. Once he was behind the driver's console, he pushed the throttle forward and headed toward the marina.

As the boat began to slide across the surface, drops of the displaced water were picked up by the stiff wind and stung Jackson in the face. His mind should have been focused on the upcoming search, but it was instead preoccupied with one man—and it wasn't Mr. McAlister.

Bobby Donaldson, the proverbial thorn in Jackson's side, was the chief ranger at the Great Smoky Mountains National Park, and Jackson's direct supervisor. To say there was a history between the two of them would be a gross understatement. Bobby was one of those guys who let everyone else do the work and took all the credit for himself. A thirty-year veteran of the Park Service, he was the stereotypical government employee—highly political in his dealings and an expert at doing nothing while making his bosses think they could not live without him. He was a real jackass, and Jackson—well, there was no other word for it—despised him.

It seemed to Jackson that Bobby had been after him ever since he had started his job at the park. Whatever Jackson did, somehow Bobby would find fault. Jackson could never please him, not that he even cared to try, but that was beside the point.

It had been a big adjustment for Jackson. His former supervisor, back in Colorado, had been awesome. They had actually become close friends and often spent off days hiking or fishing together in the park.

But Bobby was a different creature. Try as he might, Jackson couldn't figure him out. It seemed he was just always unhappy, no matter what. After the first six months of trying to stay on his good side, Jackson had given up and just said, "To hell with it." He stayed out of Bobby's way as much as possible, and when the opportunity presented itself to fill the opening at Twentymile, Jackson had jumped at the chance to get out from under Bobby's overbearing thumb.

With the new job, Jackson no longer had to work with Bobby on a daily basis, which was a huge bonus, but he still had contact with him during searches or large projects that took him over to headquarters on occasion. And, more importantly, he still had to answer to him if anything went wrong—that was what had caused their most severe clash.

About a year and a half ago, Jackson had been dispatched to assist in a search for a lost ten-year-old boy in the Cades Cove area. Located in the western section of the park, Cades Cove was a special place, tucked between the majestic, hardwood-covered mountains. Expansive green valleys, teeming with whitetail deer and black bear, were dotted with preserved nineteenth-century mountain homesteads and churches. Add to that crystal clear streams and tremendous mountain views, and it all combined to make Cades Cove one of the most beautiful, and most visited, areas within the park's boundaries.

The Cantwell family had been visiting Cades Cove in October, during the peak season for viewing the famous fall colors. They had stopped for a picnic lunch at the visitor center, located on the southwestern tip of the eleven-mile road that runs along the edge of the valley. Everything went fine until the family finished lunch. The couple's two boys, thirteen-year-old Marcus and his ten-year-old brother, Steven, went out into the field to pass a football around, while Mom and Dad rested on a picnic blanket.

After about thirty minutes, Marcus had returned without his brother. When questioned by his parents, he stated that he had passed the football to Steven, but it had gone over his head and bounced into the woods. Steven had walked into the woods searching for the football but had never returned. The Cantwells had conducted a quick search themselves but had been unable to locate Steven. Panic-stricken, the parents had alerted the authorities.

It was Bobby's standard operating procedure that during searches he was the on-scene commander, and he also managed any air assets that were being used. Another ranger, in this particular case it had been Jackson, ran the ground search.

The search had lasted almost a full week and involved more than fifty personnel conducting searches on foot, as well as numerous people on all-terrain vehicles and horseback. A helicopter had also been brought in to assist.

As usual, Bobby had taken charge right off the bat. In his typical domineering style, he made decisions without consulting any of the other searchers, some of whom had much more experience in search and rescue operations, and ignored advice from Jackson—or anyone else, for that matter—when confronted about his decisions.

Jackson was officially the ranger in charge of the ground search, but the title was little more than just that. Bobby questioned every decision Jackson made and often overruled him, sometimes in front of the searchers Jackson was supposed to be leading. That made Jackson furious.

By the end of the week, Jackson had been at his wits' end. Bobby had nearly driven him crazy, but worse than that, they had found no sign of Steven. They had searched all week, stopping for only three or four hours to sleep at night, and had covered over two square miles of territory on the ground, and much more by air. Still, there was no sign of the boy. Three consecutive nights of freezing temperatures compounded things. Warming tents were set up to provide relief from the cold and wind, but by the end of the week, everyone was exhausted and ready to call it quits.

Bobby had decided to call the search off on Friday afternoon—just six days after the boy had gone missing. And, coincidentally, just in time for Bobby to get home for the weekend.

Jackson had not agreed.

There was a drainage ditch less than two hundred yards away from the picnic area, heavily wooded and overgrown with rhododendron and mountain laurel. It had already been searched earlier in the week, but Jackson knew it warranted a second look. His theory was that Steven had gone into the woods for the football, gotten turned around, and was unable to find his way back to the field where his brother was. From the field, the terrain sloped gently down toward the drainage ditch. Jackson surmised that Steven had gotten tired and confused and then, just like electricity, had followed the path of least resistance—which meant he would have traveled downhill, toward the ditch. It was a theory he had tested in the past during other searches, and it usually turned out to be accurate.

Normally, except during periods of drought, a small stream of water flowed through the ditch due to runoff from the surrounding mountains. During the first search of the area, Jackson had noted that there was, indeed, water in the ditch. This served to bolster his belief that if Steven had made his way into the drainage ditch, simply by following the natural flow of the terrain, he would have stayed there, because he would at least have had water to drink. The problem was, the ditch was more than a hundred yards long and the vegetation was so thick, a small child would have been easy to overlook.

Jackson had wanted just one more day to try to find Steven. But Bobby had made up his mind, and once that happened, he would allow no one to change it. A very loud argument had ensued in the middle of the small tent city that served as search headquarters. Steven's parents had, of course, sided with Jackson, begging Bobby to search for just one more day. But no matter who tried to persuade Bobby, he would not budge.

Tired and beyond frustrated, Jackson had finally given in and ceased arguing. The search was discontinued.

Six months later, as warm spring temperatures drove winter's grasp away and thawed the cold mountains, Steven's body was found by a hiker who had wandered off one of the many trails that ran through the area. The little boy was curled up under a small rock outcropping—in the very drainage area Jackson had wanted to search again.

When Jackson first heard the news, he had become so sick to his stomach he threw up. He had marched into Bobby's office, irate. Fortunately, one of the other rangers saw what was going on and had followed Jackson into the office and grabbed him just before he could throw the punch.

The coroner determined that Steven had died from a combination of dehydration and exposure. But Jackson knew damn well what he had died of—stupidity and stubbornness. And he didn't need any coroner's report to tell him that.

An internal Park Service investigation was launched to determine how the boy could have gone undetected, only two hundred yards away from the visitor's center, with so many active searchers in the area.

That part didn't surprise Jackson at all. When people are lost, especially scared little ten-year-old boys, they panic. Sometimes they become so paralyzed by fear that they refuse to do something, anything, to try to make it out alive—even if it means staying in a location until they die. Others wander aimlessly, sometimes for days, before finally succumbing to the elements.

The official investigation determined that the most likely scenario was just as Jackson had concluded. Steven had wandered around the area, trying to find his way back to his family, before becoming exhausted and following the terrain down into the drainage area. Once there, he had water for the first day or so, but soon became too weak to move from under the rock outcropping. Steven had spent his last hours alone, huddled under a cold slab of stone, thirsty and freezing.

It was a horrible way to die.

In typical Bobby fashion, he had tried to pin the whole debacle on Jackson. Bobby accused him of being derelict in his duties during the first search of the drainage, which had taken place on day two. Bobby had recommended to the investigation board that Jackson's employment with the Park Service be terminated.

Jackson didn't believe Steven had been in that area when it was first searched. At least that's what he kept telling himself. More than likely, the boy had come there a day or two after the searchers moved through, but Jackson couldn't be sure. And that was what kept him awake at night. Reliving the nightmare of that little boy slowly dying—scared and alone—under a callous pile of rocks. Constantly second-guessing himself. Wondering if the whole damn mess *was* his fault.

Had he walked right by the boy and failed to see him? Was he really cut out to be a park ranger?

The investigation board had cleared both Jackson and Bobby of any wrongdoing, calling it an *unfortunate incident*. But Jackson knew better, and he had never forgiven Bobby for what he had done. One more day of searching would have saved Steven's life, he was sure of that—but now it was too late.

In Jackson's eyes, Bobby was a self-serving egomaniac who deserved to be fired. Jackson wanted nothing else to do with Bobby Donaldson—ever. But now, guiding his green and white Boston Whaler across the windswept main channel of Fontana Lake, he found himself in a similar situation. One he would love to be able to escape, but knew he couldn't.

Another search. Another run-in with Bobby.

He knew for sure that he had made at least one mistake during the search for Steven—one that cost him countless hours of sleep during the last eighteen months. He had caved and let Bobby end the search prematurely, and in the process, failed young Steven and his family. He should have gone over Bobby's head to the park superintendent and pled his case for continuing the search.

He should have done more.

As another spray of water hit him in the face, Jackson promised himself one thing. He wasn't going to let the pompous son of a bitch get away with it again.

Never again.

As he entered the cove where the marina was located, he decreased the throttle on the big outboard. As the boat slowed to a no-wake speed, Jackson was surprised to see two attractive young ladies waiting at the end of the dock.

20

It was after six o'clock when Katie pulled into the parking lot at Mountain View Resort. By the time she had packed her suitcase and Tiffany had arrived at her house, it had been one o'clock—almost two hours later than she had planned to leave. The Atlanta traffic had been horrible, as usual, and they had stopped once for gas and food at a convenience store. Tiffany was prone to motion sickness, which had forced Katie to stop several more times so Tiffany could empty her stomach contents on the side of the curvy mountain road.

It had been a long, arduous drive and the knot in the pit of her stomach had not diminished. She had packed enough clothing for a week-long stay. She didn't know how long it would take to find Cody, but she did not intend on returning to Atlanta until she knew he was okay. That was what she kept telling herself, anyway.

He was okay. He had to be.

"Thank goodness," Tiffany whispered as she released her seat belt and opened the passenger door.

One look at her face forced Katie to stifle a laugh. Tiffany's skin was pale, and sweat from her forehead had turned her auburn hair into a matted mess. "You look like hell," Katie said, feeling guilty for even wanting to smile at a time like this.

"Thanks," Tiffany replied, her eyes giving Katie the playful *go to hell* look that she was so good at.

Katie allowed herself a smile. "Sorry, Tiff. I told you not to have that day-old burrito for lunch. Greasy convenience store food and mountain roads don't mix so well."

"Well, it didn't help that you were driving like a crazy woman," Tiffany added as she rolled herself out of the passenger seat and shut the door.

"Sorry, I was just in a hurry to get up here and see what was really going on." That single statement brought the reality of the situation back to the forefront of Katie's mind and wiped any semblance of a smile off her face.

"I know . . . it's okay," Tiffany said. She followed Katie toward the lodge's entrance.

Katie had been to the lodge on a few occasions, but the beauty of the Great Room always amazed her. An afternoon chill had cooled the mountain air, and Katie heard the distinctive popping sound of burning wood. As she passed the fireplace, the warmth felt good against her goose-pimpled flesh. An older man and woman sat in front of the fireplace, drinking coffee and making small talk.

She approached the wooden registration counter on the right, behind which stood a middle-aged man dressed in brown slacks and a forest-green polo shirt.

As she rested her forearms on the counter, the attendant looked up and said, "Hi, may I help you?"

"My name is Katie Richardson." She paused when she noticed the attendant giving Tiffany a quizzical stare. "Don't worry about her. She's just been introduced to mountain curves at fifty miles an hour." She gave Tiffany another subtle smile.

"I look that bad, huh?" Tiffany asked the attendant.

The lodging attendant didn't say anything; he just shrugged and turned his attention back to Katie.

"Ah . . . shit. I feel horrible," Tiffany said. "You know, I think I'll step outside and get some fresh air, Katie."

"Okay, no problem. I'll be out in a few minutes."

After Tiffany walked away, Katie looked back at the attendant. "I need a room. Two queen beds."

"I'm sorry, ma'am, but we have no vacancy for at least the next four nights."

"What? You can't be serious. Really?"

"A big corporate convention has the place booked solid through Sunday night."

Katie looked at the attendant's name tag. Maybe a more personal touch would do the trick. "Look, Kevin . . . you don't understand the situation I'm in here. I'm looking for my friend, who's missing, and I really need a place to stay for the night. I've been on the road all afternoon. I'm tired, hungry, and I would really appreciate it if you could help me out. Can you please check again and see if you can find anything?" She was trying her best to stay calm.

Kevin sighed. Then he looked down at the computer screen and tapped a few keys. "Ma'am, I'm really sorry, but there's nothing I can do for you right now. We're booked solid. I can put your name on standby, and if we have a cancellation I'll be glad to give you a call."

Realizing that further pleading was hopeless, she simply said, "Fine, thank you." After giving Kevin her cell number, she turned and walked outside to rejoin Tiffany.

"Feeling any better?" Katie asked.

"Little bit, I guess." Tiffany was leaning against the grill of the 4Runner, taking deep breaths and brushing her hair. The color in her face had begun to return.

"You're looking better. You'll be fine, just try to stay hydrated." Katie opened the driver's door and pulled a bottle of water from the center dash, which she tossed to Tiffany. "Here . . . drink this."

"Thanks." Tiffany opened the water and drank a quarter of it before replacing the plastic cap.

"Well, Tiff . . . kinda got some bad news," Katie said, trying to keep her tone upbeat.

"Great. What's that?" Tiffany asked.

"There are no rooms available for at least the next four days."

"You're kidding."

"Sorry, I wish I was. He put us on standby . . . said he would give us a call if something opened up, but he didn't seem too optimistic."

"So let's just go somewhere else. No big deal."

"Tiffany, we're in the middle of the mountains . . . there *is* nowhere else. Nothing decent within an hour's drive, anyway."

"Well, now what are we going to do?" Tiffany asked, running a hand through her hair.

"There's a campground down by the lake, I brought a tent and some gear in case we needed them for the search. Guess we'll have to stay there tonight and try to figure out something tomorrow. Once we get settled, I'll call the Park Service again and see what the plan is for the search. Sorry 'bout this, Tiff." She paused. "But I really do appreciate you coming with me."

"Yeah, yeah. You owe me, though, girlfriend." Tiffany headed for the passenger side of the vehicle and opened the door. "Well, let's get going. I hear the campground offers complimentary cocktails to the first ten couples that show up."

The sarcasm made Katie smile. She was so grateful for her friend's presence right now. "Thanks, Tiff," she said.

"No problem." Tiffany gave Katie a wink. "Now let's hurry so we can get the primo campsite."

Just as Katie was walking toward the driver's side door, her cell phone rang. She pulled the phone from her front pocket and looked at the screen. The caller ID displayed *Unknown Number*. Normally she would have just let it go to voicemail, but instead, she tapped the screen and said, "Hello?"

"This is Janice at the Backcountry Office, calling for Katie Richardson," the voice said on the other end.

Katie felt her stomach rise into her throat. Her pulse quickened. Had they found him? Was he alive? Dead? Her mind continued to imagine disastrous scenarios, but she fought down the panic enough to speak. "Hi Janice, this is Katie."

"Katie, I was just about to leave for the evening when I heard Ranger Hart call in to dispatch. He went out to see if he could find your friend today, but didn't have any luck."

"Really? I actually drove up from Atlanta this afternoon, and I'm in the area now. Would it be possible for me to speak to the ranger in person?"

"Well, he said he was at Eagle Creek and was going back to his residence to gather a few things for the formal search. If you want to talk to him, he should be arriving back at the marina in a few minutes. Do you know where the marina is located?"

"Yes . . . I know where it is. I'm at the Mountain View Lodge right now." Katie was having a difficult time gathering her thoughts. "Is that all he said?"

"That's all I heard, ma'am. I'm sure everything is fine and they will find your friend tomorrow," Janice said.

Why did everyone insist on telling her everything was going to be all right? It sure didn't feel like everything was okay. She was worried; had been all day. And this phone call hadn't done a damn thing to calm her nerves.

"Okay. Thank you, Janice," Katie said, her voice betraying the anxiety boiling up within her.

"Well, you seemed like such a nice young lady this morning, I thought I would call and let you know what I heard," Janice replied. "You'd better get down to the marina now if you want to catch Ranger Hart before he leaves."

"Yes, we're heading that way now. Thank you again for calling me. I really appreciate it." Katie waved her arm at Tiffany to hurry up and get in the car. Katie jumped behind the wheel and reached for her seat belt.

"I'll say a prayer for you and your friend tonight," Janice said.

"Thank you, Janice. That's very nice of you. Right now, I can use all the prayers I can get." Janice's kindness touched Katie. Sadly, in today's society, finding a kind soul like this woman was not as common as it once was.

"If you need anything, I'm just a phone call away," Janice said in the same motherly tone that had comforted Katie earlier.

"I'll do that. Thank you."

Katie was already backing out of the parking spot when Tiffany asked, "What was that about?"

Katie quickly explained what she had learned from Janice as she threw the 4Runner in gear and sped out of the parking lot.

Within a few minutes, they were back on the road that led to the marina. Katie was taking the curves too fast, her tires letting out the occasional squeal on the asphalt. She looked over at Tiffany, who had a death grip on the door handle. She looked carsick again, her face pale and beads of sweat on her forehead. "You okay?" Katie asked.

"Yeah . . . fine," Tiffany replied. Her face told a different story. She was about to hurl at any moment.

"Drink some more water," Katie said.

Tiffany took a few sips of the water, and her complexion seemed to improve.

Five minutes later, Katie pulled the 4Runner over the hill that led down to the lake, thankful that she hadn't been forced to stop again for Tiffany's ailing stomach. She scanned the vehicles parked on both sides of the narrow road. "There it is." She pointed toward the Toyota pickup so Tiffany could see. "That's his truck, the red one."

Katie quickly found a parking spot and ran over to the truck to see if anything looked out of the ordinary. Nothing did. Everything was as it should be. She noticed the Park Service Suburban parked a short distance from Cody's vehicle. "Looks like the ranger is still here. Come on." She started down the hill toward the marina, with Tiffany following close behind.

Katie opened the door to the marina and asked the man behind the counter if he had seen the ranger.

"No, but Jesse told me that he went over to Eagle Creek earlier this afternoon. I haven't seen him since I came on shift, and his boat is still gone. Should be back before dark, though. He keeps the boat in the last slip on the right." The attendant pointed toward the long dock on the opposite side of the building.

"Thanks." Katie briskly crossed the floor of the store and opened the glass door that led to the boat slips.

She reached the end of the dock and stopped. The breeze coming off the water blew her blonde hair around her face. She took a deep breath and looked out over the lake, the smell of the fresh water flooding her senses. Even at a horrible time like this, the beauty of this place took her breath away. She had loved coming up here ever since she was a child. She just hoped that she could get Cody back. Otherwise, she might never be able to come here again. She still was unable to go to Eric's favorite restaurant. Too many bad memories.

Tiffany walked up beside her. "Wow, what a gorgeous view."

"Yes, it is." Katie ran her hand across her face to brush the errant hair away. "Yes, it is," she repeated.

Tiffany put her arm around Katie.

All the stress that Katie had been under came crashing down on her in one brief moment. She began to sob and buried her head in Tiffany's shoulder.

"Shhh . . . We'll find him. I promise," Tiffany said as she

rubbed Katie's back.

The sound of an outboard motor approaching caused Katie to pull away from Tiffany's arms and look back across the water. A boat was heading toward the dock.

21

Jackson guided the boat into the dock and killed the engine. The two women on the dock were watching him intently. One had blonde hair, the other red. Although they looked tired and a bit disheveled—the blonde looked like she had been crying—they were both very attractive. He made eye contact with both women but didn't speak. Instead, he gave a polite nod, a common form of greeting in the South, but got no response. He secured the forward and aft dock lines around the metal cleats that were attached to the dock and grabbed his pack. As he stepped out of the boat, the blonde approached him. The redhead followed close behind.

"Are you Ranger Hart?" the blonde asked.

"I am. And you are?" Jackson was still irritable from reliving the horrible memories of his last search with Bobby. Realizing his response was a little terse, before the blonde could answer, he added, "I'm sorry. Is there something I can do for you, ma'am?"

"My name is Katie Richardson, and my friend is missing on Eagle Creek. Janice at the Backcountry Office called me and said you had been out looking for him."

The look on the lady's face told Jackson that she did not have a good feeling about the whole situation. "Yes, ma'am, that's correct. I went up to campsite ninety-seven this afternoon to look for your friend. Cody McAlister, isn't it?"

"Yes, that's right. Did you find anything?"

"No, ma'am, I'm sorry, I didn't. I found his campsite and everything appeared normal, but I was unable to locate him. We are in the process of organizing an official search now," Jackson replied.

He could see the disappointment on her face. He had seen that look in family members' eyes before. The look of desperation, of total helplessness. It was never easy to take, and it tugged at his soul every time. When they were powerless, they always turned to him to fix everything. To find their loved ones or help an injured friend. He felt the weight of their expectations on his shoulders every single time.

Sometimes it worked out and everyone went home happy. Other times it did not—like the Steven Cantwell case. For Jackson, those were the hardest to endure. Because even if he did everything right, sometimes *shit* just happened and there was nothing he could do to change that. Still, he always felt that the family blamed him, somehow, for whatever bad thing had happened to their loved one. He tried not to become emotionally involved in these situations, but at times, it was almost impossible.

"I'm sure we'll find him tomorrow, though. This sort of thing happens all the time," Jackson lied, trying to give Katie some reassurance. It wasn't uncommon for a hiker or fisherman to go missing for a day and then turn up alive and well, that part was true, but he withheld the fact that a sick feeling had been growing in the pit of his stomach ever since he had found the broken rod and reel lying on the streambed.

"Wait." He paused and unzipped the backpack. "I did find this." He pulled out the section of broken rod with the attached reel. "Do you recognize it?"

The look on Katie's face when she saw the rod and reel told Jackson everything he needed to know. "Yes." Katie hesitated, then reached for the rod and took it from Jackson. "I do . . . I sold him this rod and reel last month. He wanted something smaller for the mountain streams, so I pointed him toward this one. It was a seven-and-a-half-foot three-weight."

"Are you sure it's his? There must have been thousands of these manufactured."

Katie turned the piece of broken rod in her hand so she could look at the silver cap at the end of the handle. "Positive. He had his initials engraved into the end cap."

Jackson bent down to get a closer look. The letters *CDM* were scrolled into the nickel cap.

Katie continued, "CDM . . . Cody David McAlister. It's his . . . no doubt about it. Where did you find it?"

"It was at the bottom of the creek at the first crossing above the campsite."

"It was just lying in the creek?" Katie asked, a puzzled look on her face.

"Yes, ma'am. Lying there on the bottom, jammed between two rocks. I thought that maybe someone had broken it and this piece washed downstream before they could recover it. But then I wondered—why wouldn't they have picked it up when they returned on the trail? If someone had lost it, they would have recovered the reel and line, if nothing else. It didn't make sense."

"No, it doesn't."

"The reel hadn't been in the water long. I checked, and it still works fine."

Katie spun the reel. "Yeah, you're right," she said. "Still feels smooth." She handed the broken rod back to Jackson and he returned it to his pack.

"What do you think happened to Cody?" Katie asked. The air was cool, but she wiped her brow with her hand to remove the beads of sweat that had popped up.

"I'm not sure. But now that we know it is definitely his rod, at least we have a starting point. He could have been injured upstream, and the broken rod washed away from him. That would explain why it was still on the bottom of the stream . . . he never walked back to the campsite."

"So what's next?" The stress in Katie's voice was unmistakable.

Jackson turned toward the water and the darkening sky. "Well, we'll get a search started in the morning. Take some guys on foot up to the campsite and search the area thoroughly. Hopefully, the weather will hold off and we can get a helicopter in the air, too." He picked up his pack and swung it over his left shoulder, then turned and began walking toward the building at the opposite end of the dock. Katie and the redhead followed him.

"What the hell do you mean, *tomorrow*?" He heard the redhead say.

Jackson kept walking at his normal brisk pace. "I *mean* tomorrow, ma'am. There's nothing that can be done tonight."

"Typical," she muttered.

The comment sent a flash of anger through Jackson, but he tried his best to suppress his irritation and remain calm. Stressful situations such as these often brought out the worst in people, but it would only complicate things if he lost his temper and participated in a shouting match. Dealing with family members and friends was often one of the more difficult aspects of search and rescue operations. He stopped and calmly turned to face her. "What's that supposed to mean?" he asked.

"It means that you government guys should get your asses in gear and go find Cody tonight," she yelled.

Jackson felt his jaw muscles tense, but he managed to speak in an even, calm tone. "Look, ma'am, searches take time to get organized. If we sent a bunch of guys into the mountains tonight just blindly walking around, we would be putting more people at risk. I promise you, we are doing everything we can. What's your name, ma'am?"

The redhead looked like she was ready to tear his head off. He cracked a smile, which he could tell only served to further infuriate her.

Katie interjected, "Sorry, Ranger Hart. I should have introduced you. This is Tiffany Colson. She's my best friend and drove up with me today."

"Oh, I see. Pleased to make your acquaintance, Ms. Colson," Jackson said.

Tiffany just stared at him with laser eyes and said nothing.

Jackson turned and continued toward the marina building. He opened the glass door and walked toward the desk, where the attendant was standing behind the cash register. "Hey, Steve. Can you let Jesse know there will be a search party here early tomorrow morning? We will need him to take the searchers across to Eagle Creek in the pontoon boat."

"Sure thing, Jackson," the attendant replied.

"Thanks, and tell the family I said hi," Jackson said.

"Will do. Have a good night, Jackson." The attendant quickly scribbled himself a note on a thin, yellow pad.

"You do the same." Jackson turned and walked out the door that led to the parking area. As he walked across the last section of dock and stepped onto shore, he could hear the two women following him.

Tiffany picked up her pace until she had caught up with him. She grabbed his elbow and spun him around. "Seriously? You're just going home and leaving Cody out there all night?"

Her pale and lightly freckled face had turned a crimson shade. Jackson could see the fury in her eyes. He sighed and rubbed his eyelids. It had been a long day—too long, really—and he didn't have the time or desire to listen to this lady second-guess him. He did enough of that on his own.

He gathered his thoughts for a few seconds and then looked back at the pretty redhead. "Tiffany, is it?" She nodded. "Look, I already told you there is nothing we can do tonight. I'm sorry, but that's just the way it is. It takes time to get a large search organized. Why don't you two go to the resort, get some dinner, and go to bed. If you want to help in the search, be back here at five o'clock tomorrow morning."

"You've got to be kidding me," Tiffany said as she put her hand on her forehead and turned her back to Jackson.

Her dismissive tone angered Jackson, and he could no longer hold his tongue. "Look, lady—"

"Tiffany, stop it!" Katie interrupted. "He's just trying to help." She paused and Jackson could see her eyes well up. "And he's right . . . there's nothing that can be done tonight."

Katie walked closer to Jackson and said in a low voice, "I'm sorry. She means well, she's just as worried about Cody as I am. I'm really thankful for all you're doing. We already stopped at the resort before we came here to the marina. They're full, so we're going to sleep down at the campground. We'll be back here tomorrow morning at five."

"Fine," Jackson responded. He resumed walking toward the Suburban, trying to ignore the voice in his head that was urging him to offer some assistance. All he wanted to do was go home, take a hot shower, crawl onto his cheap mattress, and go to sleep. But the voice kept telling him to do something. When he could no longer justify his indifference, he stopped and turned to face the women once more. They did look like they needed help, and what kind of man would he be if he just let them sleep in their car all night?

He looked down at the ground and sighed. "Dammit." He ran a hand through his hair, then looked up and met two sets of eyes. "Look, I probably shouldn't do this, I'm almost positive I'm breaking some sort of Park Service regulation, but you two can come stay at my house tonight, if you want. I live down at Twentymile Creek. It's not much, but one of you can sleep on the couch, and I have an air mattress we can put on the floor. You can ride with me if you like. Your car will be fine here overnight."

"Oh, I know where that is. I've fished Twentymile a few times. That's very nice of you," Katie said. "What do you think, Tiffany?"

Tiffany was still fuming. "I'm not going anywhere with him."

"Suit yourself. Enjoy sleeping in the car tonight, darlin'." Jackson's conscience was clear. He had offered assistance, and the ungrateful brat had turned him down. *So be it.* He turned, walked the remaining few steps to his vehicle, and unlocked the driver's door. He threw the pack into the backseat and then started to close the door.

"Wait!" Katie yelled. "We'll go . . . we'll go! Come on, Tiff." She grabbed Tiffany's arm and practically dragged her toward the Suburban. "Thank you again, Ranger Hart."

"You can just call me Jackson. No need for all the formality."

"Okay. Thank you, Jackson. I really appreciate it." Katie's eyes translated her genuine gratefulness to Jackson. She opened the passenger door and climbed inside the vehicle. "And you can just call me Katie," she added.

Her face the picture of reluctance, Tiffany opened the door behind Katie and crawled into the backseat.

"No problem, Katie. Glad I could help. So what does the pissed off one in the backseat go by?" Jackson asked.

"Her friends call her Tiff."

"Maybe I'll just stick to Ms. Colson for now," Jackson said.

Katie turned to look at Tiffany, who was staring out the

window. She wasn't smiling.

"Can you stop by the blue 4Runner over there and let me grab the luggage?" Katie asked Jackson.

Jackson pulled in front of the 4Runner. Katie jumped out and grabbed two suitcases and her backpack from the vehicle. After placing them in the back of the Suburban, she returned to the passenger seat. "Thanks, Jackson. Let's go."

22

The last hints of daylight had faded from the overcast sky by the time Jackson parked the Suburban in the short gravel driveway in front of his house. He grabbed his pack from the backseat and then helped Katie unload the two suitcases from the rear cargo compartment. Tiffany had already exited the vehicle and was walking toward the house.

"I can get these," Katie said as she slung her backpack over her shoulders.

"No, I've got 'em," Jackson replied. He hefted the two suitcases and headed toward the front porch. Tiffany was waiting to be let in. She had said nothing since the blowup at the marina. Jackson ignored her and set the suitcases down on the porch. The screen door screeched when he pulled it open. He had meant to oil the hinges last week, but had forgotten. The wind caught the screen door and slammed it against the side of the house. Jackson noticed Tiffany jump at the sound.

He fished the key out of his pants pocket and opened the front door. "Ladies first." He stood aside while Tiffany and Katie entered, then heaved the two suitcases through the door frame and pulled the screen door shut behind him. He bet the larger of the two suitcases weighed close to seventy pounds. "What have you got in this, a dead body? Thing weighs a ton."

"Sorry. That one's mine," Katie confessed. "I packed for a week-long stay. I wasn't sure how many days I would be up here."

Jackson heard Tiffany stifle a laugh. It wasn't much, but at least it was something. Maybe she had a soul after all. He closed the old wooden door and engaged the deadbolt.

He looked at the two women. They both looked exhausted. "Are either of you hungry? I don't have a lot of variety here. I'm a bachelor and eat mostly microwave meals, but I'm sure I can scrounge something up for dinner."

Katie patted her stomach. "I'm starved."

Tiffany gave only a slight nod.

"Okay then. You can put your things in the living room for now. The bathroom is down the hall on the right. Towels are in the cabinet. I suggest you take a shower tonight if you want one. If you two are going to help in the search, you might not get another chance for the next several days."

"That sounds great, thank you," Katie said over her shoulder as she pulled the oversized suitcase toward the living room. Tiffany picked the other one up and followed.

Jackson turned his attention to the kitchen cabinets. He hadn't had a woman in this house in more than a year, and it showed. His cabinets were almost bare. He opened the freezer and searched through a stack of frozen dinners. Unhappy with the selection, he turned back toward the cabinet and finally found a box of dry spaghetti that had probably been in there since the last time he had cooked for a guest. He searched through the few canned goods he had and came up with a large can of spaghetti sauce. That would have to do. Besides, it was late, and he doubted the two women would be picky.

He put a pot of water on to boil, added salt, and began

putting the only real set of plates and silverware he owned on the kitchen table. Normally he just used plastic—he hated washing dishes.

The sound of the shower running caused him to lift his head and look into the living room. Had to be Katie in the shower, as Tiffany was rummaging through her suitcase. He thought about going in and trying to smooth things over with her, but decided to leave her alone. He wouldn't push it. Besides, Tiffany didn't seem like the kind of girl who'd let anyone smooth-talk her.

He had to admit that some part of him was attracted to her. At least on some level—maybe only the superficial, physical level—he wasn't sure. She was a very attractive woman, that part couldn't be disputed. Her auburn hair and emerald-green eyes had caught his attention before he had even stepped off the boat back at the marina. She was wearing tight jeans, and he admired her well-toned figure as she pulled some clothes out of the suitcase.

But she had also been a complete pain in his ass today, which was not necessarily a bad thing—he actually preferred a little fire in his women. Otherwise, they were just plain boring.

He turned his attention away from Tiffany and back to making dinner. He dumped the entire box of pasta into the boiling water and found a small pot for warming the sauce. Then he put away the Indian chief he had been carving before he had gotten the call about Cody and swept up the pile of shavings off the floor.

His noticed his hands were shaking slightly. He was nervous. Almost nothing made Jackson nervous, not even sneaking up on poachers in the middle of the night.

But women, Tiffany in particular, made him nervous.

Tiffany adjusted the hot and cold knobs until the water running from the shower head was comfortable. She kept the temperature more to the hot end of the spectrum, as the cool and humid mountain air had put a chill in her bones. She lathered shampoo into her long, red hair and let the water wash over her naked body in hot waves that drove the coldness away.

Tiffany was not exactly happy with being in this stranger's house tonight. In fact, the whole place gave her the creeps. The pipes made a weird clanging sound when she turned the water on, and the inside looked like something from a seventies horror movie.

The house could use a good update. Paint instead of the outdated wallpaper, modern light fixtures, new countertops and a tile floor—instead of the old, stained linoleum in the kitchen—would do wonders for the place.

But she had to admit it was nice of Ranger Hart to offer his help. She had been rude to him earlier today. No one needed to point it out to her—she knew it for a fact. She wouldn't have blamed him if he had just sent them to the campground to sleep.

She told herself the reason she had been such a bitch to him was that she was just looking out for Katie, not to mention that a bad case of motion sickness had kept her puking her guts up all afternoon—but that wasn't the whole truth.

She had always had a tough time dealing with people, especially during stressful situations. Instead of working through the problem as a normal person would, she became withdrawn and lashed out at the people who were just trying to help her.

She knew she should apologize to Jackson. But that would mean she would have to admit she was wrong—and if there was one thing she hated worse than her social dysfunction, it was admitting she was wrong.

By the time she finished washing the rest of her body, the hot shower had left Tiffany feeling invigorated. She turned the water off and flung the vinyl shower curtain open. Goosebumps formed over her flesh as the cool air hit her once more. She grabbed a large cotton towel from the wooden cabinet above the toilet and dried off.

She wrapped the towel around herself and let it hang off her shoulders while she brushed her hair in front of the mirror. The glass was cracked in the lower left corner, and she wondered if the whole thing might fall out and crash on top of her. As she worked to comb through a knot in her hair, the towel parted, exposing her breasts and stomach. She allowed the towel to fall to the floor in a clump, and she stared at herself in the mirror.

The scars stared back at her.

Her right hand moved over her abdomen, as if it had a mind of its own, her index finger tracing the scar that ran from just underneath her left breast to her belly button. The flesh was smooth and a washed-out silver color. Another scar ran from the inside of her right breast to the back of her ribcage. She touched it, too. Although the doctors had done an excellent job of stitching her wounds, the scars were always there as a constant reminder of that night.

She hated the scars.

She hated seeing herself naked. It always made her think of that night—the night she had barely escaped with her life. Memories of what he had done to her flashed through her mind. The pain. The fear.

The scars were the reason she never wore a bikini at the pool or exposed her midriff at the gym. The reason she hated going to the doctor, afraid to show them to anyone. She was ashamed of what they represented, afraid that somehow letting the world see what that bastard had done to her would make it all real again.

Summon the evil back.

She had worn the scars for seven years now, and she wondered if she would ever get used to them. If she would ever be able to take them out of the dark place. Only Katie knew about them, no one else.

No one.

She wiped the single tear that was moving down her right cheek and picked the towel up off the floor. She put it in the plastic clothes hamper and then checked herself in the mirror once more to make sure it did not appear she had been crying. No one needed that now, especially not Katie. She had to stay strong for her friend.

She dressed in a pair of cotton pants and a long T-shirt that hung almost to her knees, and then made her way into the living room, where she was happy to see Jackson huddled over the rock fireplace with a lighter in his hand. Flames were just beginning to consume the ball of newspaper beneath the kindling when she walked in. She moved closer and stretched out her hands to feel the heat from the growing fire.

"How was the shower?" Jackson asked.

"Fine."

"Good. Dinner's almost ready." He gave her a smile.

Maybe she was wrong about him. Maybe she should give him another chance. She told herself she had to stop treating all men like they were her personal enemies.

Jackson couldn't help but notice how beautiful Tiffany was, standing by the fire. She was tall, with a slender build, and it looked like she spent a lot of time in the gym as well. Her legs would make a preacher want to kick out a stained glass window.

She gave him a slight smile in return, and Jackson made the mistake of letting his eyes drift from her face to her breasts—then he let his gaze linger just a moment too long. The cold air in the house had caused her nipples to become erect, and they were now clearly visible through the thin, white T-shirt she was wearing.

Tiffany looked down at her chest when she noticed

Jackson staring. She looked horrified and more than a little embarrassed, then quickly crossed her arms and turned away. She went immediately to her suitcase, took out a blue hooded sweatshirt, and pulled that on to cover herself.

I'm a complete idiot, Jackson told himself.

He placed a few larger sticks of oak on the fire, and then he walked into the kitchen to finish dinner. He placed the bowl of pasta and the pot containing the sauce in the center of the wooden dining table.

He walked to the refrigerator and grabbed three cans of soda. "I hope this is okay. I don't have a lot of beverage options."

"It's fine, thank you," Katie said. She had already taken the seat that was closest to the kitchen counter.

Jackson sat down on the end closest to the front door. Tiffany walked slowly toward the round table and took the seat to the right of Katie—directly across from Jackson. The look on her face told Jackson he had really screwed up in the living room.

The three of them were quiet for several minutes before Katie finally broke the silence. "I just want to thank you again for everything you've done, Jackson. It was really nice of you to let us stay here tonight. I know you didn't have to, and I just want you to know that I," she paused and looked at Tiffany, "both of us . . . really appreciate it."

Jackson shot a quick glance at Tiffany. She didn't seem to share Katie's enthusiasm for having a place to stay tonight.

"No problem, glad to do it." He stared at his plate of spaghetti, twirled his fork, and took another bite. After he swallowed and wiped his mouth with a napkin, he asked, "So where you girls from?"

"Just outside Atlanta," Katie said.

"Born and raised in Georgia?" Jackson asked.

"Yeah. My dad used to bring my brother and me up to

the mountains for camping trips when we were young. He taught us to fly fish up here, too. We both loved it so much that after college we went into business together and opened up our own fly shop."

Again, Jackson looked at Tiffany, who was eating with her head down, seemingly oblivious to the conversation.

"How 'bout yourself?" Katie asked.

"Grew up in Wisconsin on a dairy farm. Loved the outdoors as a kid. I was always hunting or fishing or something. During my senior year of college I applied for the Park Service, and I've been a ranger ever since."

"Do you like it?" Katie asked.

It was obvious to Jackson that Katie was trying hard to keep the conversation moving along and warm the frostiness between Tiffany and him. He took another bite of spaghetti before answering. "It has its ups and downs, like any other job, I suppose. But overall, yeah, I like it."

Just when it seemed like the conversation was about to plateau and the silence would return once more, the phone rang. Jackson knew instantly who was on the other end of the line.

Bobby Donaldson.

He took the last bite of food from his plate, then got up from the table to answer the phone.

"Jackson, this is Chief Ranger Donaldson." Bobby always referred to himself in this manner, which annoyed the piss out of Jackson. The guy had a major ego problem.

"Hi, Bobby, how's it going?" Jackson always called him Bobby. He knew the chief ranger hated to be called by his first name, which was exactly why Jackson kept doing it. Bobby let out an exasperated sigh on the other end, which brought a smile to Jackson's face. He knew he had just wounded Bobby's ego with the cheap dig, and it was tremendously satisfying. He stifled a laugh.

Bobby, the irritation apparent in his voice, continued. "I've been organizing the search efforts this afternoon."

He paused.

Jackson was familiar enough with Bobby to know that the pause was meant for dramatic effect. Bobby was about to deliver another of his famous curve balls, and Jackson knew a nauseating smile was spreading across Bobby's pudgy face.

"I've had a little problem getting the manpower put together. I called the Forest Service, and they have only ten guys they can spare for the ground search. I'm going to keep all the park employees over on this side to help with the air operation. You can run the ground search from the marina."

The Forest Service was a separate federal agency that often helped the Park Service during search and rescue operations, and Jackson had worked with them in the past. They always did a great job, but Jackson was aggravated that Bobby was not willing to commit any of his own personnel to the ground search. "Only ten guys, Bobby? I can't run an efficient ground search with that. You've got to give me more bodies."

"That's all I could come up with."

Yeah, right. Jackson wondered if Bobby was intentionally giving him fewer bodies than he needed. Bobby knew what was required to run an efficient ground search. He was a complete jackass, but he had been doing this job long enough to know ten bodies was nowhere near enough. Was he trying to hamstring Jackson, so that if he failed to find Cody, Bobby would have more ammunition to get him fired? Jackson didn't know for sure, but he wouldn't put it past him.

"I told the guy from the Forest Service to have his men out at the marina by five in the morning. Will that work for you?" Bobby asked.

Jackson knew it was pointless to bring up the subject of additional manpower again. Bobby would not give them to him, even if he could. "Yeah, that's fine. I'll be ready to go."

"Talk to you later, Jackson," Bobby said, and then hung up.

Jackson returned the phone to its cradle and walked back to the table. Bobby never ceased to amaze him. If Jackson made it through this with his job intact, he would consider it a victory.

"Who was that?" Katie asked.

"My boss, Bobby. Looks like we may be a little short on hands tomorrow. There're only ten guys coming over in the morning for the search."

"That's not enough?"

"Nowhere near enough. I would need at least thirty to cover the entire area," Jackson replied. "Bobby said that was all he could manage to round up. Personally, I think he's full of shit, but we'll just have to make do with what we have." Jackson realized he should not have voiced his doubts out loud, because a look of concern spread across Katie's face. "Don't worry, we'll make it work," he added.

"Do you think we'll find Cody?" Katie asked.

Jackson knew he should tell her the truth, but he couldn't bring himself to crush her hopes. Instead, he just smiled and said, "We'll find him . . . I promise." The moment the words escaped his lips, he wished he could pull them back in. He shouldn't have offered her such absolute assurance. In the search and rescue business, nothing was guaranteed.

Jackson decided he had suffered through enough drama for the day. Searching for Cody, dealing with Tiffany, and now the exchange with Bobby, had all left him exhausted. He needed some time alone to gather his thoughts and start planning for the search. He stretched his arms over his head and managed to fake a yawn. "Well, ladies, it's been a long day and we have an early start in the morning. I think I'll grab a shower and head to bed. There are sheets and a couple of pillows in the hall closet. Help yourselves. I'll wake you in the morning."

"Okay. Thanks again for dinner," Katie said as Jackson began walking down the hall toward the bathroom.

"You bet. Good night," he answered.

After Katie heard Jackson get in the shower, she cleared the table and placed the dirty dishes in the sink. Then she went to the hall closet and grabbed sheets and a couple of pillows.

"Ready for bed?" she asked as she walked back in the living room. Tiffany was still sitting at the kitchen table.

"Yeah, I guess," Tiffany replied.

That was the most Tiffany had spoken during the entire meal, and Katie was starting to get irritated. She didn't need all the drama right now. She needed her friend to be strong for her during this—they had to stick together so they could bring Cody home. Tiffany deliberately antagonizing the ranger was definitely not helping the situation.

"What's wrong with you?" Katie asked, her tone of voice slightly elevated. She pulled a sheet over the air mattress that was lying on the hardwood floor.

Tiffany got up from the table and walked into the living room. "Nothing," she replied.

"Tiff, I've known you for enough years to know when something is wrong. So cut the crap and just tell me."

"I just want to find Cody and get the hell out of here." She paused. "I'm sorry, Katie. I know you're worried about Cody. I shouldn't have said that. It's just that the ranger really set me off earlier today."

"Don't worry about it. Everyone's tired and I, for one, could use a good night's sleep. You want the couch?" Katie asked.

"Sounds good to me."

Katie grabbed one of the pillows and stretched out on the air mattress. "Good night, Tiff."

"Good night. And Katie . . ."

"Yeah?"

"We will find Cody."

23

*C*ody *pulled the quilted blanket up to his chin and rolled over on his side, drawing his knees toward his chest and wrapping the blanket even tighter around him. Grandma Missy had made it last year and given it to him for Christmas after he and his sister had come to live with her and Grandpa Herschel. He loved the smell of it. Hand-washed and then dried on an outdoor clothesline, it smelled of the Georgia pine trees and hay fields that surrounded the house. The old farmhouse was drafty and cold on early spring mornings such as this, and he loved the warmth the heavy quilt provided.*

His bed consisted of a worn-out twin mattress sitting atop an old army surplus metal frame. The springs squeaked when he rolled over and the mattress offered little support, but there was no other place on earth he would rather be on a cold morning than right here.

The first rays of daylight were just beginning to pierce the single-pane window above his head. His early morning chores were calling. Cody told himself he should get out of bed and get started. Instead, he kept his eyes closed and tried to get another few minutes of sleep.

The smell of bacon frying in Missy's cast iron pan made his mouth water. The aroma wafted into his room from the small kitchen where his grandma always had breakfast started before the sun was up. If Cody knew his grandmother—and he did—there would be some fresh scrambled eggs, cathead biscuits with butter and jelly, and coffee to go along with the bacon. His stomach growled.

He straightened out in bed and lifted his arms above his head. He should roll out of bed and get dressed, but something inside him told him to stay under the protection of the blanket. It was warm.

It was safe.

The sound of the bacon frying made a methodical sizzle, followed by a popping sound.

Sizzle . . . Pop . . . Sizzle . . . Pop.

"Cody, get up! Breakfast is ready!" He heard his grandmother call from the kitchen.

Sizzle . . . Pop . . . Sizzle . . . Pop.

"Cody . . . Cody . . . GET UP!"

Sizzle . . . Pop . . . Sizzle . . . Pop.

Cody opened his eyes as the sizzle and popping of the bacon grew more intense.

It wasn't bacon. What was it?

The comprehension of where he was and what had happened to him came rushing back in a surge of reality—like a locomotive barreling down the tracks in the middle of the night, the long blast of its horn waking the sleeping residents of a rundown coal town.

He was not back in the warm bed he had so loved as a child at his grandparents' house. There was no pan-fried bacon waiting for him on the kitchen table, either. But still the sound persisted.

It was pitch black, save for the faint orange glow given off by the coals leftover from the small amount of wood he had burned last night. He peered into the glow, ribbons of orange and black, dancing together in the night.

Sizzle . . . Pop . . . Sizzle . . . Pop.

He searched for an answer to the noise. Struggled to

clear the cobwebs from his mind. To make sense of the sound and the dream.

Then he saw a puff of ash rise from the coals.

Rain!

Drops of water were falling onto the warm coals and making the noise. Now he realized the ground around him was damp. He could hear the sound of raindrops hitting tree leaves, then falling to the ground. It was coming from all directions. The sound intensified as the rainfall became more intense.

He pulled himself into a sitting position against the tree trunk. The movement was too sudden—a sharp pain shot from his broken left leg, all the way up his spine, and into the base of his skull. An involuntary scream burst from his lungs as the white-hot flash of pain assaulted him. He couldn't let the agony stop him. He took a few deep breaths, gathered his strength, and then worked his way toward the outer branches of the large pine.

Except for the few drops he had gotten from the ruined bottle, he had drunk no water since the attack, and his mouth felt like a dry cotton ball. The physical exertion he had undertaken reaching the fishing vest had only added to his dehydration. He also hadn't urinated since yesterday morning, which he knew was not a good sign. In fact, it was a frighteningly bad sign. His plan to drag himself to the water bottle in the back of the vest had been an abysmal failure, and he was out of options. He needed to—no, he *had* to—get some water into his system soon, or he was going to live out his golden years right under this tree.

Once he was close enough to the end of the branches, he reached up with his right hand and grabbed one of the boughs. He placed it in his mouth and pulled, allowing his mouth to slide down the entire length of it, collecting the small droplets of water that were hanging onto the needles. The first branch yielded only a small amount of water. He repeated the process again. And again.

When he had depleted all the water that was within easy reach, he moved himself about five feet to his left, where he could reach a new set of moisture-laden boughs, and started the process over. It was difficult in the dark, and more than once he grabbed the same branch twice, but he kept at it.

This went on for about thirty minutes. He didn't know how much water he had managed to drink, but his thirst—at least for the moment—was quenched. He didn't want to put too much water into his system right now. After being without for so long, he was afraid he would make himself sick if he overdid it. But he knew he would need more water if he was going to survive until help arrived.

That gave him an idea. He didn't know for sure if his plan would work, but he had to find a way to store some of the rainwater for later. Just in case the searchers did not find him immediately. Which he desperately hoped would not be the case.

He crawled back up to the base of the tree where he had been sleeping and unzipped the back of the vest. He reached in and pulled out the damaged water bottle. He had been so dejected when he found it with holes in its side that he had almost tossed it into the forest in frustration. Now he was glad he had not.

He reached into the front pocket of his pants and pulled out the small knife from the survival kit. Using the knife and the fingers of his right hand, he cut and pulled a section of bark away from the pine tree's trunk. He wished he had a flashlight, but after feeling around blindly for several seconds, he found what he was looking for.

Sap.

He began to roll the sticky substance between his index finger and thumb. Once he had a ball about the width of a pencil's diameter, he felt for the holes the bear's teeth had left in the bottle. When he located one, he pressed the ball of sap into the hole and spread it out over the edges.

He made another ball of sap and filled the adjacent hole. Soon all four were patched. Then he took the top off the bottle and removed the filter assembly. He used the knife to poke two small holes in the rim of the bottle, and then struggled to find the small amount of fishing line in the survival kit. After several seconds, his fingers latched onto the bundle of line and he pulled it from the kit. He ran one end of the line through the holes in the bottle's rim, and then tied the loose ends together, creating a loop above the bottle's mouth.

Cody crawled back down toward the lower tree limbs and, using the loop of string, hung the bottle on one of the branches. He guided a few of the smaller boughs into the mouth of the bottle, hoping they would help funnel water into it.

He drank some more water from nearby boughs and then returned to his sleeping area near the tree trunk. He didn't know for sure if the pine-sap plugs in the bottle would hold, but he hoped so. It was all he had.

He pulled the emergency blanket around him like a shawl. He had been so consumed with getting water that he had failed to notice how wet he was. He began to shiver. He had no idea what time it was, but he hoped the sun would rise soon. Any warmth would be welcome now, no matter how minute.

He sat there under the tree, rain running down his forehead and across his lips. Aching. Shivering.

Hurting.

They would come for him today.

24

Jackson was surprised to see Katie already awake and dressed when he walked into the kitchen. She was standing at the sink, drying the dishes from last night's dinner.

"Morning," Jackson said as he walked toward the table where last night's uncomfortable meal had taken place. "I didn't expect to see you up so early."

"I couldn't sleep."

"Worried about Cody?"

"Yeah. I kept trying to make myself fall asleep last night, but every time I closed my eyes, all I could see was Cody, lying out in the woods alone. Here I was in a nice warm house, and he was probably freezing half to death or injured . . . or worse. So I ended up just tossing and turning for a few hours. I finally gave up and came in here. Figured I should do something productive if I wasn't going to be able to sleep." She wiped another dish dry with the towel and placed it in the cabinet.

Jackson could see the worry in Katie's face. Her skin had become pale, and bags now hung under her blue eyes. She looked like she was carrying the weight of the world on her shoulders. She turned her back to Jackson and put another plate away. He saw her wipe a couple of tears from her eyes. He didn't know what to do. Should he reach out and try to comfort her? Give her a hug? Instead, he just said, "I have to go feed and water the horses. I'll be back in a few minutes." Then he opened the front door and walked out. Personal interactions, especially during times of stress and difficulty, had never been his strong suit.

The truth, though, was that Jackson was worried, too. He hoped he could pull this off and bring Cody home safely—but he was beginning to have his own doubts, especially after the conversation he'd had with Bobby last night. He was going to have only ten men, in addition to himself, which he knew would be a problem. He would have the two women as well, but at this point he viewed their presence more as a hindrance than extra help. He wished he could convince them to stay behind at the marina, but he knew that wasn't going to happen. He could, of course, refuse to allow them to come with him on the search—but, then again, he didn't feel like being verbally castrated by Tiffany this morning.

The distinctive smell of hay and horses filled his nostrils as he approached the small corral. Nickel and Diablo were not used to him being out this early in the morning, so he spoke to the animals as he approached in the darkness. He gave a reassuring stroke to the neck of each one and then dumped oats in the wooden feed trough. He gave them more than usual because he didn't know for sure how long he would be gone. Hopefully, it would only be a couple of days, but when he went on searches like this, he could never be sure. If he wasn't back in two days, he would have to find someone else to check on them. He filled the large drinking basin with fresh water before making his way back toward the house.

As he opened the front door and stepped inside, he could smell fresh coffee brewing. He grabbed his travel mug and filled it. "Thanks for the coffee," he said.

"You're welcome. So what time are we leaving?" Katie asked.

"Soon. I'll grab some more supplies for you and Tiffany, and then we'll hit the road." Jackson looked down at his watch and was surprised to see it was already a quarter to four. He was supposed to be at the marina to meet the guys from the Forest Service by five. He needed to get going.

Tiffany walked into the kitchen.

"Mornin'," Jackson said over the top of his mug as he took his first drink of coffee.

"Morning," Tiffany replied. She gave a slight smile, then sat down at the table.

Jackson began to lay out his plans for the day. "There will be thirteen searchers today—ten from the Forest Service and the three of us. I wish there were more, but there's not, so we'll just have to make do with what we have. My plan is to divide the Forest Service guys into two groups of five, then the three of us will make up the last group. Bobby will be coordinating the air search from the park's headquarters in Tennessee. Does that sound okay to you two?" In truth, Jackson was not going to change his plan based on what Katie and Tiffany thought. He was the one in charge, and the search was his responsibility, but he thought if he made them feel like they were involved in the process, things would go more smoothly for everyone.

He was relieved when both women nodded in agreement.

"Okay, then. I'll get everything ready and we'll be on the road shortly."

A few minutes later, the three of them were leaving the house and walking toward the Suburban. Each carried a backpack containing food, a water bottle, some extra clothing, and other items essential for survival in the wild.

Jackson was in the lead, with Tiffany following close behind. Katie was bringing up the rear. Jackson wondered if Katie had faith in him. Wondered if she believed he could do as he had promised and bring Cody back to her alive.

As he climbed into the truck and started the engine, he didn't know if he even had faith in himself anymore.

25

Cody sat huddled in a ball, his back against the base of the pine tree, the small emergency blanket wrapped tightly around his shivering body. He tried to prevent his teeth from chattering so violently, but was unable to quell the spasms coursing through him. The rain had fallen uninterrupted since he had first been awakened by it several hours ago. He had tried to fall back to sleep, but every time he was about to doze off, a raindrop would run down his forehead and into his eye.

He shifted his body again, trying to remain as comfortable as possible under the circumstances. Still, he wasn't complaining. Yesterday, he had been suffering from severe dehydration. Now, water was falling all around him. The rain had been a life-saver.

The makeshift collection device he had fashioned out of the ruined water bottle had worked well. He had made two trips down to the hanging bottle over the last three hours, each time getting a sufficient amount of water. He knew he needed to keep drinking, because if the rain stopped and he wasn't rescued soon, dehydration would once again become a threat. So he had decided to hydrate himself as much as possible while he had the opportunity, even though every short trip to the water bottle was excruciatingly painful for him.

Hunger was becoming a problem as well. He hadn't eaten since just before the attack, almost three days ago now, and his stomach had begun to growl almost nonstop. Yesterday, while he had been focused on reaching the fishing vest, he had not noticed any hunger pangs—but now, given the forced inactivity, his mind was consumed with the thought of food—any food. The harder he tried to focus on something else, the more insistently his stomach told him he needed to eat.

He raised his head and peered out from underneath the blanket. Water ran off the edge of his makeshift shelter and onto his face in an uninterrupted stream. The first tinges of daylight were just breaking through the thick tree canopy, allowing him to make out indistinct shapes along the forest floor. Off to his right, he spotted the fallen log where he had found the vest. He remembered watching one of those survival shows on television, where the host ate grubs and worms he had found in a rotten log. Cody decided it was worth a try. He gently moved away from the tree trunk and began to pull himself along the ground toward the fallen log, just as he had yesterday.

His body protested the initial movements with ferocity. Every muscle seemed to seize up, like an engine running with no oil. He took a few deep breaths and stretched out the best he could, allowing the blood flow to return to his extremities, but now the pain increased as well.

He began to move across the ground, pulling himself along on his right side, while trying to protect his left side as well as he could. It was slow going, and the rain made the process of crawling along the ground even more unpleasant, but he knew he needed to find calories—in whatever form he could.

He tried to block the surges of pain that moved up and down his broken leg with every movement he made. The entire left side of his body felt like it was on fire.

In about ten minutes he had reached the log. Then, for the next several minutes, he simply remained motionless next to the rotting wood, resting. He was amazed at how much his once athletic and muscular body had deteriorated. Just three short days ago, he would have been able to cover the distance from his shelter to the log in a few seconds, and now it had taken him what seemed like an eternity, and he was so exhausted from the trip, he considered not even returning to the pine tree.

Maybe he should just stay here and wait for rescue—or death.

Once he regained his strength enough to move again, he pulled the upper half of his torso onto the log. The persistent rain had softened the already rotting wood, and he found it easy to pull hand-sized chunks of the log free. He quickly found a few small, white grubs crawling underneath the surface and collected them into a small pile on top of the log. He soon had gathered about ten grubs. He picked up one of them between his fingers and held it in front of his face. It was writhing, trying to break free. Cody hesitated. Was he really about to put this dirty, slimy grub in his mouth? He needed to eat, though, and he no longer had the luxury of being picky. He decided it was best to get it over with quickly. In his mind, he slowly counted to three, and then popped the grub into his mouth, trying to imagine it was popcorn or some equally palatable morsel, and then smashed it with his back molars. He was pleasantly surprised by the taste. It had a nutty flavor, similar to an almond. The worst part was the gooey texture, but once he overcame that, they weren't bad at all. He ate the other grubs and began to search for more. He would gather extra and save them for later.

After working for fifteen minutes, he had around thirty of the small, white grubs. He divided the group and put half of them in each hand, then began the slow trip back to the pine tree.

The rain was still falling, not a downpour like he had experienced last night, but instead, a light and steady drizzle. He was soaked through. The small portion of his body he had managed to keep dry under the emergency blanket was now wet as well. The clouds had lowered significantly overnight, and they now appeared to be just above the tree tops. Tendrils of fog wove through the trees, their ghostly white vapors decreasing visibility and giving the forest an eerie feel.

The physical exertion needed to travel to the log had warmed his body somewhat and reduced the shivering, but now, as he began his return trip, he noticed that the shaking had returned—the damp, frigid ground once again sucking the heat out of him. He had to find a way to get warm and stay warm. He decided to try to start the fire again once he reached the shelter. He doubted he would have much luck, as everything was now soaked, but he had to at least try. Maybe he could find some dry material close to the base of the tree.

He continued his slog up the hill toward the pine tree, which had now become his new home. Water was dripping from his torn scalp and running down his face. His whole right side was caked in mud. The bitter chill was driving straight through to his bones.

Cody was about two-thirds of the way back to the pine when he had to stop and take another break. He lay flat on the ground for several minutes, catching his breath. He turned his head to look back at the log and was glad he had taken the chance to get some food. He would return tomorrow for more grubs and, if he could get a fire going, he might even try to roast some of them. Just the idea of a hot meal made him smile a little. Maybe he would get out of this alive after all.

He looked past the log and focused on the location where the bear had left him to die, about fifty yards past the log and slightly to the right. The spot where he had almost lost his life. It sent a chill through him, one colder than the falling rain that now surrounded him.

Just as he was about to turn his head and continue his journey back to the pine tree, a quick movement behind some distant bushes caught his attention. His left eye was still swollen shut, which hindered his depth perception, but he was sure he had seen something move. He continued to stare.

Nothing.

Maybe his mind was just playing a trick on him.

Then another movement—a black flash this time—near the attack area.

Cody did not want to admit to himself what he was witnessing, because if what his eye was telling him was true, his situation had just become much more serious. Finally, the large black mass moved from behind a rhododendron bush and his worst fear—what he desperately wanted not to be true—was realized.

The bear had come back.

Cody was frozen with fear—afraid to make the slightest movement. He kept his gaze locked on the massive beast. Its head was to the ground, as if smelling for any remaining trace of him. It licked at the blood-soaked leaves.

His mind began to race. What should he do? Try to move unnoticed to the pine tree? If the bear saw him, it could charge and be upon him in just a few seconds. But if he stayed in his current position, the bear would almost certainly see him. He was unprotected and exposed.

He continued to watch as the bear smelled around the area and began widening its search. *Why had it returned?* From everything Cody knew about black bears, they generally weren't aggressive. The attack itself was out of the norm, and the fact that the bear had remained in the area further puzzled him.

Cody didn't know what was going on, but he hoped all the rain had diluted his scent enough that the bear would be unable to follow his trail. He needed to get back to the relative safety underneath the pine tree. At least he would be hidden. If the bear was going to track him down, Cody wanted to make it as difficult as possible. He didn't want to serve himself up on a platter by lying out in the open, exposed. He decided to make a move for the tree at his first opportunity.

He kept his eye on the bear as it continued to move away from the attack site, slowly following the route Cody had taken to the fishing vest. Then the bear stopped and turned, its big black nose still to the ground. It began to walk in circles.

It's lost my scent.

The rainfall increased and another patch of fog moved over the area, momentarily reducing the visibility between Cody and the bear. This was his chance. It was now or never, he told himself.

He gritted his teeth and moved faster than he had since the attack. Every thrust forward sent a shooting pain through his broken leg. He felt as though he were being repeatedly stabbed, the attacker twisting the blade for maximum effect. He was within a few feet of the tree now—his body desperately begging him to stop and rest—but Cody forced himself to move on. The fog was beginning to thin and drift away. Soon visibility would improve, leaving him vulnerable once again. But he was having difficulty gaining traction on the rain-slickened ground. He was not going to make it! In just a few more seconds the fog would be gone, and the bear would see him. Then it would be over.

He struggled to keep the panic at bay. To keep moving forward. To save himself.

He was having difficulty breathing, his respirations shallow and rapid. But he kept pushing. Willing himself toward the tree. His heart racing. His fingers clawing frantically at the muddy ground. The pain becoming almost unbearable.

He summoned what little strength he had left, and with one final burst of energy, pulled himself under the tree limbs just as the last of the fog cleared.

Then he collapsed.

26

Cody awoke choking, struggling to catch his breath. He was lying face down in a small pool of standing water, where he must have rolled while he was out. The rain was still falling, not a downpour, but a good, steady soaker. He wasn't sure how long he had been unconscious. Maybe a few minutes or even a few hours, he couldn't tell. It was the first sleep he had gotten since the rain started, but he hardly felt rested. It wasn't genuine sleep, anyway; more an unavoidable consequence of his ordeal—his body refusing to continue any further. He felt as though he was becoming weaker by the hour.

He raised his head and looked around for any sign of the bear, listening intently. Relieved when he saw and heard nothing, he returned his lips to the standing water and sucked the muddy mixture off the ground. Even with all the rainwater he had been able to gather during the night, he was still thirsty. He pulled himself across the ground until he reached the hanging water bottle on the other side of the tree and was pleased to find it almost half full. He quickly gulped the water down and replaced the bottle on the limb.

He moved back to the base of the tree and pulled the

blanket around him. The shivering returned with a vengeance. He was freezing. Then his stomach growled and he remembered the grubs he had collected. He looked down at his hands.

They were empty.

"Dammit!" he yelled. He looked frantically on the ground for the missing grubs, but found nothing. Frustration turned to sorrow.

All the grubs must have been lost during the frantic escape from the bear, or during his blackout. He wasn't sure. Not that it really mattered either way. The fact was, he was now without food once more. He should have put them in a pocket or something. He sure as hell wasn't going back to the fallen log anytime soon—not with the bear still hanging around the area. No way.

But why had the bear returned? The question still haunted Cody.

Was it stalking him? Had it come back to finish the job?

Cody decided he needed something for protection. He searched his surroundings and spotted a large stick to his left, just beyond the outer branches. He crawled until he was able to reach the piece of wood with his right hand. He did not want to expose his entire body again in case the bear was still around. He thrust his arm out quickly and retrieved the stick.

Once he was back in the center of the canopy, he pulled the knife from his pants pocket and unfolded the blade. He placed the wood in between his legs as best he could and began to sharpen one end of the stick. With a broken leg and one arm in a sling, it wasn't an easy job, but after a few minutes he had a crude spear that was roughly three feet long. Not much in the way of a weapon, but it was the best he could do for now.

He laid the spear next to his right thigh and then turned

to face the tree. Using the blade of the knife, he cut the bark away from the trunk in the area just above his head. Then he carved three vertical lines in the top left corner.

Three days he had been trapped.

27

Katie stared at the glowing embers in the fire pit. She was struggling just to keep warm, even with the fire only a few feet away. The rain-laden skies had blocked any warmth the sun had to offer. Tiffany sat beside her, shivering.

Katie's mind was wrecked, completely devoid of any coherent thought. She had hoped they would find Cody quickly and be back to civilization before dinner. Instead, she was sitting at the very same campsite Cody had used just a few days before. His tent was staring at her from across the flames. It gave her an eerie feeling.

The day had gotten off to a rotten start. By the time they arrived at the marina, a steady rainfall had commenced. The bad weather had grounded the helicopter in Tennessee, which meant no air search until the low clouds and rain moved out. To make matters worse, the ten searchers from the Forest Service had shown up two hours late—their supervisor had given them the incorrect rendezvous point. Jackson had once again asked Bobby to send some of the Park Service personnel he was holding for the air search over to give their group some reinforcements, but Bobby had refused—despite the obvious fact that the air search was not going to happen anytime soon. Jackson had been furious. After getting the news, he had cursed and thrown the radio into the floor of the Suburban.

Still, Jackson had continued with the search, leading the Forest Service employees, along with Katie and Tiffany, into the wilderness. It had been slow going ever since the group left the lakeshore. The weather had grown progressively worse, and Tiffany had lagged behind for most of the hike, forcing the rest of the group to stop often and wait for her to catch up. Katie, used to being in the outdoors, had kept up with the men with no problem.

About two miles from campsite ninety-seven, Tiffany had fallen into the water at one of the many creek crossings. Totally submerged, all of her clothes and equipment had become drenched. She had begun to shiver badly after they continued walking, and Jackson had pushed the group to hurry to the campsite so he could get a fire started.

Once they arrived, Katie had helped Tiffany strip out of her wet clothes and wrapped her in a lightweight blanket while Jackson went to work on the fire. Somehow— Katie didn't really know how—he managed to get the water-logged wood burning. He had told Katie to keep Tiffany by the fire and let her warm up. He had said the last thing he needed was a case of hypothermia to screw things up even more than they already were.

After he had prepared Tiffany a warm electrolyte drink, he had taken the other searchers and headed up the trail. Katie was afraid he was regretting his decision to allow her and Tiffany to come along in the first place. She hoped he wouldn't insist they return to the resort.

Sitting next to Tiffany by the fire, Katie felt useless. She should be out looking for Cody, too, not back at camp babysitting Tiffany. She was angry at her friend for falling into the water in the first place, even though it had just been an accident. But at least Tiffany had the fortitude to make it all the way. Katie was grateful for that. A lot of people she knew would have turned around after the first mile or two on the trail.

Katie went to her backpack and grabbed a T-shirt and a pair of cotton pants. She walked back to Tiffany and handed the dry clothing to her. "Here, put these on."

"Thanks."

Tiffany looked like she was on the verge of breaking. Her hair was matted to her forehead, and beads of rainwater were rolling down her face. She stood up and removed the blanket, put on the clothing, then wrapped herself in the blanket once again and sat back down.

Katie picked up some more of the wet wood Jackson had piled up before he left and placed a few more sticks on the fire. A thick, white smoke rose as the soaked wood came in contact with the flames, and the acrid smell of burning wood filled the air. The rain had almost stopped now, but heavy drops continued to fall from the tree limbs above them.

Katie remained by the fire for the next couple of hours, talking to Tiffany occasionally, but mostly just staring into the flames and worrying about Cody. Every thirty minutes or so, she added more wood to the fire.

"Katie?" Tiffany said.

"Yeah?"

"I'm really sorry I screwed things up today. I should have just stayed back at the house. I'm not an outdoor person like you. I just wanted to be here for you, that's all. Just like you've always been there for me. Even after . . . well, you know."

Katie did know. The subject of what had happened was still too fresh and painful for Tiffany to talk about, despite the seven years that had passed. Katie had almost lost her back then, and it had scared the hell out of her. Sure, she got mad at her from time to time, but when two people had been friends as long as they had, they couldn't stay angry for very long. She wrapped her left arm around Tiffany and gave her a hug. "Nonsense. I don't know what I would do without you, Tiff, and I am really glad you came with me," she said.

"Really?" Tiffany asked.

"Really." Katie gave her a kiss on the cheek. "Love you."

"Love you, too," Tiffany replied.

Behind the hard exterior that Tiffany often projected, Katie knew there was a very warm and loving person. Once anyone got to know her, they saw that, too. But it was the getting to know her that was the hard part. Katie knew the reason Tiffany was so harsh to people she first met was because of what that horrible person had done to her all those years ago. It was her way of protecting herself. But that terrible chapter in her life was over now, and she knew Tiffany would eventually, when the time was right, come out of her shell.

It was getting late in the afternoon when Katie finally heard Jackson and the others coming back down the trail. She stood to meet them—to see if they had any news. One look at Jackson's face told her the answer was *no*. She asked anyway. "Any sign of Cody?"

"No, sorry. Nothing."

Katie went back to her seat next to Tiffany. She thought it was strange that not much was said between members of the group for the next several minutes. They just went about setting up camp for the night. In thirty minutes, several tents had been erected and the group started preparing dinner, which consisted of a variety of dehydrated meals. Katie had pitched in the best she was able. But for the most part, she felt as if she was just in the way. Tiffany remained huddled under the blanket, still shivering.

Katie now knew, without a shadow of doubt, that Jackson regretted bringing the two of them along.

After dinner, Jackson conveyed his plans for the next day to the group. Five of the Forest Service men would fan out and head upstream from the creek crossing that was just above the campsite. The other five would head downstream. Jackson explained that his gut told him Cody was somewhere upstream from the trail crossing, but he wanted to make sure he covered all the bases. Katie and Tiffany would stay with him, walking the trail on the off chance that Cody was there, and also to see if they could find another hiker who might have some useful information.

Katie knew the real reason Jackson was keeping them with him in the relative safety of the trail—and after the way today had gone, she couldn't say she blamed him.

After hashing the plan out for a few more minutes, most of the searchers retired to their respective tents, exhausted from a long day in less than ideal weather conditions. Katie, Tiffany, and Jackson were left alone, lingering around the campfire.

Jackson looked up at Katie. "We'll do the best we can tomorrow. I'm not making any promises, but I'm going to give it everything I have. Hopefully," he paused and looked into the darkened sky, "this weather will break and Bobby will be able to get the helicopter up. That would help out a lot." He stood and began to turn toward his tent, then added, "You girls better get some sleep . . . we have another long day ahead of us tomorrow."

28

It was raining. Again.

Cody was thankful for the water to drink, but now he began to worry that the bad weather would hamper the search that was surely underway.

He hadn't slept in more than a day now. He found that the wet, miserable conditions were not conducive to sleep. His entire body was cold and wet—he could find no escape from the constant and maddening drop-drop-drop of the rain. The skin on his left leg had gotten noticeably warmer over the past several hours, and he was afraid that meant an infection had set in. To make matters worse, he had developed a nasty cough. He didn't know if he could survive another day without help.

He had managed to urinate again this morning, which was good news. The rainwater had provided enough hydration that his urine had returned to a more normal color. But his hunger had grown so intense that at times he felt he was on the verge of passing out. He had debated trying to make another trip to the log where he had collected the grubs yesterday, but decided the risk it posed was not worth a few measly grub worms. It was just too dangerous.

He wondered why he had ended up in this situation.

What had he done to make God punish him like this? He had not always been on the *straight and narrow*, but he didn't think he deserved this. Maybe Grandma Missy had been wrong all along—maybe God was not in Heaven watching over everyone.

All he had wanted was to come up to the mountains for a few days and enjoy some fly fishing. Get away from the job he had come to loathe. And now it had turned into a battle for his life. A battle he feared he was losing.

His thoughts turned to the mess he had made of his life. Wasn't that what dying people were supposed to do, anyway? Come to peace with all the bad things they had done just before they go to meet their maker? He didn't really believe it, and he sure didn't need a *feel good* therapy session. If he was meant to die out here alone, then so be it. But he couldn't help but wish he had done at least a few things differently during his thirty-two short years on earth.

His mother had not done him any favors, but that was no excuse. Missy and Herschel had given him a good, loving home. He had been given opportunities during his life that he couldn't afford on his own and, quite honestly, a few that he didn't deserve. And what had he done with all those opportunities? Become a selfish and conceited person—that's what. Allowed his career to come before his family. Finally, he had lost his wife.

Sure, he had tried to save his marriage, but Cody knew he could have done more. After college, he should have moved to a small town, opened up a private practice, and left the big money, the big city law firms, to others. He and Amy could have bought a nice house on a cul-de-sac— maybe started a family. Even if Amy had been unable to have kids, they could have adopted. But now he would never know. His obsession with financial success and social standing had driven him to put himself and the firm in front of everyone and everything else in his life.

It was not entirely his fault, he knew that. Amy had cheated on him, which was almost unforgivable in his eyes, but he knew that would never have happened if he had not put his career before his own wife. He had screwed the whole thing up. He was responsible.

He was not proud of some of the business practices he had engaged in, either. Being a corporate lawyer could be a somewhat dirty business. Behind the crisply starched white shirts and power ties lay the darkness of greed and power. His partners in the firm demanded new and ever-expanding revenue streams. And the clients were no different. It was all about the money. Always had been—always would be.

Cody was far from innocent in the whole matter. He had done some pretty callous shit, in and out of the courtroom, just for the win. Winning ranked second only to money in the hierarchy of importance at the firm. And how you played the game? That didn't matter. Those television shows where the lawyer diligently searches out the truth, the innocent are never punished, where the guilty always pay, and truth and justice prevail, were total bullshit. Cody had found that, in the real world, nothing could be farther from the truth.

He doubted Missy and Herschel would be very proud of the man he had become.

Maybe he deserved to die out here after all.

He coughed again. A violent, heaving cough that shot bolts of pain through his racked body. He needed to get warm. He opened the survival kit and retrieved the matches and fire starting material. He took the knife from his pants pocket and carved a small piece from the stick of fire starter. There wasn't much of the material left, and he wanted to be careful not to waste it. Then he gathered some small twigs and pine needles into a pile in front of him—everything was soaked. He placed the chunk of fire starter at the bottom of the pile of kindling and struck the match. The fire starter caught first. Then a small, determined flame slowly spread through the needles and sticks. Cody blew softly, fanning the flame, and placed more kindling on the pile. The warmth felt good on his face.

But a problem soon became evident. All the larger kindling was so wet that once it came in contact with the flame, it just smoked for a few seconds and then—nothing. Once the piece of fire starter was exhausted, the whole pile extinguished.

Cody wanted to save as much of the fire starting stick as possible; he didn't know how much longer he would be in the wilderness, but he decided to try once more. He repeated the whole process and, for a couple of minutes, thought that he had been successful, but then the fire died again, despite his frantic efforts to keep it alive. Discouragement flooded through him.

Dejected, he picked up the knife and carved another notch in the tree above his head. This made day four. He couldn't help but wonder if he would live to see day five.

He turned around and faced the worthless pile of blackened twigs and pine needles. He wrapped the emergency blanket around himself again. It did little to keep him warm anymore, but it was better than nothing. And it did, at least, keep some of the rain away.

He desperately needed sleep. His eyelids were heavy, but every time he thought he was about to doze off, a rain drop or a sudden chill or sharp pain startled him awake. He felt as if he was on the verge of death. *No, don't think that way.* The rain picked up again, and he pulled the blanket over his head as best he could manage.

Millions of water droplets, hitting the leaves of a thousand trees and then falling to the ground, created a symphony in his ears that was both relaxing and infuriating— he was tired of being cold. He longed for a hot shower and dry clothes. A nice steak dinner would be icing on the cake.

He felt himself about to doze off again when he heard something in the distance, something that seemed out of place in the constant rattle of the rain. It sounded like a human voice. Could it be—? He pulled the blanket from around his head. Then he heard it again, off to his right. This time, it sounded like the voice called his name.

He quickly threw the blanket off and started to scoot toward the edge of the tree's canopy. It was the fastest he had moved since he had evaded the bear for the second time—the pain dulled by the surge of adrenaline coursing through his body. He pushed himself. Moved with everything he had left. He heard the voice again.

"Cody! Cody McAlister!"

"Over here!" Cody tried to scream just as he reached the edge of the tree limbs, where he could get a clear view. He saw a man about seventy-five yards away, walking in a straight line from the creek up toward the trail. The man was continuing to call his name.

"Help! Please help!" he screamed. But Cody was so weak the scream he heard in his mind was, in actuality, little more than a whisper, barely audible above the rainfall. He tried again. "Stop! Please help me." The rain increased in intensity, and his voice would not carry above it. He grabbed a small stick and waved it as best he could with his right hand. Standing up was not an option. Another patch of mist was moving through the mountains, reducing visibility. He could barely make out the man now.

He began to panic. "Help me! Please, help me! I'm over here!" he cried as he waved the stick frantically above his head.

No response.

Cody heard the man call his name again—farther up the mountain this time—and moving away. He was desperate. He tried again, "Help! Help! Help! Please stop, I'm down here." But the searcher kept moving away from him, never even pausing.

Realizing all hope was lost, Cody began to sob. The moisture of the few tears his body could spare ran down his cheeks and fell to the ground. Now the adrenaline rush departed as quickly as it had arrived, leaving him completely drained. The intense pain he had lived with for the past four days returned with a vengeance.

He collapsed to the forest floor, sobbing.

Everything went black.

29

Jackson was regretting his decision to let Katie and Tiffany come along. The hike from the lakeshore to the campsite yesterday had taken almost twice as long as it should have because Tiffany had not been able to keep up. Then she had damn near become hypothermic after falling into the creek.

The weather had been horrible since the start of the search. Jackson had hoped it would break today so he could try to convince Bobby to get the helicopter in the air, but daylight had revealed the same low clouds and relentless rain they had been battling since the search began.

Early in the morning, he had divided the searchers into two groups of five men each. He sent the more experienced group upstream, because he felt that was the most likely location for Cody. The other group went downstream.

He had taken Katie and Tiffany upstream, but unlike the searchers, who were working a grid pattern between the creek and the trail above, the three of them stayed strictly on-trail—he wanted no further incidents that would slow down the search, so he had decided to keep the two ladies close by his side. Katie didn't seem thrilled with her diminished role in the search, but right now, Jackson didn't give a rat's ass what she thought. His job was to find Cody

McAlister. End of story.

And he had given up trying to read Tiffany—she was an enigma to him.

The three of them had been walking the trail for a couple of hours, taking things slow, looking for any sign of Cody. So far, they had found nothing. Jackson had also been in radio contact with the other searchers all morning, but they hadn't found any sign of the missing man either.

Whatever had befallen Mr. McAlister remained a mystery.

Jackson wondered if the mountains would give up their secrets this time, or if Cody's case would end up like so many others—with no answers.

He continued forward through a rocky, narrow portion of the trail. He slowed and turned around to make sure Katie and Tiffany were still following him. Just as he was about to issue a warning to the two of them to be careful, he saw Tiffany get too close to the edge.

"Stop!" he yelled, but it was too late. The shoulder, softened by the heavy rain, gave way and she slid down the slope, dirt and rocks falling more than a hundred feet to the boulders below. Jackson saw Tiffany grab an exposed tree root and a large clump of grass just before going over the edge. She was barely hanging on.

"Help!" she screamed.

"Tiffany!" Katie gasped.

Jackson rushed toward her, pushing Katie out of the way. He could see Tiffany's hands starting to slip. A few more seconds and she would be gone. He threw himself onto the ground in front of her and grabbed her backpack with his right hand. Tiffany was kicking her legs wildly, trying to find solid footing. All the movement was threatening to pull her away from Jackson's grasp.

"Stop moving! Just be still and let me get you."

Tiffany stopped thrashing and hung still below him,

pleading with him. "Please, help me!"

"I've got you, just calm down and do what I say, okay?"

"Okay," she responded. Tears were starting to roll down her cheeks.

"Katie! Come lay across my feet. I need an anchor to keep me from going over too," Jackson said.

A second later, he felt Katie's body weight spread over his calves and ankles. He moved his left arm from under his chest, reached down, and grabbed Tiffany's forearm. "Let go of the root and grab my arm," he instructed.

Tiffany was frozen with panic. She didn't move.

"Tiffany, listen to me, you have to turn loose and grab my arm. I won't let you fall . . . I promise." He locked his eyes with hers and tried to speak in the calmest, most reassuring voice he could manage, but it didn't seem to be working.

She didn't respond, her eyes distant and detached.

"Dammit, Tiffany! Listen to me! Grab my arm . . . now!" Jackson felt his grip on the backpack beginning to slip. His shouts snapped Tiffany out of her fog and she released the tree root, then grabbed Jackson's arm.

"Okay, good. Now I'm going to pull you up, okay?"

Tiffany nodded.

Jackson pulled hard, inching his way back along the ground. He started to make progress—then stalled. "Give me a hand, Katie!" He felt her grab the back of his belt and pull. After a few seconds, Tiffany's torso was back on the trail. Jackson released her arm and grabbed the top of her blue jeans. He slid his fingers around her belt for more leverage. Then, with one final heave, he pulled her safely back to solid ground.

"Oh, thank God," she whispered.

Katie ran over and helped Tiffany sit up. "Are you okay?"

Tiffany was still trying to catch her breath. "Yeah . . . I think so."

The whole episode had taken less than a minute, but Jackson felt like he had been punched in the gut. When he finally stood, his legs felt like Jell-O.

"Thank you," Tiffany said, looking up to meet Jackson's stare.

Jackson was still shaken and gave her only a slight nod. "Let's turn around and head back toward the creek crossing."

Katie protested, "But we've already covered that. Shouldn't we keep going the way we were?"

Jackson sighed, tired of having to explain himself to the two women. "Look . . . the trail turns up the mountain about a hundred yards ahead and moves farther away from the creek. It's steep and more dangerous, too. If Cody is up here, I doubt he made it this far upstream. We'll spend the rest of the day walking the trail back and forth . . . *and take our time.*" He looked at Tiffany to emphasize the point as he walked past her, starting back down the trail.

An hour later, the three stopped for lunch at a wide spot in the trail. The lightweight poncho he wore did a decent job of keeping the rain away, but as Jackson prepared to eat, he noticed his fingers looked like prunes. He pulled a pack of cheese crackers, a Clif bar, and an apple from his backpack. As he ate in silence, he again berated himself for getting into this situation. Now he just hoped he could get out of it with no one else getting hurt. It was obvious that Tiffany had little or no experience outdoors—he should have known better than to bring her along in the first place. Katie seemed to be able to hang with everyone else, but Tiffany had constantly fallen behind yesterday, and had almost taken a one-way trip down the mountain just an hour ago. Still, there was something about her he liked. He wasn't sure what it was, because she had pretty much annoyed the hell out of him ever since arriving on Thursday. But it was there—whatever it was.

After lunch he stood, donned his backpack once more,

and started walking down the trail again. He had gone no more than a hundred feet when he noticed something in the loose dirt on the right side of the trail—something he had failed to notice this morning, when he had first passed by. Or it had occurred between then and now, he wasn't sure. He bent down to take a closer look.

Katie moved in behind him. "What's that?" she asked.

"Bear track," he replied. He heard Katie gasp behind him. "I wouldn't worry about it, though. The black bears we have in the Smokies are not usually aggressive." He paused. "Just keep an eye out."

Jackson stood and examined the area. He found two more tracks, a faint one in the center of the trail, and another off the left edge. The tracks were leading up the mountain, away from the stream below. They also looked fresh, which told him that the bear had crossed sometime this morning. He couldn't be certain they were not present when he passed earlier—but he didn't think so.

Could the bear have something to do with Cody's disappearance? He doubted it, but with no sign of him yet, he had to keep all options on the table. He radioed his findings to the crew leaders of the two search parties down at the creek and told them to stay alert.

Jackson, Katie, and Tiffany resumed their march back down the mountain.

30

When Cody regained consciousness, his mind was clouded and he was unsure of where he was. It took him a minute to remember how he had ended up lying face down in the rain-soaked leaves. The memory of the lost opportunity to be rescued burned in his mind.

The rain had slacked off again, a light drizzle now fell over the mountains.

He pulled himself back to the large pine tree. Just moving that short distance left him worn-out. He collapsed once he was back to his spot under the canopy, where he had spent so many hours huddled in a fruitless attempt to stay dry.

He was defeated. His only chance of survival had slipped through his fingers. He had been too weak to signal the searcher, and now he would spend the rest of what remained of his life under this lonesome, indifferent tree.

He pulled himself back into a sitting position with his back to the tree trunk. He began to sob. It was over. He could not go on another day—another hour—another minute. He was done.

Finished.

Why was his life going to end this way? Miserable and

alone.

The one thing he had found saddest about his mother's death was that she died alone. No one was with her. No one to give her a comforting squeeze of the hand, or a kiss on the cheek. It must have been horrible. And now he was in the same position. It didn't seem fair. He had always thought he would die an old, wealthy man. But life had thrown a wrench into his plans, and he had to accept that fact. It was over.

He hoped Grandma Missy had been right, and that a band of angels would take him to Heaven. But if he was honest with himself, he had his doubts.

A drop of water ran from his wet hair into his eye. A shiver ran through his body. A pain shot through his injured leg. Anger began to boil inside of him. Why had this happened to him? What had he done to deserve it?

He spotted the pocket knife lying on the ground next to him, the blade still opened from when he had used it to carve another notch in the tree behind him earlier. He had cut four lines in the tree now—four days of hell. Why should he carve a fifth one? Or a sixth? Or a seventh, for that matter? Why should he prolong the inevitable? As much as he didn't want to admit the obvious, he knew how this was going to end for him.

Not good.

It made no sense, really. Why should he continue to suffer until his body and mind finally gave out and he died? What was to be gained in that? A more honorable death? That seemed a little trivial at this point. He began to consider the possibility of using the knife to expedite his departure from this wretched situation.

At first, he tried to fight the idea. He tried to tell himself that was not the answer, but the thought would not go away. And the longer he allowed it to linger, the more plausible it became. The idea of committing suicide last week, before he had been trapped, would have been ludicrous to him. But now, it seemed not only a viable option—but the only option.

He picked up the knife and examined the blade, now caked in mud. He wiped it off on the fabric sling around his left arm. He felt the edge. It didn't seem very sharp. He picked up a small, round stone that was lying next to his leg and attempted to sharpen the blade by drawing the edge across the flat rock. After a minute or two of this, he felt the edge again. Not great—but better.

Holding the knife in his right hand, he pushed the fabric of the sling away from his left wrist. His right hand began to shake as he placed the blade against his flesh.

A tear fell from his eye.

He could not believe what he was about to do. The idea that random circumstances led him to such a desperate measure was almost incomprehensible to him.

Almost.

He began to apply more pressure to the blade.

He wondered if it would hurt. He had once heard that people who slashed their wrists simply went to sleep; that it was almost a painless way to die. He doubted that, too.

Should he do it slowly? Quickly? He did not know.

More pressure. Pain at the tip of the knife. He began to draw it across his wrist—the blue veins glaring back at him.

It was now or never—a quick ending to his misery or prolonged despair with very little chance of survival. The moment of truth had arrived. The choice was his.

He was going to do it. He gritted his teeth and gripped the knife handle as hard as possible. A drop of blood flowed from beneath the blade.

Another tear.

Then out of nowhere, Katie's face flashed in his mind, just as it had during the bear attack. What would she think when they eventually found his body? That he was a quitter? A coward?

He dropped the knife.

And sobbed.

31

Cody woke to another cloud-laden sky. The rain had continued off and on through the night, but at the moment it had slackened. He was thirsty again, so he crawled back to the water bottle that he had used to collect rainwater for the last several days. His movements had slowed yet again, and he could feel the life draining from him with even the smallest amount of physical exertion.

When he finally reached the water bottle, he was disappointed to find it only a quarter full. Just one good swallow of water. After drinking, he repositioned the bottle to another spot, hoping to catch more of the rainwater. He pulled several of the evergreen boughs that were within easy reach and ran them through his mouth, sucking down every drop of moisture he could.

He crawled back to the base of the tree and pulled the blanket around his shoulders. Ever since he had failed to signal the searcher yesterday, his desperation had reached a new level.

He looked down at the knife again. The blade was still open. He picked it up and stared at the metal edge. He spun it back and forth in his hand, causing the small amount of available light to bounce off the steel. He contemplated trying again. Then, in a flash, he remembered why he hadn't gone through with it yesterday.

He had thought of Katie.

She was the one bright spot that remained in his life. He had grown to hate his job and where he lived. And except for his sister, he had no family left. A strange thought slammed into his mind. Who would come to his funeral? His sister? Yes, she would surely show up. His partners at the law firm and a few other people he knew from the practice would be there. To do otherwise would reflect badly on them—and they couldn't let that happen. His clients, for whom he had worked so hard and won massive settlements? He doubted it. Friends? He had none outside of work. His ex-wife? Hell no.

As he began to take an inventory of the attendees, he sadly realized only two people would be there because they truly loved and cared for him—his sister and Katie. And the more he thought about it, the more he realized they were the only two people he truly cared for.

He had once heard someone say that what really matters when you die is the dash between the two years on your tombstone. That dash represents everything you accomplished, all the people whose lives you touched, all the people you loved, and, more importantly, the ones who loved you. A man's life was reduced to one small dash carved in a piece of granite. That seemed somewhat unfair to Cody, but he couldn't help wondering what people would think of his dash. That he was a good lawyer? That was true enough, he supposed, but it was hardly the way he wanted to be remembered.

He regretted that his life had, in the grand scheme of things, counted for very little.

He wished he had done more. Wished he had made a genuine difference in other people's lives. Sure, he had made lots of people lots of money, but that would seem trivial when they threw the first shovelful of dirt on top of him.

He had little to be proud of.

He determined then and there, sitting under the massive pine tree that now served as his home, that if God—yes, deep down, he still believed there was a God—allowed him to survive this, he would make a change in his life.

Start over.

The idea of quitting his job and moving away from Atlanta became more than a mere fantasy. And he wouldn't just look for a vacation property in the mountains. It would be a permanent move. It was something he *must* do. He had to change. Had to see what else life had to offer. Had to be important to someone other than himself.

He yearned to see Katie again. To hear her voice and feel her touch.

If he was going to live long enough to make the changes in his life he so desperately wanted—so desperately craved—he was going to have to fight with everything he had.

He held the knife firmly and examined the blade once more.

Then he turned around and carved a fifth notch in the tree.

32

Cody decided he would start making decisions again—start trying to figure a way out of this mess.

But he also had to be realistic. He had to be judicious about the energy he expended. No matter how determined his spirit was to live, his body was severely injured, and his physical limitations made doing even the mundane tasks necessary for survival daunting. He began to make a mental list of things he could do to increase his chances of making it out alive.

The water situation could be better. With the steady rain decreasing to just a constant drizzle, he would be able to collect only about two good swallows a day in his water bottle—not great, but it should be enough to sustain him for a few more days at least.

Of greater concern was his left leg, which was still very warm, leading him to believe an infection was almost a certainty. There was little he could do about it, though. He had taken the last dose of Tylenol from the survival kit two days ago. All he could do was hope and pray he was found before the infection killed him.

There wasn't much he could do about any of his other physical injuries, either. He had done the best he could, us-ing his own torn pants to make a dressing for his detached scalp and a makeshift sling for his left arm. But, beyond that, he was pretty much helpless, so he decided to move on to other concerns.

He had not eaten anything since the handful of grubs he had managed to take from the rotten log on Friday. It had been much longer since he had eaten anything substantial. He knew his body desperately needed nourishment, but he was hesitant to try another trip to the log after seeing the bear back in the area last time. But if he was going to do everything he could to survive—and he intended to—he needed more food. What was the worst that could happen, anyway? The bear would find him and finish him off? It would at least be faster than dying from starvation or an infection. So he decided to make another attempt to get food.

He picked up the pocket knife and the makeshift spear he had fashioned after the last trip to the log. If it came down to a three-foot-long wooden stick and a cheap pocket knife against a 350-pound black bear, he would be screwed anyway. But he decided if he was going to die out here, then he would at least go out fighting. His grandfather, who rarely used coarse language, used to tell him before every one of his high school football games to go out and *give 'em hell*. Cody had often thought of that maxim before important events in his life: court cases, divorce proceedings, dealing with car salesmen; you name it.

As he moved out from the protection of the pine tree, holding the spear in his right hand and the knife between his teeth, he whispered to himself, "Give 'em hell, Cody . . . Give 'em hell!"

33

Jackson kicked one of the logs burning on the campfire. A shower of glowing embers rose into the air like fireflies. The damp morning air sent a chill through him, and he pulled his jacket collar close around his neck. He grabbed a fresh piece of wood and threw it on the burning pile, then took another sip of coffee. It was now Wednesday morning, and he was more than discouraged. Cody had been missing for a week, and, other than a perfectly normal campsite and a broken fishing rod, no sign of him had surfaced. Jackson had used every trick in the book to try to find him, but to no avail.

To complicate the situation, the weather had been horrible all week. The rain had continued off and on, and the persistent low cloud cover had thwarted any airborne search. The forecast for today was for gradual clearing, and Jackson hoped he could convince Bobby to finally get the helicopter in the air. He doubted it, though. He had talked to Bobby yesterday and had gotten the feeling that Bobby wanted to begin to wrap things up. Jackson figured he had two more days of searching before Bobby pulled the plug on the whole operation. It just wouldn't be right to keep searching past Friday and spoil Bobby's precious weekend.

Jackson was not going to let that happen until they found out what had happened to Cody—not this time.

Not again.

He knew Bobby couldn't wait to hang another failure around Jackson's neck. One more reason to get rid of him. One more chance for Bobby to remove a thorn from his side.

He took another sip of his coffee and, over the top of his mug, noticed Katie emerging from the tent she shared with Tiffany.

"Morning," he said.

"Good morning," Katie replied. She gave him a faint smile.

He noticed that she looked run-down and defeated. He had promised her that they would find Cody and, so far at least, he had failed to keep his word. "Hungry?" he asked.

"No thanks. I haven't had much of an appetite lately." She walked toward the campfire, her arms folded in a self-embrace. Jackson saw her shiver and rub her arms in the cool morning air.

Jackson wasn't sure how to respond. After an awkward silence, he finally said, "I'm going to radio Bobby again today and see if he thinks we can get the helicopter in the air."

"Looks like the weather's clearing some, maybe he'll send it over today."

"Yeah, maybe." Jackson didn't want to tell Katie about his personal problems with Bobby. He didn't see what could be gained by telling her, and it would just give her something else to worry about. By the looks of her, she had enough to worry about already. But he knew what Bobby was going to do. He would manufacture some crisis, or come up with some other horseshit reason to justify not using the helicopter.

Jackson was not going to let him get away with it.

After a breakfast that consisted of instant oatmeal and

dried fruit, Jackson got the members of the search team to-gether for the morning meeting. Only three of the original Forest Service guys remained. The rest had been swapped out for fresh men after the fourth day. Bobby had man-aged to come up with only two of the seven replacements. The others had, once again, come from the Forest Service.

Bobby was an expert at doing just enough to cover his ass if things went south, while at the same time, not enough to offer Jackson any substantial help.

Jackson unfolded the map and spread it across the ground. He knelt down as the other searchers gathered around, then drew a circle with his index finger around the area just upstream from their campsite. He spoke in a raised voice so everyone could hear him. "We are going to concentrate on this area today . . . and this area only." He tapped the map for emphasis, paused, then looked up at the ten men surrounding him. Many looked haggard and just ready to go home, their eyes beginning to show the exhaustion their bodies were feeling. Jackson had worked with some of the men before, and he could tell by the looks on their faces that they knew time was running out. The longer the search went without resolution, the longer the odds were that it would have a favorable outcome.

His finger still on the map, Jackson took a breath and continued, "It was searched Friday afternoon and all day on Saturday, but I have a strong feeling that if Cody is still in the area," he paused and again tapped his finger on the map, "this is where he is." He looked back up at the men. A few heads shook affirmatively, while others remained motionless.

Jackson was once again thinking of the broken rod he had found in the stream last Thursday. It was the only clue he had found, and in his mind, it was pointing him up-stream toward Cody. He was so sure that Cody was there that he had been surprised when the search had gone past the second day.

He stood back up, and the group of men stepped back to give him space. "Look . . . we all know time is running out on this. The weather is forecast to clear some today, so I'm going to work my contacts back at park headquarters to see if I can get a helicopter up here. But I need each and every one of you to give everything you have today . . . one hundred percent. I want you to take your time and look around every rock and tree you come across. Remember that Mr. McAlister may not be able to move or speak, depending on his injuries, so work slowly and look everywhere you can think of, and if you find anything or run into trouble, radio me immediately." He paused and looked briefly at each man. "Any questions?"

No one voiced any concerns, so Jackson turned to the two group leaders. "Jeff, you and your guys take the trail as far up the creek as you can, then drop off into the basin near the headwaters. Spread out so you can cover both sides of the creek, then start working your way back down. Got it?"

"No problem," Jeff responded. He turned and led his men toward the large pile of backpacks that were waiting near the edge of the trail.

Jackson turned his attention to the other group. "Tim, I want you and your men to start here at the campsite and work your way upstream, fan out so you can cover as much ground as possible, and walk until you meet up with Jeff's group."

"We'll do," Tim said.

Jackson looked at Katie and Tiffany, who were sitting next to the campfire. He could see Katie wiping away tears from her eyes. He hoped she had not heard his comment about time running out. He probably should have spoken in a more subdued voice. Tiffany was rubbing Katie's back and whispering something in her ear.

Tiffany had really surprised Jackson over the last several days. She had been completely out of her element at the beginning of the search, but she was a fast learner and now seemed an old pro at living in the wilderness. After the first day, she had not complained at all, even after she was almost killed when the ground gave way on the cliff. He was impressed.

Tiffany had also proved invaluable in helping to keep Katie's spirits up. She had worked hard to stay positive and to keep Katie encouraged and motivated. Jackson had often observed her speaking to Katie quietly, usually away from the group. He was never able to hear what they were talking about, but their body language revealed a deep and long-lasting friendship.

He walked over to the two women. "Everything okay?"

"Yeah, we're fine," Tiffany replied. Katie continued to drink her coffee in silence.

"Good. I'm going to radio headquarters and check on that helicopter. Then we'll be on our way. Be ready to go in ten minutes."

"Thanks, we'll be ready," Tiffany said, and gave Jackson a slight nod and a smile. She was still rubbing Katie's back.

Jackson noticed Katie's hands were trembling as she lifted the coffee cup to her mouth. He was afraid she was breaking. He had seen this happen before to family members of missing people. Once they lost hope of finding their loved one, they became withdrawn and solemn. He felt like he should say something, but wasn't sure what. Instead, he just turned and walked away. Why in the hell had he allowed himself to get so personally involved with these two women?

He walked down the trail until he was out of earshot of Katie and Tiffany, then called into headquarters. After several attempts, he finally reached Bobby. "We really would like to get that helicopter in the air today and see if we can spot anything. We've searched the area thoroughly on foot, but you know how dense these woods are . . . a bird's-eye view would really help. Looks like the weather is supposed to clear some today, too. When do you think you'll be able to get the helicopter up here?" Jackson waited nervously for Bobby's reaction. He hoped this would go smoothly and not devolve into a shouting match—but he was determined not to let Bobby run him over again.

After a lengthy pause, Bobby responded, "I don't know, Jackson. We're certainly doing everything we can on this side. The weather is still crap over here. I talked to the mechanic this morning, and he said he needed to do some scheduled maintenance on the chopper today, so I'm not sure if we can get it up there or not. I doubt it."

Jackson knew Bobby was just making excuses. Hell, Bobby probably insisted the mechanic take the helicopter out of service, just to make things difficult for him. "Listen, Bobby. We need that helicopter up here *today*. We're running out of time on this. You know that. Look, if this is some personal vendetta you have against me, don't do it. A man's life is riding on this."

"You better watch your mouth, Hart!" Bobby shouted. "Are you accusing me of letting my personal feelings get in the way of a search? You are walking on some very thin ice, Ranger Hart, and I advise you strongly to reconsider your last statement."

It was obvious to Jackson that he had touched a nerve with Bobby. Maybe he was getting too close to the truth. But he could not stop himself, and he pushed back at Bobby a second time.

"I just know that ever since the Cades Cove fiasco, you haven't exactly bent over backward to offer me any assistance. Hell, you sent only two men over to help in the ground search. I swear, if Mr. McAlister dies because of your stonewalling, I'll go directly to the park superintendent and tell him how this whole situation went down."

Bobby let out a sigh. "Threatening me, Jackson, is not an advisable course of action for you. Do you understand what I'm saying?"

Jackson wanted to spew a string of profanities into the radio, but instead, held his tongue and said nothing.

"I told you, we are doing everything possible to find Mr. McAlister. Perhaps, if you feel otherwise, I should send another ranger to replace you and take over the search?" Bobby added.

Jackson could tell by Bobby's tone that he was fuming. "Don't worry about it, Bobby. I'll find him myself."

"You do that," Bobby said.

Jackson heard him stifle a laugh before the radio transmission ended. Jackson was so angry that he almost threw the radio to the ground, but thought better of it, and returned it to his belt instead. He knew Bobby had no intention of sending the helicopter over today—or any day. How someone could be so petty and cruel eluded him. Bobby was trying to destroy him. And if Bobby wanted to ruin Jackson's career with the Park Service, that was one thing. Jackson could take care of himself. But putting an innocent man's life in jeopardy, just to settle a personal score, made his hatred of the man even more palpable. He was not going to let Bobby get away with this. Somehow, he would make sure Bobby paid the price for his actions.

Somehow.

He began the short walk back to the campsite. When he arrived, he found Katie and Tiffany standing next to the fire with their backpacks on, ready to go.

"What did they say about the helicopter?" Katie asked.

"They're going to try to get it in the air later this afternoon," Jackson lied. He didn't want Katie to know the truth. He needed her to remain focused on the search, not get involved with an internal government squabble. When Katie wasn't looking, Tiffany caught his eye and asked him silently if what he had just told Katie was true. He shook his head.

"Ready to go?" he asked them.

Both women nodded.

"Okay, we're going to walk upstream again . . . like we did on Saturday. Maybe we'll find a clue we missed the first time. I'm going to be in constant contact with the other search leaders and, if they find anything, we can drop off the trail and go down to assist."

"Sounds good," Tiffany said.

Jackson looked at Katie, but she said nothing. Her gaze seemed unfocused and lifeless. It heightened Jackson's worry for her. Even the lie about the helicopter had not lifted her spirits. She was losing hope.

The sad thing was—he was, too.

34

By the time Cody carved another notch into the tree, his hand barely had enough strength to pull the blade across the wood. He counted the marks above his head. There were eight notches in the tree now, and their appearance told the story of his slow, agonizing demise. The first four were distinct, deep cuts in the wood. The last four had grown progressively weaker—the eighth barely visible, not much more than a surface scratch.

A violent cough racked his body. He was afraid it was the beginning stages of pneumonia. He coughed again. And again.

The grubs he had managed to collect when he had dared another trip to the fallen log on Sunday were long gone. He had made it to the log and back without having another encounter with the bear, but he barely remembered eating the small amount of food. He had become so weak that trips to the water bottle had become infrequent. The rainfall had decreased, too, and when he was able to travel the short distance to the bottle, he considered himself fortunate if there was one good swallow of water waiting.

By his count of the notches in the tree, it was now Wednesday, although he couldn't be certain. His mind had become clouded and unreliable due to the lack of food and water.

He was wet, cold, and starving.

He coughed again.

He had the worst headache he had ever experienced in his life. A shiver ran through his body and his teeth chattered. He sniffled—then coughed again. He pulled the now well-worn emergency blanket tighter around his body.

When he looked up, he was surprised to see his grandfather sitting in front of him. A pipe hung from Herschel's mouth, and Cody could smell the fragrant tobacco smoke as his grandfather took a long puff. It smelled wonderful, a mixture of cherry and apple tobacco, just like he remembered. It caused a rush of warmth to flow through his body—the first warmth he had felt in days. Memories of the many nights he had spent sitting with Herschel next to the old rock fireplace in their rural Georgia home came flooding into his mind. His grandfather would smoke his pipe as they played dominoes together. One time, Herschel had taught Cody how to play poker, but they could only play when his grandmother was not around. His grandfather had said the game offended her *Christian sensibilities*. Cody hadn't understood what that meant at the time, but he had listened to his grandfather and kept the clandestine poker games just between the two of them.

Herschel was dressed in his usual flannel shirt, bib overalls, and a John Deere cap—the same clothing in which he had been buried. His boots looked worn and muddy. He sat atop his old Sears and Roebuck tackle box, holding his fiberglass fishing rod in his left hand. He looked like he was ready for a trip to one of the Georgia farm ponds the two of them used to fish together.

"How are you doing, Cody?" Herschel asked.

"Not too good." Cody's vision was blurring, and his grandfather was fading in and out of focus.

"I know that, son. That's why I'm here," his grandfather responded.

Cody was confused. "What do you mean, Grandpa? Are you here to take me to Heaven?"

Herschel slapped his knee and laughed with the same boisterous laugh that Cody recalled from his childhood. "No, son. I'm not here to take you to Heaven."

"Am I dead? Is this Heaven?"

Herschel chuckled and rubbed his chin. "No, Cody, you are not dead." He paused and looked around, carefully examining his surroundings. "And Heaven is a might bit prettier than this place, if I do say so."

Cody coughed again, and an intense sensation of pressure assaulted his head. It was worse than any headache he had ever experienced. His head was down, and he was barely able to open his eyes. "Then what are you doing here?"

Herschel avoided the question. "Say, that's a mean sounding cough you have there. How long has that been going on?"

"I dunno, maybe a couple of days." He coughed again. This time harder than before. White flashes of light appeared in his vision. When the coughing spell subsided and he was able to lift his head enough to see Herschel again, he noticed a look of concern on his grandfather's face.

Herschel rubbed his chin once again, as if in deep thought. "Cody, we need to get you warm. Have you built a fire yet?"

"Had one." Cody paused to cough. "It went out." He coughed again. "Too wet."

Herschel grunted. "You need to get warm, Cody . . . now. Do you understand what I'm saying?"

"Yeah." Cody's speech was now little more than a whisper.

"Why don't you look around and see if you can find a piece of that fire starting stick?"

"How did you know about that?" Cody asked.

"Don't worry about how I knew, Cody. Just do it. You're running out of time, son . . . you need to hurry."

"I think I used it all up a while back. There's not any left."

"Just try, Cody."

More violent coughing. "Can you do it, Grandpa . . . please? I can hardly move."

"Sorry, son. I wish I could help, but I'm afraid you'll have to do this part on your own." Herschel stood from his tackle box and walked closer. He squatted in front of Cody. The blackened soil of the long dead campfire lay between the two of them. "Look around on the ground here. Maybe there's a piece left."

"All right, Grandpa. I'll try."

"Good job, son. Just try," Herschel said.

Cody leaned forward to get a better look at the ground. He was dizzy and things seemed to be spinning out of control. He lost his balance and toppled over onto his side.

Cody felt his grandfather's hand on his shoulder. "Cody, are you all right?"

"No . . . I think . . . I'm dying."

"Stop that talk right this second. You have to fight, Cody. Get yourself up. You need to get a fire going. You're running out of time, son."

All Cody wanted to do was close his eyes and go to sleep, but his grandfather continued to shake him awake. He finally pulled himself back up and started to look for a piece of the fire starting material. "Why are you here, Grandpa?" he asked again.

"Don't worry about that now . . . just find what you're looking for, Cody. Concentrate."

Cody's vision was blurring again. "I can't see very well, Grandpa."

"You're doing great, son. Just keep going."

Cody searched the ground with his right hand, feeling for the last piece of fire starter. Then he felt his fingers run across something in the pile of wet pine needles that felt familiar. He picked it up and held it close to his face. It was small, but it was what he was looking for. "I think I found a piece."

"Good job, Cody!" his grandfather replied. "Now, do you still have the matches?"

"Yeah, I think so." Cody dug the matches out of his pants pocket and showed them to Herschel.

"Okay, good. Now, listen to me . . . you need to go to the edge of the tree, away from the limbs, and start a fire."

Cody was confused again. "Why? I can just build a fire here. I don't have the energy to move anymore, Grandpa."

"Dammit, son! Listen to me, and just do what I say. Please?"

His grandfather's insistence that he move away from the tree to start the fire didn't make sense to Cody, but he couldn't remember the last time he had heard his grandfather curse, and that caught his attention. He decided further argument was useless, so he began to slowly crawl toward the edge of the tree limbs.

Cody heard his grandfather offering encouragement. "That's the way, Cody. Keep going. You're doing fine."

When he finally reached the outer edge of the tree's canopy, he collapsed.

"Just a little farther, Cody. You're almost there," Herschel said.

"I can't, Grandpa. I need to . . . go to . . . sleep."

"Come on, Cody! Just a little farther!"

Cody made one final push and moved another few feet, just past the outer edge of the tree limbs.

"Good . . . good. Now, grab some pine needles and sticks and put them around the fire starter."

"Can you get them for me, Grandpa? I'm so tired."

"You have to do this part yourself, Cody. Just keep trying."

Cody's hand was shaking uncontrollably, but he managed to collect a small amount of pine needles and twigs. He placed the piece of fire starter in the center of the pile, then set the clump of material on the ground in front of him.

"Good. You're doing great, Cody," Herschel said. "Now, take a match and light it."

Cody tried to strike the match, but his hand was so weak he dropped it into the leaves.

"Pick it up and try again, Cody. You have to," Herschel said.

"I can't," Cody responded, his voice trembling. He felt his grandfather's hand on his shoulder again.

"Yes, you can. You have to believe in yourself."

Cody picked up the match and tried again.

Nothing.

"Dammit," Cody whispered.

"That's okay, son. Just try again," Herschel said.

Cody tried a third time, and a small flame sprang up.

"Now, light it," Herschel said. His voice had a measure of calmness about it now.

Cody touched the flame to the fire starter, his hand shaking so badly he thought he was about to drop the match again. Flames began to slowly spread over the pile. He blew a weak breath over the fire to keep it going.

"Now, Cody, this is very important. Take a handful of the wet leaves and place them on the fire."

"Won't that just put it out?" Cody asked. But before the question was even out of his mouth, he had grabbed a small handful of the wet leaves that littered the ground and placed them on the flame. Dense, white smoke began to rise into the air. "Is that good, Grandpa?" He turned to look at Herschel, seeking his approval.

His grandfather had vanished.

35

Cody turned his head to the right, then back to the left, looking for Herschel—but he was nowhere to be seen. "Grandpa! Grandpa!" he yelled. "Where did you go?" The scream caused a painful burning sensation in his throat. Then the wind shifted, and Cody choked on the thick smoke that blew over his face. After a severe coughing spell, he looked up again, still searching for his grandfather.

What he saw instead scared the hell out of him—the bear was standing a mere stone's throw in front of him.

It began to walk slowly toward Cody, and he could hear the same low, guttural growls emerging from the animal that he had heard prior to the attack. It looked massive, even larger than he remembered. Its broad shoulders moved up and down as it continued its march toward Cody.

He was defenseless. Too weak to move. Too weak to even attempt a defense. He had left the wooden spear behind when Herschel had urged him to leave the relative safety of the tree. Not that it mattered much, anyway—in his weakened state, he could do little to stop the bear, even with the spear.

So this is it. This is how everything is going to end, he

thought. He felt some sadness, a small amount of fear, but surprisingly, a great deal of relief, too. Sadness for the fact that his life was going to end unfulfilled. All his hopes for the future, destroyed—the possibility for a second chance at life extinguished.

His dash on the granite slab would be found lacking.

He experienced a flash of fear when he first saw the bear approaching, a natural instinct—but he knew instantly there was nothing he could do. Whatever was going to happen was out of his control. He was lying on the ground, wounded and defenseless. He wondered why his grandfather had been so insistent that he leave the tree. *Why?* So he could come out here and be finished off by the bear? Maybe Herschel was being merciful—a swift death, versus another day or two of agony before he finally succumbed to his wounds and the elements. Whatever the reason, it didn't matter now. Cody accepted his fate and found himself welcoming death.

A rush of relief flowed through him. At least this hellish nightmare was about to be over. Though he feared the pain of another bear attack, he supposed it was the most expedient, and therefore the preferable option.

The bear was still approaching. Slowly. Methodically.

Cody closed his eyes and said a silent prayer—not for deliverance, but rather that it would be over quickly.

The bear had drawn to within a few feet of him. It would not be long now.

The bear was so close that Cody could smell the putrid stench of its breath. A musky odor wafted up from its thick fur coat. He looked up once more, directly into the cold, black eyes staring down at him. The beast's lips were parted, exposing its jagged teeth. He wanted to face his destiny like a man, head-on, with no reservations or fear. He had made a lot of mistakes in his life, but he still had control of one thing—the way he faced death.

And he intended to die like a man.

36

Jackson kicked a stone as he walked along the trail. Katie and Tiffany followed behind. The three of them had been walking back and forth on the trail that ran along the mountainside above Eagle Creek for almost an hour when they paused to take a break. He removed his pack, leaned it against a tree, and took a drink from his water bottle.

So far, he had heard nothing significant from either of the two search leaders, Tim and Jeff, although he had been checking in with them on a regular basis. He let out a lengthy sigh.

"You don't think we're going to find him, do you?" Katie asked.

Jackson saw the desperation written on her face—trying to hold on to the little hope she had left. He thought about lying again, like he had earlier about the helicopter, but he decided to tell her the truth this time.

Jackson ran his fingers through his thick, black hair. "Katie, I wish I could tell you that we were definitely going to find him, but the truth is, I'm not sure anymore. I haven't given up yet, and neither should you. But the longer this search goes on, the less the chances are for a . . ." He tried to find the best word, something that would convey the seriousness of the situation, but not seem insensitive. ". . . favorable outcome," he finished. He knew instantly that he had chosen the wrong words. Too mechanical. Too distant.

Too cold.

He saw the tears begin to form once more in her eyes. She quickly wiped them away and turned around.

"I'm sorry, Katie, I—" Jackson began, but he didn't know what else to say, so he just remained silent. He took another drink of water, then stood up and put his pack back on. Tiffany was giving Katie another hug. The sight of it tore at Jackson's heart. He had been so sure this time would be different. That this search *would* have a favorable outcome.

Jackson peered down the mountain, toward Eagle Creek and wished that he could have delivered what he had promised. He felt like a failure. He was just about to turn away and resume walking, when he noticed a small puff of gray smoke drifting up through the trees. He moved closer to the edge of the trail to get a better look. He saw nothing. Maybe he had just imagined the whole thing. He turned to start walking again, but then, out the corner of his eye, he saw it again. It was definitely smoke—not fog or a wisp of mist moving up from the cold water below—but smoke. The distinct smell of burning wood hit his nostrils. He pulled his radio from his belt. "Tim, this is Jackson. Did you or any of your men start a fire?" he asked. There was a lengthy pause while Jackson waited for Tim to respond.

Tiffany and Katie stood up and walked to Jackson. "What's going on?" Tiffany asked.

"Just a minute," Jackson said.

Finally, the radio crackled back to life, and Tim replied, "Jackson, that's a negative. We haven't started a fire."

"Do you see any smoke? It should be just upstream from you."

Another pause.

"Sorry, Jackson, but it's so thick down here, we can't see very far in front of us. We haven't found anything yet."

"Okay, thanks."

Although Tim's group should be nearer to the source of the smoke than Jeff's, Jackson wanted to be sure, so he called Jeff on the radio. Jeff responded that his group was still well upstream, far away from the source of the smoke.

Jackson keyed the radio again. "Jeff and Tim, I'm about a mile upstream from the creek crossing. I'm going to make my way down the mountain and investigate the source of the smoke. I'll call back when I know something, so pay attention to your radios."

Both men quickly acknowledged what he told them, and then Jackson turned to Tiffany and Katie. "You two stay here. Tiffany, do you still have the radio I gave you yesterday?"

"Yes . . . I've got it, but shouldn't we come with you?" she asked.

"No. It's probably nothing, and you'll be safer up here. If I need you, I'll call you on the radio. Make sure it's set to channel three. I'll be back in a few minutes."

Both women looked like they were about to protest being left behind, but before they had a chance to voice their displeasure, Jackson stepped off the trail and started down the mountain. He didn't want them coming along because he saw no reason to get their hopes up. Most likely, this was just a backpacker camping where they weren't supposed to. All campers were supposed to stay only in designated campsites, but often, someone seeking more isolation would camp wherever they wanted. Jackson was sure this was probably the case this time, too. However, if there was any chance it was Cody, he could be in very bad shape, and Jackson didn't want Katie and Tiffany to have to witness that.

He made his way rapidly down the steep slope, almost jogging, slowing his descent when necessary by grabbing hold of bushes and tree trunks. He lost sight of the smoke for an instant, but then saw another puff rise from the ground about two hundred yards away.

More than anything, he wanted Cody to be sitting down at the bottom of the mountain, alive. He wanted to find this man, not just for himself, but for Katie and Tiffany, too. Although he had met the two women only recently, he had grown fond of both of them, and the idea of having to carry a body bag out of the mountains with the two of them in tow was unbearable.

He was still wishing he hadn't let them come along.

He slowed his approach once he was within about seventy-five yards of the smoke. The last thing he wanted to do was run haphazardly into an unknown situation. The smoke could be coming from poachers, or a fugitive, or a thousand other possibilities.

Carelessness could get you killed on this job.

The dense foliage made it difficult to get a clear view of the situation. The smell of the smoke was stronger now, but it was not overpowering. He started to call out for Cody but didn't, deciding it was better to remain silent in the event it was someone not expecting company.

As he drew nearer, the foliage thinned, and what he saw was not at all what he had been expecting—or what he was hoping for.

A huge black bear—the largest Jackson had ever seen in the wild—was standing over a man's body, growling.

Jackson did not have time to think. He just had time to act.

He drew his Glock and fired two shots at the bear's head.

37

When Katie heard the two shots ring out in rapid succession, her heart jumped. "What was that?" she asked.

"I don't know. It sounded like gunshots to me," Tiffany replied.

"That's what I thought, too. We've got to get down there."

Before Tiffany could try to stop her, Katie had dropped off the trail and was practically running down the mountainside.

"Katie, slow down! Wait for me!" she heard Tiffany yell from behind her, but Katie kept charging forward. She was moving as quickly as possible, bushes and small tree limbs whipping against her body as she descended. Her mind had a single focus—finding Cody—and to hell with everything else. If she tripped and broke her leg, so be it. Something inside her told her Cody was at the bottom of this mountain, and she had to get to him *now*. She could hear Tiffany stumbling behind her. Once, she thought she heard her fall, but she didn't slow down to check.

"Cody! Cody!" she yelled, as she drew closer to the smoke. When she finally emerged from the thick foliage, she could not believe her eyes.

Jackson was holding his gun and standing over a dead bear.

And Cody was lying dead in front of him.

38

Cody was unsure of what had just happened. He felt the little energy he had left leave his body all at once, and he allowed his head to fall back to the earth.

The next thing he knew, a man was standing over him. The man told him his name was Ranger Jackson Hart and that everything was going to be fine.

Cody had serious doubts about that.

Then something happened that Cody had thought would never again be possible—he saw Katie's face. His vision was still blurring off and on, but he knew without a doubt that it was her. She was bending over him and crying.

"Thank God," she said. "I thought you were dead!" She grasped his right hand and rubbed it in between her own.

Cody heard the ranger begin to talk into his radio.

"Tim, Jeff . . . we have him! Get everyone down here ASAP! Have someone bring the backboard and the medical kit from camp. And contact your supervisor at the Forest Service, and see if they have a search and rescue helicopter available. Explain the situation and let them know the park service helicopter is currently out of service. He needs to get to a hospital immediately, so we need to hustle on this . . . do you understand?"

"Copy that, Jackson," one of the other men replied. "I'm sending two guys for the backboard now. We thought we heard gunshots. Is everything okay?"

"Yeah, everything is fine. I'll explain later. Just hurry and make that call, then let me know what you find out."

"Got it," the other man said.

"But I thought the park service helicopter was going to be up here today?" Katie asked Jackson.

"Look, I'll explain later. Right now, I just need you to help me with Cody."

Now Jackson was over him again. "Hold on, Cody. We're going to get you out of here, but I need you to keep fighting. Okay?"

Cody tried to talk, but the words would not come. Instead, he just nodded.

"Don't try to talk," Katie told him. "Just be still and hold my hand. You're going to be fine."

Tears were flowing freely from her eyes now. Cody wondered if they were all tears of joy, or if some—maybe most of them—were tears of fear. Fear that he might not make it. He imagined what Katie was seeing. His appearance must have been horrible because she would not stop crying.

"Here, Cody, drink this," Jackson said.

He drank the liquid the ranger slowly poured over his lips. He thought it was water, but it had a funny taste.

"This is an electrolyte solution, Cody. It should help you feel better," Jackson told him.

A few minutes later, another group of men came up and they helped place him on the backboard. They secured him with three straps; one across his chest, another across his waist, and a final one across his legs. The whole process hurt like hell.

"Any word on the helicopter?" Jackson asked one of the men.

"Both helicopters are away on other missions right now. They can recall one of them, but it will take at least three hours to get on-scene here."

"Dammit!" Jackson shouted.

"What about the National Guard or another agency?" the other man asked.

"It would take too long to coordinate . . . we don't have time to wait around. Plus, the cloud cover could move back in at any minute and stop an air rescue. We'll just have to carry him out on the backboard. If we hurry and take shifts, we can be back to the lake in a couple of hours. I'll radio ahead and have a boat waiting for us."

Cody heard some more talking back and forth, but his mind was having a difficult time focusing on anything long enough to gather any additional information.

Jackson leaned over him. "Cody, I'm going to give you something to ease the pain, okay?"

That sounded like the best idea Cody had heard in days. He felt a needle stick in his right arm, then the men lifted him off the ground and began carrying him through the woods.

Katie was still holding his hand. He looked into her beautiful blue eyes, wanting to say something. Wanting to tell her how much he cared for her, and how things were going to be different from now on, but he still could not find the strength to verbalize anything.

He didn't need to say anything.

"I love you, too," she said.

Cody watched as the pine tree that had been his home disappeared in the distance. It had been both his hell and his heaven.

Where he had almost lost everything.

Where he had truly found himself.

Cody felt the pain medication begin to take effect, and he became sleepy. After eight days in the wilderness, his body finally felt at rest. His left eye was still swollen shut, but he kept looking up at Katie with his right eye until he could no longer keep his eyelid open.

Then he drifted off to sleep.

39

By the time they reached the lakeshore, Jackson was exhausted. It had taken less than two hours to make the trip, which was a lot faster than he had expected. They had broken into smaller groups and alternated carrying the backboard. While one group was carrying Cody, the others would rest and then catch up later. Even Katie and Tiffany had taken their turns helping carry the backboard. On the smoother parts of the trail, some of the men broke into a slow jog. Everyone had done all they could to make sure Cody made it out of this alive.

Cody had remained unconscious for most of the trip, only moaning when they jostled him a little too much at a creek crossing or a rough spot in the trail.

Jackson was happy to see Jesse waiting with the pontoon boat. They quickly loaded Cody onto the boat, and then everyone else piled in. Before everyone was even seated, Jackson yelled at Jesse, "Let's go!"

Jesse turned the boat around and headed for the marina.

The pontoon boat was no speed machine, and Jackson was wishing he had made some of the men stay on shore to lighten the load. It was too late now. He motioned for Tim—who, besides being one hell of a searcher, was also an EMT—to check Cody's vital signs again. Jackson breathed a sigh of relief when Tim gave him a thumbs up.

Fifteen minutes later, Jackson spotted the marina. Flashing emergency lights dotted the shoreline. Jesse never let off the throttle, not until just before they reached shore. Jackson and three other men grabbed the backboard and carried Cody to the waiting ambulance.

As they loaded him in the back of the ambulance, one of the paramedics pushed Katie aside when she tried to get in the back with Cody.

Jackson saw what was happening. "No, it's okay. Let her go with him," he told the paramedic. The man just shrugged and waved Katie forward. Once she was inside with Cody, the doors were closed and Jackson heard the big diesel engine howl as the ambulance began to move up the steep hill.

"Where are they taking him?" Jackson asked a sheriff's deputy, who was standing nearby and talking into his radio.

"They're landing a medical helicopter at the abandoned golf course, just up the road. They're flying him to Asheville."

Jackson nodded. "Thank you." He turned to Tiffany and smiled. "He's in pretty rough shape, but I think he's going to make it."

She moved forward and gave Jackson a warm hug and a kiss on the cheek. "Thank you so much. He would have died out there if it weren't for you."

Jackson shrugged off the thanks. "You're welcome. Glad to do it." He started to walk up the ramp toward his Suburban. He stopped, then turned around and looked at Tiffany. "I'm heading back home. Do you want to come with me and get cleaned up? You can gather the luggage the two of you left at my house, and then we'll go up to the hospital and pay Cody and Katie a visit tomorrow."

"Sounds great," Tiffany said. "I need a shower in the

worst way." She smelled her shirt. "I stink!" She smiled then said, "You know something?"

"What's that?"

"I've never even been camping before."

Jackson laughed. "Really?"

"Really."

"Well, I think you did a wonderful job, Tiffany."

"Thanks. And you can call me Tiff." She paused. "All my friends do, anyway."

"I'd be honored. Thank you, Tiff," he replied.

They both continued walking toward the Suburban. Jackson's muscles felt like they were going to give out at any moment. He could only imagine how Tiffany felt.

Something off to his left caught Jackson's attention. A news crew had set up and was interviewing someone. With all the flashing emergency lights, he hadn't noticed it before. He walked closer to get a better look and was shocked to see none other than Bobby Donaldson standing in front of the cameras. He was using his fake politician's smile and describing how they had pulled off such an impossible rescue.

The anger boiled up inside of Jackson as he walked closer. Bobby saw him approaching, and Jackson caught a hint of fear in his eyes.

"Here's one of our heroes now," Bobby said to the cameras, motioning for Jackson to come over. "Come on over, Ranger Hart, and tell us exactly what happened."

Jackson could no longer contain his anger. He was going to do something he had wanted to do ever since Steven Cantwell had been found dead in Cades Cove. Something that would most likely cost him his job, but he didn't care anymore—he walked straight up to Bobby and slugged him as hard as he could, right on the end of his jaw.

Bobby fell to the ground in a heap. He moaned and wiped blood away from his lips as he tried to stand back up. His lower lip started to quiver. Was he going to cry?

He looked like a middle-school bully who had just had someone fight back for the first time. The reporters gasped. Jackson just turned and walked away without saying a word. He heard Bobby yell, "Jackson, I'll have your job over this!"

He just kept walking.

When he rejoined Tiffany, she asked, "What was that about?"

"He's the reason we had no helicopter today. I thought he needed a little attitude adjustment."

"Oh . . . Well, I guess he deserved it then."

"Yeah, you could say that." Jackson opened the doors to the Suburban, climbed inside, and started the engine. He looked over at Tiffany, who was sitting next to him in the front passenger seat. "Let's go get a warm shower and something hot to eat," Jackson said.

"Agreed," she replied.

EPILOGUE

Cody's nerves were on edge. His hands were sweating, and he wiped them on his blue jeans to dry them.

The irony of the whole situation was not lost on him.

It had been a year since he had been pulled from the mountains only half-alive. He thought of everything he had been through—the six weeks spent in a hospital bed, followed by four more months of rehabilitation at an out-patient facility.

When he had first arrived at the hospital, the doctors were astonished that he had survived. He had four broken ribs, a dislocated shoulder, three cracked vertebrae in his lower back, a large piece of his scalp was detached, and he was severely malnourished. The most serious injury he had, though, was the infection in his left leg. The doctors had pumped him full of strong antibiotics to counteract it. He had been in ICU for a full week, and when he spiked a high temperature on day three, the members of the medical staff weren't sure he would survive. Cody remembered none of this. He had been unconscious for most of the first two weeks following his rescue. Eventually, the drugs were effective and the infection was eradicated.

While the antibiotics saved his life, they had not been able to save his leg. He ran his hand down his thigh until he felt the titanium prosthetic leg he now wore, remembering the loss he had suffered.

The rehab staff had been extraordinarily patient with him, teaching him to walk with his new leg and helping him through the emotional trials he had faced. For the first few months, he awoke every night screaming—reliving the bear attack in his dreams.

Katie had been there, too, helping him through every phase of his recovery. Comforting him when he awoke in a panic.

His partners had assured him that his job was safe and he would be welcomed back as a full partner once his recovery was complete. But Cody had decided that being a corporate lawyer was not for him. He liked most of his coworkers, but his heart just wasn't in it anymore. He had promised himself on the mountain that if God allowed him to live, he would make changes in his life.

And he did.

The day he was released from the hospital, he had turned in his letter of resignation. The McAlister family name was no longer on the big law firm in Atlanta—and that was just fine with him.

The day he finished rehab, he made another big change. He put his townhouse up for sale and left the city for good. He had moved to the small mountain town of Sylva, North Carolina, and taken a job in a local fly shop. He worked for minimum wage, something he hadn't done since college, but for the first time in years, he had found happiness.

Three months after he started his new job, the fly shop was put up for sale. With the money he had been able to save after the divorce, coupled with a nice profit on his townhouse, he was able to purchase the shop. He finally loved going to work every day.

So, for all the struggles he had been through, he thought it ironic that he found himself back in a hospital. Sitting outside an operating room. Once again hoping that everything would turn out okay.

He wiped his hands on his pants again. He felt nauseous.

A nurse dressed in operating room scrubs ran through the large double doors.

"Mr. McAlister, your wife is ready. Come on!"

Cody stood slowly, being careful not to lose his balance. He was still getting used to the prosthesis. He hobbled as fast as he could toward the nurse. She put a covering over his hair, helped him get into the gown, and then handed him a mask and a pair of sterile gloves, which he quickly donned.

He walked into the room and saw Katie lying flat on the gurney, the doctor and a group of nurses surrounding her.

Katie's abdomen was covered with iodine, and the doctor was holding a scalpel in his hand. He looked up when Cody entered the room. "Mr. McAlister, are you ready?" he asked.

Cody felt like his legs were about to come out from under him—both of them. This was harder than his experience in the mountains. Then, he had been concerned only with keeping himself alive. Now, he was worried about Katie.

"Yeah . . . I guess so," he replied, his voice shaking.

"Somebody get that man a chair," he heard the doctor say.

A nurse shoved a chair behind his legs and helped Cody sit down. Then she wheeled him over to Katie. He grabbed her hand and held tight, rubbing it comfortingly—just like she had done for him a year ago in the mountains.

"I love you, Katie," he said.

"I love you too, Cody," she replied.

"Okay, Mrs. McAlister, you're going to feel a lot of pressure," the doctor said. "Are you ready?"

"Yeah, ready," Katie replied.

A large sheet had been placed between Katie's head and her abdomen, blocking her and Cody's view of the procedure. He was thankful for that.

"Here we go," the doctor said.

Cody squeezed Katie's hand. She grimaced, and then it was over.

Cody kept his eyes on his wife. He didn't want to chance seeing anything below that sheet. He was afraid he would faint right then and there, but he took a few deep breaths and felt the dizziness abate. He heard the doctor and nurses making some sort of commotion, but he kept looking directly into Katie's beautiful blue eyes. He stroked her blonde hair. "I'm so proud of you," he said.

"Thanks, Cody. I'm so glad you're here." She smiled and a tear ran down her cheek.

"Congratulations, Mr. and Mrs. McAlister!" Cody heard the doctor say. He finally looked up and saw the doctor holding the most beautiful thing he had ever seen.

Tiny.

Perfect.

His daughter.

The doctor asked if he wanted to cut the umbilical cord and Cody agreed, although his hands were shaking so badly, he was afraid he would accidentally hurt the baby. With the help of the doctor's guiding hand, he was finally able to complete the task, and then he took his daughter into his arms.

One of the nurses helped him wrap the baby in a blanket, and then he took her to meet her mother. He laid their daughter on Katie's chest and gave his wife a kiss on her cheek.

They both cried.

Cody was watching the six o'clock news, still holding

Katie's hand, their daughter resting comfortably on his wife's chest, when the door to their hospital room cracked opened.

"Heard there was a new McAlister in the world," Jackson said.

"Hey guys, come on in," Cody said, standing to greet the visitors.

"Congratulations!" Tiffany yelled as she entered the room. She was carrying a bouquet of flowers, a new baby blanket, and a balloon with *It's a Girl!* printed on it. She gave Cody a quick kiss on the cheek as she passed, and then headed straight to Katie with a huge smile on her face.

Cody reached out and shook Jackson's hand. Cody had not seen the man that saved his life since he left the hospital in Asheville. "Thanks for coming, Jackson. It's great to see you again." He could hear Katie and Tiffany doing all the usual *oohs* and *ahhs* that inevitably came with a new baby.

Cody offered Jackson a seat. "How's everything been going?"

"Good," Jackson replied. "How are you doing? I see you're up and walking around again."

"Things are going well. I had a hard time getting adjusted to my new metal friend," Cody tapped his prosthesis before he continued. "But to tell you the truth, I'm just happy to be alive. I just want to thank you again for everything you did, Jackson. Without your help, today would never have happened. I can never repay you, but I just want you to know that I am forever grateful."

"You're welcome, Cody. I'm glad everything worked out well for you and Katie. You two deserve it. Hey, sorry I couldn't make it to the wedding, but I had a training seminar in Montana I had to attend. Tiffany said it was a great wedding, though."

Cody looked over at his wife and Tiffany, who were

still talking about the new baby. "Yeah, it really was." He turned back to Jackson and motioned with his head toward Tiffany. "So how are things going with you and Tiffany?"

"Well, ever since she moved up from Atlanta about four months ago, we get to see a lot of each other. She works at the resort now, so we get to have dinner together a few times a week." He paused and smiled. "Things are going well. She's still the same fireball she always was, but I wouldn't have it any other way."

Cody smiled. "Good, I'm glad to hear that. So you're still working at Twentymile?"

"Yep, sure am. I had an opportunity to move back over to headquarters a couple of months ago, but I turned it down. Twentymile is a nice place, not much goes on, and I like the solitude."

"That's great," Cody said. "Listen, I hope you didn't get into any trouble on my account. I heard about the run-in you had with the other ranger at the marina."

"Don't worry about it. Everything's fine." Jackson laughed and rubbed his chin. "To tell you the truth, I thought my career was finished when Bobby hit the asphalt, but things have a way of working themselves out, I suppose.

"Ever since Bobby was forced to retire, things have gotten a lot better. Several of his friends in the Park Service were really pissed after I testified against him at the inquiry, and they tried to make things hard for me, but I didn't care. It was the right thing to do. The new guy is a lot better, and easier to work with, too."

"That's good to hear. Glad everything worked out okay."

Tiffany broke up their conversation when she asked, "So what's her name?"

Cody looked at Katie and smiled. "We named her after

my grandmother, Missy."

"Oh, that's so sweet," Tiffany said. "I know your Grand-ma Missy meant a lot to you, Cody."

Jackson stood up. "Well, Tiffany, we've kept them long enough. We'd better get going."

"Yeah, you owe me dinner and a movie, mister," Tiffany said.

"For what?" Jackson asked.

"Just for putting up with you. Isn't that a good enough reason?"

"I guess so." Jackson winked at Cody and Katie, then laughed.

Tiffany gave both Katie and Cody a goodbye hug, and then she and Jackson made their way to the door.

As the group said their last goodbyes, Jackson paused at the door. "And Cody . . . your grandmother did a hell of a job."

That statement brought a tear to Cody's eye. It meant so much coming from a man he admired as much as he did Jackson. "Thank you, Jackson."

When they were gone, Cody took Katie's hand again. It felt wonderful to be sharing this moment with her. She had saved his life twice on the mountain. Once during the bear attack, when he was within seconds of drowning and the memory of her face urged him to keep fighting, and again, when his desperation was so great that he was about to take his own life, her face changed his mind. He would never be able to repay her. All he could do was love her for the rest of his life.

God had granted him a second chance.

Cody squeezed his wife's hand and kissed her on the forehead.

Looking into the glowing face of a new mother, he de-cided moments such as these were what life was all about. It wasn't about money or power or fame. It was about love and family. That was what made life special and worth living. What made you smile when you woke up in the morning. What made you want to come home at night.

What sustained you during tough times.

Author's Note

I began writing this novel several years ago, after the idea for the story came to me following a backcountry fly fishing trip of my own to Eagle Creek. It has been both frustrating and fulfilling to write. I would complete a few chapters and then put it aside for an indeterminate amount of time. After I made the decision to pursue a career in writing, I dusted it off and finally found the motivation to finish it. As any story does, it evolved over time. For example, the idea of Tiffany's scars came to me during the last weeks of writing. I purposely left the details of that situation out of *this* book.

One of my favorite characters in this story, although he plays a relatively minor role, is Herschel. He is a mixture of my own grandfathers, Billy and Richard, who taught me to love the outdoors, how to fish, and a lot about life. Thank you.

I have heard it said that no one writes a novel by themselves; no truer statement could be made. I owe thanks to many, many people.

First, to my wife, Janice, and daughter, Grace, who make *me* want to get up every morning and come home every night. I love both of you more than you can imagine.

I would also like to thank my PR and marketing firm, Mike and Jeannie Stewart (aka Mom and Dad), for all your love, support, and encouragement. Keep spreading the word!

I am so thankful for my wonderful team of editors, Sharon Jeffers, Winslow Eliot, and Melissa Gray. Without your suggestions and corrections, this book would be sorely lacking. Thank you for everything!

Thanks to Travis at probookcovers.com for the awesome covers he creates for me. To my book designer, Amy Siders, and her team at 52 Novels, thanks for all your help and the great work you do!

Finally, I want to thank all my friends and family members who have read my work and offered words of encouragement during the last year. I love hearing from you, and your support keeps me writing. I am forever grateful.

J. Michael Stewart

About the Author

J. Michael Stewart was born in the Smoky Mountains of North Carolina in 1978. He is the author of two novels, along with other works of short fiction. An avid fly fisherman, he loves to go to the mountains and spend time on a trout stream whenever possible. He currently lives in Nebraska with his wife and daughter.

To contact him, or for more information about J. Michael Stewart, please visit:

www.authorjmichaelstewart.com.

Also by J. Michael Stewart

A WINNING TICKET

Twin brothers Benjamin and Harrison Zimmerman are struggling just to keep their heads above water. Low crop prices and a recent drought have driven them to the brink of bankruptcy. The family farm is on the verge of foreclosure, and the mounting debt seems overwhelming. In the midst of a Nebraska blizzard, their luck suddenly changes when they hit it big by winning the lottery. In an instant they become multimillionaires. Now richer than they ever dreamed possible, all their problems seem to be solved. But before the night is over, the brothers' true feelings about the farm and each other will be revealed and their relationship changed forever.

DOSE of VENGEANCE

Everyone has secrets.

When the rich and powerful in Big Creek, Montana, are in danger of having their most private and embarrassing secrets exposed, they call Sean Foster. He gets paid to make other people's problems go away. And he's good at it. Very good.

But when a simple morning jog goes horribly wrong, Sean is the one who needs a fixer. In the struggle to survive and return to his wife, he forgets the most important lesson he has learned in his business.

Everyone has secrets.

And sometimes, they will kill to keep them hidden . . .

FIRE ON THE WATER

(Ranger Jackson Hart Book 2)

**Sometimes to live for the future, you have to defeat the
past . . .**

For ten years, Tiffany Colson has struggled to reclaim
her life, but it finally seems to be on track for a bright future. She has moved to a small cabin tucked deep in the
heart of the Great Smoky Mountains. She's surrounded
by wilderness and solitude, and her job at a small resort
as an outdoor guide has been the best therapy she could
have asked for.

And she's in love with the man who may just be the one—
U.S. Park Ranger Jackson Hart.

But there is a part of Tiffany's past that still haunts her. It's a
story only a handful of people know. A story she keeps hidden away deep inside her soul.

Ten years ago, Tiffany Colson killed a man.

At least . . . she thought she did.

Now, all her hopes for the future are jeopardized by the
ghost of a man she thought was dead and buried. As the tenth

anniversary of his death approaches, frightening things are happening. Things that threaten Tiffany's own sanity.

Soon, she will find that ghosts from her past are not just fleeting shadows moving through the halls of her mind.

They're real . . .

Following is a Preview of Book 2 in the
Ranger Jackson Hart Series

Fire on the Water

1

"*You ever seen water burn?*" *he asks, his words dripping off his tongue in a cutting southern drawl that, despite the warmth of the bath water, sends an ice-cold shiver up her spine. Goose bumps form over her exposed arms and breasts. He stands above her, his short brown hair and thick mustache visible even in the dimly lit bathroom. Two large candles flicker on top of a small wooden stand behind him. The left side of his mouth turns upward in an evil grin, spreading across his face as his gray eyes inspect her nude body.*

She sinks below the waterline to hide her nakedness, the water now up to her chin. Her long auburn hair floats around her. "No . . . no, I haven't," she says so softly it's almost inaudible.

"Well, I have," he responds. "My dad used to work on old cars in our garage. He always had a few cans of oil lying around. One day, I took one of the cans down to the small pond behind our house. My buddy from school, Willy was his name, but I guess that's not important to you right now." He smiles at her again, that same lopsided, chilling grin. "Anyway, Willy was with me, and he didn't

believe me when I told him that I could make water burn, so I proceeded to pour the full can of oil into the pond." His smile widens at the memory as he reaches down to the floor and picks up a large, red gasoline container. He swishes it in front of her; she can hear that it's almost full.

Her hands tremble beneath the water, and her legs begin to quake. Her breaths come in short, fearful gasps.

The fear, the torment, the confinement she's lived with for the past six months boils up inside her. She tries to hide her emotion, tries to deny him the satisfaction of seeing his power over her again, but it's no use. A single tear trickles down her right cheek.

He removes the cap from the container and tosses it next to the marble bathtub. He laughs softly as he sees the terror consume her. "Then I pulled a book of matches out of my pocket and lit the oil as I backed away from the pond. Willy and I watched as the fire spread over the surface of the water, like some invisible dragon was breathing across the pond . . . our eyes must've been as big as silver dollars." He chuckles and tilts the nozzle of the can down until a large stream of thick, dark oil flows into the bathwater.

"Please . . . please don't," she cries, but watches helplessly as the black goop enters the tub.

"Dad beat my ass for that one, but as I stood there, watching the water burn, watching the black smoke roll into the air, I felt absolutely invigorated . . . I was hypnotized by it. It was worth the whipping I took."

He pours the oil faster now, causing it to splash wildly as it makes contact with the surface of the water. She feels several drops land on her forehead and cheeks. Soon, the entire surface of the water is covered with a coal-black sheen. "You ever had something like that happen to you? Where you couldn't look away, even if you wanted to?" he asks.

"Paul, please don't hurt me. I'm sorry . . . for whatever I've done . . . I'm so sorry."

"Shut up!" he yells, his voice suddenly filled with rage. He pours the last of the oil into the bathtub and throws the container behind him. She watches it skid across the tile floor and slam into the opposite wall. He pulls a wadded ball of newspaper from the left pocket of his jeans, and then from the right, a gold-plated cigar lighter. He flips the top open, and a long flame dances back and forth. He moves the newspaper near the fire.

"No . . . stop! Please! Stop!" She begins to sob uncontrollably.

"You should've never betrayed me. I warned you, but you wouldn't listen, would you? Don't you remember what happened the last time you disobeyed me?"

"I'm sorry. I really am. I'll do better next time, I promise I will. Just don't hurt me, Paul. Please, I'm begging." She tries to silence her cries, to hold on to what little dignity she has left—the little that hasn't been slowly stripped from her during the past six months—but she can't.

She screams as he lights the newspaper and drops it . . .

She watches the glowing ball float toward the oil-laden water. Everything is in slow motion now, and even though she feels herself continuing to scream, she can no longer hear her own pleas.

The room is enveloped in silence.

Her eyes wide with panic.

Tears running down her cheeks and into the contaminated water.

She tries to lift her arms out of the tub to catch the orange orb of fire before it touches the water, but her arms won't move. She's paralyzed by fear.

The flaming ball of newspaper reaches the surface, and the water begins to burn . . .

Tiffany Colson gasped as she sat up in bed. She felt as if she were smothering, not able to draw a single breath. Her heart was racing so fast she thought for sure it would explode and she would die right there in her own bed.

Calm down, she told herself, *it was only another dream.*

She struggled to pull oxygen into her lungs, to calm her runaway heartbeat. Her blue silk pajamas were soaked with sweat, and she ran her hand through her hair, clearing the matted clumps away from her forehead. At last, she felt her pulse slow and her breathing return to normal, but she was burning up, her flesh hot and clammy.

She threw the covers back and rolled out of bed, then walked to the small window on the outside wall of the cabin. She turned the latch and raised the window, letting the cool October air flow into the room. A stiff breeze whipped her auburn hair away from her face. She just stood there, staring up at the bright stars and drawing deep breaths of the mountain air into her lungs. Her hands were still trembling, her stomach roiling with anxiety.

When would it ever stop?

Would it ever stop?

It had been almost ten years since she had escaped the demon she had been foolish enough to fall for. November 10th had been her independence day, and she always marked the anniversary with a combination of joy and trepidation.

Afraid that, somehow, he would come back.

Come back to finish what he started.

With the ten-year anniversary less than a month away, it seemed her nerves had been more on edge than usual. The nightmare that had just awakened her was only the latest in a series of terrifying memories that haunted her nights, and sometimes even her days.

They played over and over in her mind like a movie reel. Just as if it had happened yesterday.

Her body still bore the scars from that night. The night he had tried to burn her alive.

The night she had barely escaped with her life.

And the night Paul had lost his.

Her hand slipped under her pajama top, as though it had a mind of its own, just as it had done countless times before. The silk gently caressed the back of her hand as her fingertips found the smooth, silvery skin. She traced each mark—each reminder—carefully, slowly. One ran from underneath her left breast all the way to her belly button, another from the inside of her right breast to the back of her ribcage.

The outside air chilled her sweat-covered body, and she slid the windowpane back down, locking it in place with the metal tab on top. She looked back across her bed, toward her alarm clock. It was 4:30 a.m. She did not have to be at work until 7:30. She should lie down and try to go back to sleep. But she knew sleep would not come, no matter how hard she tried.

It never did.

She sighed and looked out the window once more, the beams of soft light cast by the full moon streaking through the giant oak tree in her front yard and creating elongated shadows outside the cabin. She again thought about crawling back into bed, but instead turned and walked from her room toward the bathroom that lay just a short distance down the narrow hallway.

She let her damp pajamas fall to the floor and climbed into the shower. As the hot water streamed over her body, she tried to push all the horrible memories that seemed to have been dogging her lately out of her mind. But, once again, she failed.

She still didn't understand how she could have been so blind. How she hadn't seen the evil lurking behind the handsome face. She guessed that's what made psychopaths so dangerous, though—they looked completely normal on the outside.

She remembered the first time she had met Paul. She had been walking toward her car late one afternoon. It had been a long day, and she was still pissed she had gotten a C on her last English Comp paper. She only had a few more months until graduation. Then she would be finished with college and could find a real job and leave the late-night waitressing at the local truck stop behind for good.

If she made it a few more months.

Between work and classes, she felt like she was barely hanging on, the daily grind of her schedule exhausting her. To make matters worse, six months prior, she had been forced to bury her parents after a late-night car crash. They had been returning from a dinner party at their friends' house. The police said her father had fallen asleep at the wheel and drifted off the road before crashing head-on into a large pine tree. She had spent the last several months organizing her parents' financial affairs. Much to her surprise, her family had been deeply in debt, and by the time all the bills were paid with the money from the meager life insurance policy her father had carried, she was left with only a few inexpensive mementos to remember them by. So she had been forced to not only deal with the stress of school, work, and a rapidly shrinking bank account, but also the grief of losing the two people who meant the most to her in life. She was emotionally drained.

As she approached her car, she noticed that her rear driver's side tire was flat. "Damn," she whispered. *A perfect end to an already bad day*, she thought.

As she stared down at the deflated tire, she considered calling a service to fix it for her, but money was tight, and she just wanted to get back to her small one-bedroom apartment, have a glass of Merlot, and go to bed. Besides, her dad had taught her how to change a tire before she had even gotten her driver's license. It had been several years since she had actually changed one, but she was pretty sure she remembered how.

She opened the driver's door, threw her backpack inside, and popped the trunk open. She walked to the back of the car and stared into the trunk at the mound of items covering the carpeted bottom where the spare tire was stored. Frustrated, she huffed and began clearing the area. She removed her gym bag and set it down on the asphalt, then a pair of jumper cables, a large blanket, and a few other items that were in her way. When she had cleared out the trunk, she removed the panel that covered the spare tire and jack. "*You can do this, Tiff,*" she told herself as she looked down into the compartment.

"Excuse me, Miss?" she heard someone say behind her. Startled, she spun and found a young man approaching her. He was tall, maybe six feet, with brown hair and gray eyes that had just a hint of blue in them. "Looks like you have a flat tire there," he said.

"Yeah, I just finished my last class and was on my way home when I found it. It's been one of those days, you know?" Tiffany replied.

The stranger laughed softly. "Yeah, I know what you mean." He stuck out his hand. "My name's Paul."

Tiffany shook his hand and said, "I'm Tiffany. Nice to meet you, Paul."

He smiled. "Are you a student here?"

His warm demeanor put Tiffany at ease. "Yes, dental hygiene. Only a few more months and I'm finished. I can't wait, either. It's been a rough semester. How 'bout you?" she asked.

"Business administration, which, by the way, I have found to be incredibly boring. But my dad insists that if I want to take over the family business, I have to get an education first. I wish I had only a few months to go. I've got two more years of this shit." He laughed.

Tiffany found herself laughing along with him. She welcomed a little levity on what had otherwise been a pretty crappy day.

Paul pointed at the flat. "I can give you a hand with the tire if you like."

"No, no," she replied, waving her hand dismissively. "I think I can handle it."

"Don't be ridiculous." He paused and grinned. "I insist," he said as he began to roll up his sleeves.

Tiffany considered the stranger's offer. She didn't really want him to have to change her tire, but she was so tired, and a hot shower and that glass of Merlot were calling her name. With only a few second's hesitation, she motioned with her hand toward the trunk. "Okay. Thank you, Paul. That's very nice of you."

He didn't say anything in response; he just got right to it. She watched as he removed his backpack and went to work, lifting the tire and jack from the trunk. She offered to help, but he assured her he could handle it.

Fifteen minutes later, Paul was loading the jack and old tire into the back of her car. He slammed the trunk lid and smiled. "There you go. Should be fine now."

"Thank you. Thank you, so much." She ran her hand through her hair and smiled.

"No problem." He picked up his backpack, turned, and started to walk away, then stopped and spun around. "Would you like to have dinner with me sometime?" he asked, the inflection in his voice indicating he had just come up with the idea on the spur of the moment.

Tiffany smiled again, flattered by the invitation. Paul looked nervous, and that made her even more attracted to him. She had definitely noticed his good looks and athletic body while he was changing the tire, and dinner with a handsome man seemed like the perfect thing to take her mind off of school and her miserable waitressing job. After several seconds of contemplation, she replied, "I'd like that. Just a minute, let me give you my number." She leaned into the car and retrieved her purse. She pulled a pen and piece of paper from it, quickly wrote down her phone number, and handed it to him. "Give me a call. I'm free this Friday."

"Thanks," Paul said with his warm smile again on display. He folded the torn piece of notebook paper and stuck it into the front pocket of his blue jeans. "I'll be looking forward to it," he said as he turned and walked away.

That's how it had all started: as a simple, seemingly coincidental, meeting after a bad day at school. If Tiffany could have seen the future, she would have called a tire repair service, locked herself in her car, and refused the stranger's help.

If only . . .

But she hadn't.

Everything was good at the beginning. Paul was funny, polite, and treated her like a woman should be treated. But only a month into the relationship, he began to change. He became controlling, constantly calling, demanding to know exactly where she was and what she was doing every minute of the day. She had tried to break it off after only six weeks of dating, but Paul refused to even consider the possibility of losing her. He apologized profusely and promised to do better. Maybe if she could be patient, he would change, she had told herself.

But he didn't change.

Instead, things just kept getting worse. He became even more controlling, wrapping his tentacles around her like a boa constrictor smothers its prey—slow, but steady. After one argument, he backhanded her across the cheek, and she picked up the phone to call the police. He grabbed the phone and threw it to the floor, smashing it to pieces. Then he had whispered in her ear that if she ever tried to leave him again, she would be sorry.

He made sure she understood that he and his family were among the powerful elite in Georgia and could make her and everyone she cared about simply disappear—and no one would ever find them.

She knew he was telling the truth.

Tiffany turned the water off and stepped out of the shower. She wrapped herself in a towel, the feel of the soft cotton against her skin comforting, and she pulled it extra tight, wishing it were a pair of reassuring arms holding her.

She walked into the kitchen and grabbed her favorite mug and a coffee filter from the wooden cabinet above the corner countertop. The kitchen was a no-frills version, but it served its purpose. The counters were a baby blue laminate, and the white cabinets that hung above gave the place a clean feeling, which was good since she was a bit of a germaphobe.

Paul had always used fresh-ground French roast. She had hated it, but drank it anyway, afraid any minor disagreement would lead to him becoming uncontrollably angry. Right after she escaped, she had sworn to herself she would never drink French roast again. She picked up the canister of Folgers from the countertop and added three heaping spoonfuls of the pre-ground coffee to the paper filter. She filled the coffeemaker with tap water— Paul had always insisted on bottled water—and turned it on, then returned to the bathroom to dry her hair.

A few minutes later, the smell of fresh-brewed coffee wafted through the house, helping to drive the need for sleep from her body. Tiffany inhaled the smooth aroma deeply into her lungs as she walked back to the counter and filled her mug with her favorite morning drink. She added a splash of cream, then went into the open living area adjacent to the kitchen and curled up on the couch, wrapping herself in the heavy terrycloth bathrobe she now wore. She picked up the remote control and started to turn on the TV to check the weather, but then threw it next to her on the sofa, deciding instead to enjoy the early morning silence.

She stared into the cup of caramel-colored coffee and blew across the top as she lifted the mug to her lips and took the first sip. It went down smoothly and warmed her inside. As she drank, she wondered if she would ever get over the memories Paul had left her with.

Wondered if she would ever get a peaceful night's sleep again.

After Paul died, she had somehow managed to move on with her life, although it wasn't easy. She had taken a job as a dental hygienist in an Atlanta suburb and worked there for years, yet she never seemed quite at peace. She always felt on edge, often looking over her shoulder. Afraid that, somehow, he would come back. He always said that if he couldn't have her, no one would. She wondered if his reach stopped at the six feet of dirt that now rested on top of him.

That was ridiculous; of course it did. He was gone. Forever.

All that was behind her now. She had made a clean start, and things were going well. In fact, things were going great. She took another sip of coffee, the mug warming her chilly hands, then looked out the small window to her right and stared at the moon-drenched landscape that lay just beyond the front porch of her small cabin.

It was still hard for her to believe she was now working at a small mountain resort in Western North Carolina. The cabin she now called home was a world apart from the brick and marble mansion Paul had promised her all those years ago.

The cabin was provided to her as part of her employment contract with the resort. It was small, with only one bedroom, one bathroom, a tiny kitchen, and a small living room. It was nothing fancy at all: the walls were drafty, the pipes made noises when she turned on the water, and the old wooden floors in the living room and hallway creaked when she walked on them. But she loved it, and she was happy.

Finally.

As she stared at the giant oak outside her cabin, she remembered the first time she came to Mountain View Resort. It had been almost two and a half years ago, when she had traveled to the heart of the Smoky Mountains to help her best friend, Katie, search for her boyfriend, Cody, who had gone missing during a backcountry fly fishing trip. They had found him several days later, almost at the point of death. He had been attacked by a large black bear, and Tiffany still found it hard to believe that he had found the courage to survive. But he had somehow pulled through, and he and Katie were now married with a young daughter. They, too, had moved from the Atlanta area and were now living their dream of owning a fly fishing shop and guiding clients on the many trout streams that flowed through the surrounding mountains.

Tiffany didn't understand their obsession with fishing, but she admired them, both of them, for leaving their old lives behind and following their dreams. And if Cody could survive a bear attack and find the will to keep going when all hope seemed to be lost, surely she could put the haunting memories of Paul behind her.

Tiffany would never have guessed that leaving the suburbs of Atlanta in a mad rush to find a missing fisherman would end up changing her life as drastically as it had. She had come along with the intention of helping her best friend during a difficult time, and then returning to Georgia and resuming her life. But something happened on that trip that she hadn't expected at all.

She met Jackson.

Jackson Hart had been the park ranger in charge of Cody's search and rescue operation, and, at first, Tiffany reacted to him the same way she reacted to most men she met—with suspicion and fear. She had been cold, even rude. She was still surprised he hadn't sent her and Katie back to Atlanta at his first opportunity. Tiffany smiled to herself. It couldn't have been easy for Jackson, putting up with her temper and Katie's sad face every day, especially in the midst of a stressful search and rescue operation—but thankfully, he had.

At one point in her life, she had been an outgoing, friendly person. But Paul had changed all that, and the old carefree Tiffany seemed to have been lost. She now thought of her life in two distinct parts—before Paul and after.

After Paul, she found social interactions challenging, if not downright impossible, especially with men. So she had treated Jackson the same way at first; he got the same cold, distant Tiffany every other man did.

But as the search for Cody continued, she had found herself falling for Jackson. He was kind, and his dogged determination to find Cody made her love him even more. She could see that he really cared about finding a man he had never even met. He could have called the search off after the first couple of days, but he didn't. He persevered until Cody was back with Katie.

After the search was over, they kept in touch, and their relationship slowly grew. He traveled to Georgia to visit her several times, and she had made the trip to the Smokies. After several months of long-distance dating, she had decided to move to North Carolina and take the job at the resort. There had been no pressure from Jackson to move; otherwise, she would have bolted like a scared rabbit. But she had been ready to leave the Atlanta area for some time anyway, and the job offer at the resort seemed like an opportunity for a fresh start. She had hoped leaving Georgia and moving to the solace of the mountains would help her forget Paul, but, so far, that had failed.

She had worked for the resort for almost two years now, and her relationship with Jackson had continued to blossom over that time. It was not the white-hot fire of a new twenty-something romance, but rather the slow sizzle of more mature adults.

Still, she was in her thirties now and couldn't help wondering what the future held for her. She hoped to someday get married and have a family, but every time she had that particular longing, flashes of her past always intruded.

But maybe Ranger Jackson Hart was the one she had been waiting for. The one who would be able to open her soul and love her despite all the emotional baggage that was still tied around her neck like a millstone.

Much to her relief, Jackson had been understanding and supportive when she had finally opened up to him about her past. Just summoning the courage to mention Paul's name to him had seemed an impossible task. She was afraid Jackson wouldn't want someone with so much damage, so many hang-ups.

But the first time they had made love, when Tiffany had revealed the scars on her body that she had never shown anyone, other than Katie and her doctors, Jackson had proved her wrong. He had just kissed her and held her tight, even as she trembled with fear and uncertainty in his arms. She could still hear him whisper, "It's going to be all right, Tiffany. I promise. I'm here, now."

She took her last sip of coffee, tilting the cup upward to make sure the last drops flowed into her mouth, then got up from the couch and walked into the kitchen. She washed and dried the mug, then placed it back in the cabinet. She hated coming home to dirty dishes, so she always made sure everything was cleaned and put away before leaving for the day. Paul had always left a dirty plate, bowl, or glass in the kitchen sink for her to wash, and she had resented it.

The caffeine had failed to give her the jump-start she was hoping for, and she yawned deeply, stretching her arms over her head. Now, she wished she had gone back to bed after the nightmare had awakened her. Today was Wednesday, which meant she would be leading a hike on one of the many trails that surrounded the resort. It was rather short, only a three-mile out-and-back, but she was already tired, partly from the lack of sleep, but primarily, from the energy-draining dream.

She sighed and walked into her bedroom, where she dressed in a comfortable pair of jeans, a long-sleeved cotton shirt, and a fleece jacket. She pulled her hair into a ponytail and did her makeup, applying just enough to highlight her natural beauty. She hated the caked-on look some women wore. She grabbed her backpack and headed toward the front door.

As she bent over to put on her hiking boots, she glanced at her watch. It was only 6:45 a.m., which meant she was running way early this morning. That was all right, though. She would rather go in early than sit in the cabin thinking about Paul.

She opened the door and stepped into the new day.

2

"That's it," Jackson said. He held the ring between his thumb and index finger, rolling it slightly. The solitaire diamond sparkled under the white lights of the jewelry store. The stone cast multi-colored rays that danced on the surface of the glass counter where he leaned. "How much?" he asked, looking up and holding his breath.

"$3,400," Charlie Hetherington replied.

Jackson whistled sharply. "Whew, Charlie. You trying to break me or something?"

"Hey, you already told me that was the one. Seems to me like I've got you by the short hairs now," Charlie said, his large belly shaking with laughter.

A crooked smile appeared on Jackson's face. "Yeah, I guess that's about right." He glanced back down at the diamond. There was no doubt about it; the ring he now held in his hand was *perfect*. "I'm not a very good poker player, Charlie, in case you couldn't tell," Jackson added, laughing softly.

Charlie ran a hand down his short white beard. "Tell you what, if you buy it today, you can have it for $3,200. Sorry, but that's the best I can do, Jackson."

Jackson hesitated for a moment, trying to make it seem as though he were in serious debate with himself, considering whether or not he would accept Charlie's price. He was hoping the old jeweler would knock another couple hundred bucks off in order to seal the deal, but after several seconds of silence between the two men, Jackson finally relented. "Deal," he said as he offered his hand across the counter.

Charlie grasped his hand with a firm grip. "Deal," he repeated. "You want it wrapped?"

"No, just the box is fine."

"Okay, I'll get it ready. Be right back." Charlie took the ring from Jackson and disappeared into the back room.

Charlie had operated the jewelry store on Main Street in Sylva for years. Jackson wasn't exactly sure how long he had been in business, but he had been here since Jackson was first stationed at the Twentymile Ranger Station five years ago.

Jackson had liked Charlie from their first meeting. He always enjoyed haggling with the genial old man whenever he was in the shop picking out a gift for Tiffany, even though Jackson seldom ended up on the better end of their haggling.

He relished trying to get the best deal possible, whether buying a new car or an engagement ring. He saw it as a challenge, and it was just part of who he was. He loved Tiffany and would have paid full price for the ring if it had come down to it, but he didn't see any harm in trying to save a few bucks.

A couple of minutes later, Charlie reappeared and handed Jackson a small, gray paper bag with U-shaped nylon handles. "Thanks," Jackson said as he handed his credit card across the counter.

Charlie ran the card, and once the receipt printed, he tore it off and pushed the slip of paper and a pen across the counter toward Jackson. "So who's the lucky lady, if I might ask?"

"Her name's Tiffany. I met her a while back. I might bring her in sometime . . . but then I'd probably leave here owing you another three grand." Jackson chuckled, then added, "She's one hell of a woman, Charlie."

"Must be to put up with your cheap ass," Charlie said, his deep laugh once again echoing off the walls of the small store.

"You know that's right," Jackson replied, grinning. He shook Charlie's hand again. "Thanks for the ring."

"Thank you, Jackson. Come back anytime," Charlie replied, genuine gratitude evident in his eyes now.

"You know I will." Jackson turned and walked out of the store, then stepped onto the concrete sidewalk that ran the length of Main Street.

As he stepped from beneath the jewelry store's awning, he paused and took notice of his surroundings. He loved fall. It was his favorite time of the entire year. He was thankful that the long, tiresome dog days of summer, filled with their oftentimes oppressive heat and humidity, were long gone.

Now, the trees were changing colors, painting the mountainsides surrounding the small town in hues of flaming orange, burnished gold, and the deepest, brightest red he had ever seen. A cold front had pushed through the area the day prior, ushering in clean, crisp air and deep blue skies. The sun was bright, warming Jackson's face, and a breeze was blowing out of the north, tossing his thick black hair around his forehead. He took a deep, invigorating breath of the fresh air, then continued walking toward his pickup truck.

He stopped at his vehicle momentarily to lock the ring inside the glove compartment, then continued west on Main Street. He had some extra time today, so he had decided to stop in and see Cody and Katie at their fly shop. But he didn't want his friends asking any questions about his recent purchase at Charlie's. For now, he wanted to keep that little piece of news all to himself.

As Jackson strode toward the fly shop, he felt the urge for an autumn fishing trip coming on.

70297466R00183

Made in the USA
Columbia, SC
03 May 2017